I0703803

DRAWING DEAD

A LIZZY BALLARD THRILLER

MATTY DALRYMPLE

WILLIAM KINGSFIELD PUBLISHERS

For Lisa Regan, with deep appreciation for your expert eye and generous spirit.

Drawing dead: A situation in which a player has absolutely no chance of winning a hand. This means that even if the remaining cards to be dealt are theoretically the best possible for that player's hand, they still will not beat the opponent's hand. This often occurs when the opponent already holds a hand that is unbeatably superior, rendering any draw futile.

From Blinds to Bets: Poker Basics for Beginners by Thomas Koenigsfeld

1

———

Lizzy Ballard glanced around the casino's parking garage from her vantage point in the SUV's passenger seat. On this June midafternoon, there was only a scattering of cars, and no people were visible.

She opened the glove compartment and removed a small case, unzipping it to reveal a glass vial and syringe.

She rolled up the sleeve of her T-shirt. She no longer bothered with the dress, high heels, and makeup she had worn to the casinos back in Phoenix. Experience had shown that her fake ID was bullet-proof enough to pass even a careful inspection by casino staffers. Especially in her more casual clothes, they might suspect she was closer to her actual age of seventeen than the ID's claim of twenty-one, but no one had challenged her on it.

They did sometimes comment on the fact that she had a different haircut: not the sun-bleached gold tipped with bright red as it had been back in Arizona, but a mousy blond pixie.

She had decided she should let her look be guided by her usual mantra: avoid notice.

She filled the syringe and injected herself in the bicep.

It would take her no more than a few minutes to reach the

poker table. The juice, as she referred to the drug, might not have taken full effect by then, but if not, she'd bide her time until it kicked in. She didn't feel like hanging out in the parking garage. She was conditioned to assess every environment for danger, and she couldn't help but consider every car that stood between her and the casino entrance to be a potential hiding place for an attacker. Of course, she was armed with her own special defense, but soon the juice would deprive her of that defense. Maybe she should go back to her previous practice of injecting herself in the casino restroom.

She returned the syringe and vial to the case and put the case in the glove compartment, then climbed out of the SUV. As she crossed the garage, she could tell that the juice was starting to take effect—the *tick tick* of a cooling car engine like nails tapping on granite, a sequin sparkling like a diamond against the dirty concrete floor. This heightened sensory perception was as annoying as ever, but at least it confirmed that Owen had complied with her instruction not to tinker with the concentration of the steroid-based drug.

She found her godfather, Owen McNally, standing outside the door to the casino.

"I thought you were going to go to the bar," she said.

"Thought I'd wait for you here." He opened the door for her and followed her into the casino's cavernous central atrium. "I figured you were just giving me an excuse not to stay in the car with you while—" He shuddered. "—you know."

She laughed as they stepped onto the escalator. "How did you ever get through medical school?"

He laughed with her. "It wasn't easy ... although the professors did what they could to save me from giving injections. Or," he shuddered again, "drawing blood. No one wants to deal with someone fainting in a class, especially if they weigh three hundred pounds."

Owen, as best he could, had also adopted Lizzy's goals of flying under the radar appearance-wise, although at six-four, there was only so much he could do. He had shaved off his wispy beard and mustache, and his usually untidy hair was now cut short. The biggest change, however, was his weight. The rigors of the past year—a drug-induced heart attack and a stab wound to the thigh—had slimmed him down, his weight now closer to two hundred than three hundred pounds. His step was firmer, his complexion rosier, his expression more cheerful. He was looking good. If he turned heads now, Lizzy thought it was for the right reasons.

They passed the second floor, Lizzy grimacing at the sensory assault of the beeps, buzzes, jingles, and flashes from the slot machines, and continued to the poker lounge on the third floor.

As was usual at this time of day, the casino was sparsely populated. Most of the chairs, upholstered in orange faux leather, were empty. There were more patrons at the bar than at the tables, but their conversation was desultory.

"Want me to come to the table with you?" Owen asked.

"No, you can wait at the bar." She gestured to the folded copy of *NeuroFrontiers: Advances in Human Potential* he carried under his arm. "A little light reading, I see," she said with a smile.

He opened the magazine and riffled through the pages. "They have an article on 'Neural Adaptations in the Auditory Cortex of Superhuman Hearing: A Case Study.' Thought it might give me some ideas for reducing some of the side effects."

"Don't mess with the formulation too much. I don't mind putting up with the noise as long as the juice does what it's supposed to do."

After all, she wouldn't be spending her afternoon at a casino if it wasn't to earn some money by reading her fellow poker players' thoughts.

LIZZY PLACED her cards face-down on the green felt of the poker table. "Fold." The juice was performing its work but knowing what cards the other players held didn't help her if the hand she was dealt had no chance of winning. Drawing dead, as her fellow players would say.

The hand ended, the winning player pulled in the pot, and the dealer dealt the next hand.

Lizzy was following her usual strategy of folding losing hands to minimize her losses. During this game, one of the players—the dealer had called him Stan—was harder to read than the others, so she had lost some money to him. She consoled herself that it was smart to make sure that not all her hands were either a fold or a winner.

She checked her cards, scanned her fellow player's thoughts, and folded again.

She wondered idly about the cause of her difficulty in reading Stan's thoughts. It might be because he had some natural mental barriers up, as was the case with some people. Or it might be her own distraction based on his topic of conversation.

"Shelby will be going to Europe in a couple of weeks with her mom, her aunt, and her cousin," Stan said, "then she'll be starting at Kutztown in the fall."

Stop your bragging, thought another player, a man in his fifties wearing an Eagles jersey.

Shaking his head, Stan continued. "Man, I wish I had been able to go to Europe when *I* was a teenager." He tossed in some poker chips and laughed. "For that matter, I wish I had been able to go to *college*, although I didn't think that at the time." He grinned. "But Daddy's got to bring home the bacon to pay for the trip and tuition, so don't be too hard on me, guys." He winked at Lizzy. "And gal."

Hitting on a girl not much older than his daughter. Scumbag, thought Eagles.

"How about you, sweetheart?" Stan asked Lizzy. "You in college?"

Earlier, when another player had asked Lizzy that question, she had told him she was a student at William Penn University, where Owen taught neurobiology. However, when the questioner turned out to be an alum and began quizzing her about her favorite classes and professors, she quickly realized the downside of mentioning a local school. She had also learned not to say that she hadn't gone to college at all, because people inevitably tried to convince her to give it a try. She scanned the other players' thoughts to see if anyone was thinking about their own alma mater but got nothing.

"I went to a little college in Arizona for a semester," she said, "but I didn't like it."

Should have stayed out there, thought another player, a man in his thirties wearing a Flyers jersey. *Maybe Arizona players don't mind girls who fold every goddamn hand.*

"What brought you to Philly?" asked Stan.

Lizzy suppressed a sigh. Evidently any answer she gave was an opening to an unwelcome conversation. "Family." At least she wouldn't fall into the trap of giving him any details that would form the basis for another question.

He nodded sagely. "Family's the best reason to come home."

You haven't met my family, thought Flyers.

Suddenly, she felt tears prick her eyes. In a way, she *had* come back East to family. In addition to being her godfather, Owen had been her father's best friend in college. Owen's younger brother Andy was like a considerably older brother. And Ruby DiMano, Owen's majordomo, was like the world's most badass grandmother. But they could never fill the aching space of her dead mother and father.

Stan looked stricken. "Sorry, honey, I didn't mean to bring up a sore subject."

You wouldn't have hurt the girl's feelings if you just kept your mouth shut, thought Eagles.

She sensed Owen's presence at her shoulder. "How's it going ..." She heard him mentally adding his nickname for her: ... *Pumpkin?*

"I think I'm ready to call it quits." She had won almost no money—and she wouldn't be spending time in the stupid casino if it wasn't to earn money—but she suspected that her upset wouldn't help her ability to sense the other players' thoughts.

About goddamned time, thought Flyers.

Poor little thing, thought Eagles. *Wonder if the big guy's her dad.*

As the dealer closed her out of the game—*If one of them was leaving, wish it wasn't her ... she's a lot easier on the eyes than these old farts*—she drew a deep breath, trying to hold the tears at bay.

After cashing in her chips, she and Owen headed for the parking garage.

"What happened, Pumpkin?" Owen asked when they had climbed into his SUV.

Lizzy knew that, regarding the death of her mother, Owen felt grief but not guilt. But she also knew that he held himself partially to blame for the death of her father, and she didn't want to remind him of that by mentioning Stan's comment about coming home to family.

"One of the players was talking about how his daughter was traveling in Europe this summer and then was going to college in the fall." She paused. "I wish I could do that."

Owen patted her shoulder. "I know, Pumpkin. I don't think it's a foregone conclusion that you can't—we just haven't found the right way to approach it yet. We'll keep thinking."

She marshaled a smile. "I know we will."

He started up the SUV, and they exited the garage and headed north on I-95.

Lizzy turned her gaze out the window. The sun was periodically disappearing behind scudding clouds, and it was cool for June. As they passed the airport and the Navy Yard, she thought about the three things she needed in order to engage in the activities most seventeen-year-olds took for granted, like traveling and going to school.

She needed to earn more money than she was likely to get playing poker.

To do that, she needed a real job, and that would require an identity backed up by data like a social security number.

And she needed a way to guarantee that the people she encountered wouldn't become victims of "the squeeze," as she called her ability to cause strokes in others when frightened or angry ... as angry as she had been as a sickly and feverish seven-year-old when her mother, already somewhat incapacitated by the effect of the many small strokes little Lizzy had inflicted, had refused her daughter the beagle puppy she so desperately wanted. It was the last argument Charlotte Ballard had with her daughter. Lizzy still sometimes woke in the middle of the night, her teeth clenched, her body slicked with sweat, her hand frantically patting the covers, just as it had patted the hand of her dying mother.

Owen interrupted her gloomy reverie. "Stop somewhere for a late lunch?"

She summoned a laugh. "We already had lunch."

He smiled, happy that he had made her laugh. "An early dinner, then."

"It would be a pretty early dinner. And I think Ruby is making spaghetti for dinner."

"Ah, good! I love her sauce." He adopted a grumpy expression that looked out of place on his usually cheerful face. "Although I'd like it more if she let me have more than one serving."

"I'll try to sneak you some extra spaghetti when she isn't looking."

"That's my girl."

Lizzy turned toward the window again, hoping Owen didn't notice her smile fade as she thought how unlikely it seemed that she'd ever be able to live the life Stan's daughter was enjoying.

She wished she could talk it over with her mentor, Philip Castillo ... but she hadn't seen Philip for two weeks.

2

───────

Philip leaned against a wall of the room that served as Billy Chapel's command center. The walls were black lacquer, and despite—or maybe because of—the fact that they reflected the light from the mid-century modern chandelier suspended from the vaulted ceiling, even in the middle of day, it felt like midnight in the room.

The window Philip stood next to looked out on a sweep of green lawn leading down to a pool and pool house and the thick woods that lay beyond them. He had never seen anyone in the pool, and the only people he had seen outside were the men who patrolled the property. Another contingent patrolled inside, beefy men with bulges under their jackets where a shoulder holster would lie, wandering the halls or lounging by the front door.

He could catch a glimpse of the roof of another house over the trees, and based on its location, he calculated Chapel's property to be at least a dozen acres. He knew from the signs he had seen during the drive from the compound that they were close to Baltimore. A house this big on a property this large must have cost a fortune ... but Chapel had plenty of income from his off-the-books operation. Philip wondered what Chapel's well-heeled neighbors must think of living next door to the crime kingpin of Baltimore.

He had seen the outside of the house only once, when he arrived here from the compound two weeks earlier with Chapel and his men. He had not been allowed outside since then, and of course he didn't have a phone. He was still in the probationary period as an ostensible member of Chapel's entourage, living in a dorm-like room on the top floor. For clothing, Philip had been issued what was practically a uniform: a down-market version of Chapel's own outfits of subtly-colored leather jackets, tight T-shirts, designer black jeans, and highly polished boots. Most of the men wore their hair crew-cut short, as Chapel did, but at least no one had demanded that Philip cut his longish black hair, although one of the men had asked with an unpleasant laugh if Philip wanted a couple of feathers to stick in it.

Chapel sat behind a massive desk. Everything in the house was massively proportioned—a good match with its owner. Chapel reminded Philip of the mesas of his native Arizona—a column of granite-like hardness.

The top of the desk was as black as the walls and empty except for a mobile phone. Chapel leaned forward and tapped *Replay* on the voice memo app.

Louise Mortensen's voice came from the speaker.

"He's not aware of your presence. I need some information from him. I'll ask questions, and you'll relay to me what you can gather about his answers. Don't say anything unless it's to convey what he's thinking. In the course of our conversation, I may mention the work we did at Vivantem, but he won't remember any of what we discuss. Your friend Philip could confirm that for you."

Next came Lizzy Ballard's whispered response. "I'm sure Philip could tell me all sorts of things ... if I could talk to him."

Chapel stabbed the audio off and sat back. *"Your friend Philip."*

Philip was silent.

"Thought you didn't know her."

"I ran into her at the compound. I believed her when she said she was Viklund's niece."

"So how come you pretended you didn't know her when she came to my suite?"

"She's underage. I didn't want any hassle."

"You and her hooked up?"

Philip shrugged.

Chapel wagged a finger at Philip. "Bad boy, Phil."

Hooking up with the seventeen-year-old Lizzy was not even a consideration for Philip, but there was no harm in Chapel believing it. "Hey, she was game. But that didn't mean Viklund—who I thought was her uncle—would have liked it."

"Viklund was dead."

"I didn't know that."

"You sure? You didn't have anything to do with ol' Uncle Theo ending up in a freezer?"

"No."

"You think Mortensen did?"

"That's my guess."

"And what was Mortensen doing at the compound?"

"Research for Viklund."

Billy gestured toward the phone on his desk. "That research?"

"That's my guess."

"You don't have anything better than guesses?"

Philip shrugged. "Mortensen and I weren't pals."

"Were Mortensen and Viklund pals?"

"My understanding was that she went to the compound on her own but became Viklund's prisoner."

"And why did she go in the first place?"

"Thought it was a better alternative than whatever the Pennsylvania Attorney General had in mind for her."

Chapel stared at him for a few long seconds, then stood and ambled over to the window where Philip stood. "It looked to me like Ballard didn't plan to get onboard that helicopter when everyone was leaving the compound like rats from a sinking ship. She looked like she was just trying to get Andrew McNally in. What do you suppose that was all about?"

He shrugged again. "No seats left."

"If I were in her shoes—unarmed and a bunch of guys shooting at me—you can be damn sure I'd find a way to get on the chopper, even if it meant tossing McNally out."

"Lucky for McNally it was Ballard there and not you."

Billy ignored Philip's comment. "You told me at the helipad that McNally was the valuable one. That's the only reason I stopped the boys from firing at the chopper."

They had been through this so many times before. Now all Philip could do was continue repeating the story he had given Billy the first time he had been asked the question, even if 20/20 hindsight suggested a better one. "I thought he was. Mortensen mentioned to me that McNally was a medical doctor and that he was staying in the lab. I assumed he was helping her out with whatever she was doing."

Chapel rubbed his chin. "Mortensen's muscle, Lucas, had a gun on McNally when I ran into them in the lab. Doesn't sound like how you treat an ally."

"Sounds like even *you* don't believe an ally needs to be willing to be useful."

Chapel snorted out a laugh. "True enough." He returned to the desk, slipped off his jacket—today's was fern green—and hung it over the back of the chair. He sat down, leaned back, and laced his fingers behind his head, elbows splayed. The sleeve of his T-shirt hiked up, revealing a piece of gauze taped over his bicep—his souvenir of the gun battle that had raged at the compound's helipad two weeks earlier.

If only the bullet had been a foot closer to center mass, thought Philip.

"Your buddy Liz appears to be a mind-reader," said Chapel.

"Or at least pretending to be."

"She'd have to be a pretty smart cookie to know all that medical jargon—and if she's pretending, she's fooling Mortensen." Chapel gestured to the phone on the desk. "It sounds like this guy Ballard is talking to is drugged."

"It does." Philip assumed that Edmund Rinnert, the man whose thoughts Lizzy had been conveying to Mortensen in the recording, had been given a dose of Rohypnol, but he wasn't about to share with Billy that his assumption was based on personal experience.

"You still claim you didn't know about this mind-reading thing."

"I'm still claiming that."

"You didn't sense that your underage girlfriend had an idea about what it was you liked, beyond any instructions you might have been giving her?"

"Jesus, Billy," muttered Philip.

Chapel laughed, then his expression darkened. "I don't appreciate being lied to."

"I don't appreciate being forced to take a job I didn't ask for."

Chapel shrugged. "Better than the alternative. If Theo Viklund hadn't thought you were worth a little trouble, you'd be at the bottom of the Patapsco right now, missing a few key body parts." He arched an eyebrow. "Pre-mortem."

"Sounds unpleasant."

Chapel spun the phone on the desktop. "Unpleasant. Yeah, you could say that." He pushed himself to his feet and crossed to the window again. He thrust his hands in his pockets and looked out. "You know, I've got plenty of guys that would be happy to slit a guy's throat or put a bullet in someone's head, just like you did. But they're bigmouths, show-offs." He looked back at Philip. "That—and the fact that Viklund, who didn't vouch for many men, vouched for you—is why I'm willing to keep you around." He cocked an eyebrow at Philip. "Despite the fact that you've been holding back on me—at least about knowing the girl."

"I appreciate it."

"The Sedona cops still want you for the Hanrick killing."

"I don't imagine they'll think to look for me in Baltimore. And I don't see you turning snitch."

"I'm not necessarily above having one of my boys place an anonymous tip to the cops, if it suits me. But as far as I'm concerned, it's a case of good riddance—Hanrick sounds like a bastard."

"He was."

"Killed a buddy of yours in prison?"

"Yes."

Chapel waited for more. When Philip was silent, he continued. "I appreciate a man who's willing to avenge a buddy's death."

After a beat, Philip replied. "The man Hanrick had killed was more than a buddy—he was like a father to me. The fact that I was willing to kill Hanrick to avenge that man's death doesn't mean I'm going to be the right guy for murdering people because they piss you off."

"Doesn't mean you're not—or couldn't be, with the right incentive."

Philip gazed back at him, stone-faced.

Chapel waved a hand. "Philosophical discussions bore me. If

I need you to do something for me, I'll find a way to get you to do it." Without waiting for an answer, he strolled back to the desk and looked down at the phone. "Don't suppose you can make heads or tails of what Mortensen gets Rinnert to talk about—or think about—in the rest of that recording. *Electrophysiology*? *Neural interface augmentation*? *Diagnostic elucidation*?"

"Not a clue."

Chapel laughed. "You know, Phil, that I *can* believe. I think I'm going to need to bring in some specialized help on this one."

Philip raised an eyebrow. "You know someone who's an expert in electrophysiology and neural interface augmentation?"

Chapel waved a hand. "Close enough. That whole conversation is about using electricity to make people be able to cause strokes or read minds. What we need is someone with electrical expertise." He dropped into the desk chair. "But the person I *really* want to talk to is Mortensen. Lucas told us she went to Philly to pick up her fake ID and that she's going by *Louise Gerard* now. We need to find her ... and find out what she knows."

"Like you found out from Lucas?"

Chapel grinned. "Pretty much."

"And then what?"

"Might have to think of something a little more inventive for Doctor Louise Mortensen than a bullet in the back of the head." He raised his arms in a stretch. "And unlike Lucas, the good doctor is likely to lose a couple of body parts before she ends up in her final resting place."

"Pre-mortem?"

Chapel dropped his arms and slapped his stomach with a sound like slapping a length of board. "You know it. And also unlike with Lucas, where you got to do the honors, I'm going to take care of that bit of work myself."

3

Louise Mortensen sat at a window table, a shaft of late afternoon sun glinting off her untouched glass of Sauvignon Blanc. The restaurant, across the street from the Philadelphia Center City high rise that housed the Vivantem fertility clinic, was almost empty, giving her server the bandwidth to be a little oversolicitous. She noticed with a twinge of irritation that he was approaching her table, no doubt to ask again if he could bring her something other than the glass of wine. She waved him off. She'd leave him a tip sufficient to compensate him for the time she was spending there.

She turned back to the window, her eyes on the high-rise entrance.

She wondered where Lucas and Maja—the late Theo Viklund's head of security and housekeeper—were now. No doubt back in Sweden, which, Louise hoped, was too far away for Billy Chapel to bother pursuing them. She herself would have appreciated having an ocean between herself and Chapel.

However, Philadelphia was where Louise had asked Lucas to send the documents supporting her new identity as Louise Gerard, and it was to Philadelphia she had come to retrieve them. Lucas hadn't made it easy, dropping her off unceremoniously at an airport not far from the compound, almost literally with just the clothes on her back. She had orchestrated a ride to a pawn shop, pawned her wedding ring, and purchased an Amtrak ticket to Philadelphia's 30th Street Station and then a SEPTA ticket to the Main Line stop closest to the post office where the documents awaited her.

Now she not only had her identity documents in hand but had used them to tap into the offshore accounts where she had transferred her portion of Theo Viklund's millions.

She had also had her hair dyed back to its natural auburn, although the stylist hadn't bothered resurrecting the threads of silver that had run through it before Louise had dyed it a drab brown in preparation for her escape from the Viklund compound.

Now she could leave Philadelphia if she wanted to. But against the disadvantage of its proximity to Billy Chapel's base in Baltimore, it had the advantage of being the part of the world she knew best. She had decided that familiarity with her environment was more important than distance from Chapel, and she had settled into a suite in a boutique hotel in Wayne.

What she really needed, though, was a laboratory, and she was there to find out if her Vivantem lab might be an option.

Twenty-five minutes after the time she had requested, a florist's truck pulled up in front of the high rise. The driver got out, carefully lifted a large vase of flowers out of the back, and disappeared into the building. One minute ticked by, then two. Louise's phone rang.

"Hello?" she answered.

"Hey, Ms. Gerard, I'm trying to deliver the flowers you ordered this morning, but the guy at the security desk says that the Vivantem offices are closed down. No one's there—haven't been there for a couple of months."

"If there's no one in the Vivantem *offices*, perhaps you could deliver them to the Vivantem *lab*."

"Hold on, let me check." There was some indistinct conversation, then the man was back. "Lab is closed, too. In fact, the guy says there's some kind of investigation into the company. The whole facility's been sealed—no one allowed in without an escort from the attorney general's office."

"My, what a surprise." It was far from a surprise, but disappointing, nonetheless. "Well, feel free to leave the flowers at the security desk—perhaps the guard can enjoy them."

"Sure thing, Ms. Gerard."

She ended the call. She had known it was unlikely that the lab was still operational, and even more unlikely that she'd be able to find a way to get in, but she had needed to know for sure.

She wondered if the Pennsylvania Attorney General had discovered any documentation of the experiments she had conducted on some of the women who had come to Vivantem for fertility treatments. She was fairly certain she had removed any incriminating documents before the investigation began. And, she thought with a scowl, most of her documents were now in the hands of Lucas, who wouldn't even know what to make of them. At least she had retained the records related to Elizabeth Ballard, which she had smuggled out of Theo Viklund's compound on a flash drive taped to her ankle.

But even if she had the records Lucas had taken, it probably wouldn't make much difference to her current situation. What she needed was not simply to initiate a pregnancy in an unsuspecting test subject that *might* result in a baby with extraordinary abilities, as she had in the case of Ballard's mother. She couldn't afford the decades it would take for such babies to grow into useful allies.

She had always pursued her goals with the support of others: her late husband, Gerard Bonnay; her late enforcer,

George Millard; the no doubt Sweden-bound Lucas and Maja. And with Billy Chapel no doubt on her trail, she needed useful allies now.

What she needed was the ability to create those abilities in otherwise normal adults.

At one time, Louise had thought that electricity might be the key to her goal, but she had eventually accepted that she herself didn't have the expertise needed to pursue that approach.

No, Louise's expertise was better applied to a pharmaceutical approach. But she needed a lab.

And with the Vivantem lab unavailable, there was only one other facility she knew of that would meet her needs.

She raised her finger, and the server was at her table in a moment. "May I bring you—"

"Just the check," Louise said. "There's somewhere I need to be."

4

As Owen turned the SUV off 95 toward Andy McNally's Center City apartment, Lizzy got out her phone to check her online alerts for any updates about the three people whose activities she was most interested in and whose activities she knew the least about: Billy Chapel, Louise Mortensen, and Philip Castillo.

There was no lack of information about Chapel. Authorities knew he controlled drugs, prostitution, and gambling in Baltimore, but arrests and prosecution had been repeatedly derailed by informers and witnesses changing their stories ... or dying.

There was nothing new about Louise Mortensen. The Pennsylvania Attorney General's office was still investigating her Vivantem fertility clinic and still wanted to question her about the fire that had burned down her Pocopson home. Louise had fallen off any official radar when she fled Pocopson to take refuge in Theo Viklund's Western Maryland compound, and she had not reappeared after her escape from the compound.

And the Sedona police still wanted to question Philip about the deaths in Oak Creek Canyon of three of his fellow former inmates of the Williams Correctional Facility. Lizzy thought back to the last time she had seen Philip. He had been standing next to Chapel, who, seconds before, had been firing at the helicopter carrying her and Andy. The fist Philip had raised as the aircraft rose from the helipad—an echo of the fist bump that was their usual goodbye gesture—had been enough to convince Lizzy that he hadn't changed sides. But she also knew that her other allies—Owen, Andy, and Ruby DiMano—weren't as convinced as she was.

Dragging her thoughts out of this depressing groove, she recalled the first time she had seen Philip. She had gone to his "psychic counseling" office in Sedona, hoping she might come away with some insight that would help her control the ability she called the squeeze. The name of his business was meant to appeal to the tourists, but although Philip wasn't psychic in any usual sense of the word, he had shown an innate understanding of the terrible situation her ability had put her in and of the grinding guilt she felt about the deaths of her parents. And in the course of their relationship, he had come to her rescue so many times. She had to do what she could to come to his rescue now.

Baltimore, as Billy's base of operations, seemed like the most likely place to go looking for Philip. But so far, Owen, Andy, and Ruby had talked her out of it, arguing that her appearance there might prove more dangerous to Philip than helpful if Billy caught her snooping around.

She and Owen reached Andy's apartment building, and Owen maneuvered the SUV into a space in the underground parking garage. Lizzy was grateful he was at the wheel since she found the concrete pillars on either side of the space intimidating. She also as a rule didn't drive for some time after taking the juice, despite the relatively mild side effects of Owen's formulations. He had reduced the concentration until it began interfering with Lizzy's mind-reading ability, at which point she insisted he increase it again. She knew he was unhappy with the idea of her taking *any* concentration of the steroid-based drug.

They took the elevator up one floor, then crossed the elegantly appointed lobby toward the elevators that provided access to the apartments.

"Doctor McNally," said the security guard at the desk. "Miss."

"Hey, Sherman," said Lizzy.

"Good afternoon, Sherman," said Owen. "How's your little boy doing?"

"Lots better, thanks. The cortisone cream you recommended really seems to be helping. My wife and I appreciate your help."

"Not at all. Glad to hear the little guy is feeling better."

Owen and Lizzy stepped into the elevator, and Owen pushed the button for the top floor.

"What happened to Sherman's little boy?" asked Lizzy.

"Eczema. Quite common in young children."

She smiled. "You've been chatting with Sherman?"

Owen shrugged. "Not much else to do."

It was true—they were all going a little stir-crazy. "Sherman must wonder what's going on in Andy's apartment these days, with all the extra people staying there."

Owen laughed. "I'm sure we're in violation of some condition of his lease, but I imagine Sherman doesn't care as long as we're not causing trouble for other tenants."

"And as long as you're helping him out with his little boy."

"Never thought of it that way, but I guess it can't hurt."

The elevator doors dinged open, and they followed a short hallway to Andy's apartment. They entered, and Lizzy heard voices coming from the kitchen.

"I could have gotten it myself—I just went to look for a step stool." Ruby, remonstrating.

"I don't *have* a step stool—I can reach everything in my apartment." Andy, irritated.

They found Ruby and Andy standing next to an open cabinet door: Ruby's fists on her hips; Andy, nearly a foot taller, holding a can of tomato sauce. The other hand, its middle fingers splinted, was pressed to his side.

"What's up?" asked Owen.

"Nothing's up," said Andy.

Ruby crossed her arms. "The younger Doctor McNally overexerted himself getting the tomato sauce off the top shelf."

"If I can't get a damned can of tomato sauce off the damned shelf ..." Andy's voice trailed off, evidently uncertain how to complete the sentence. "Anyhow," he handed the can to Ruby with exaggerated gallantry, "there's your sauce."

Ruby took the can. "Thank you," she said frostily.

"Are you okay?" Owen asked Andy.

Andy pulled out one of the stools from the kitchen island and sat, trying to disguise a wince. "I'm fine."

"Did you—?"

"I said I'm fine."

An uneasy silence fell over the kitchen.

After a few moments, Andy pushed himself to his feet. "I'm going to lie down for a few minutes."

He left the kitchen, and his steps receded down the hall to the bedroom. Lizzy, Owen, and Ruby had at least prevailed on Andy to sleep in his own bed rather than ceding it to one of them. A moment later, the bedroom door closed—a little more firmly than was necessary.

"I shouldn't have let him get the can down for me," Ruby muttered. "I knew it might pull at the stitches."

It had been two weeks since Andy and Lizzy had escaped

from the compound, but a Band-Aid still covered the cut over one of his eyes, and both eyes were still surrounded by a yellowish tinge, a reminder of his broken nose. The wince was probably from the gunshot wound in his side ... or maybe from the two fingers that Lucas's men had dislocated as a warning to Lizzy.

But his physical condition was less worrying than his mental state. Lizzy had spoken to Andy on the phone just before Lucas's men kidnapped him and took him to the compound, and he had been his normal, cheerful, teasing self. When he regained consciousness after the operation to repair the wound in his side, he had been sullen and short-tempered, snapping at even the prettiest nurses and doctors.

When he had been discharged and returned home—the close quarters in his apartment not improving his mood—he had been the most adamant objector to Lizzy's proposal that she go to Baltimore to look for Philip.

"He's the reason we're in this boat," Andy had said.

"Actually, Andy, *I'm* the reason we're in this boat." Lizzy resisted adding that Philip was the person who had arranged to get Andy to the helipad and was probably the reason Chapel had ordered his men to stop firing at the helicopter that had flown her and Andy to safety.

Andy and Philip's relationship had always been strained. Andy hadn't approved of Lizzy sharing living quarters with Philip back in Sedona—this despite the fact that Philip's girl-friend, Olivia, was a frequent visitor to the apartment—and Philip had resented Andy's lack of trust. More significantly, it had been a request from Philip that had led to Lizzy being kidnapped by Tobe Hanrick, and that had ended in the deadly showdown in Oak Creek Canyon.

"If he was thinking about how his disappearance was

worrying you," Andy grumbled, "he would have found a way to get in touch with you by now."

That was the thought that kept Lizzy awake at night: the gnawing dread that Philip hadn't gotten in touch with her because he was dead ... or worse.

And, scraping at the corners of her mind, the corrosive fear that perhaps she was being naive about Philip's true allegiance.

Lizzy turned to Ruby and Owen. "I know Andy's not *fine*," she whispered, her voice tight with emotion, "but do you think he's *okay*?"

Owen sighed. "He just needs some time." Then added, almost to himself, "At least I hope that's all he needs."

They were silent for a few moments, then Ruby roused herself. "Well, dinner isn't going to make itself." She got a can opener out of a drawer, snapped it onto the can of sauce, and began twisting the handle with what seemed like unnecessary vigor.

Owen opened the fridge and removed a beer. "Want anything, Pumpkin?"

"Maybe some iced tea," she said.

When Owen had poured her a glass, Lizzy briefly thought of settling down in her sleeping quarters—an air mattress in the living room, next to where Ruby slept on the couch—then decided she'd hang out on the condo's balcony until the mood lightened.

Four people in the condo really wasn't practical, and she had allowed her three apartment-mates to believe that she was staying there because of the possible impact on Philip of her doing anything else. In fact, her primary reason for staying as long as she had was that she felt a responsibility to do what she could to keep Owen, Andy, and Ruby safe. After all, she was equipped with a weapon—the squeeze—that they didn't have.

However, despite Andy's mood, he was in much better physical shape now than when he had first come home from the hospital, and although Owen wasn't a natural bodyguard, Lizzy knew from personal experience that Ruby was.

Lizzy couldn't just keep hanging around Philly hoping that Philip would get in touch. She needed to go looking for him. Baltimore was the most likely place for him to have ended up, assuming he had left the compound. She'd go there and see what she could find out.

And maybe on the way she'd make a side trip to Bethesda, where Philip's girlfriend Olivia was on temporary assignment with the Bureau of Indian Affairs, and see how she was doing.

She got out her phone and dialed Olivia's cell phone number. The call went to voicemail, so she tried Olivia's work number at a D.C.-area office of the BIA.

That call rang to a recorded message: "The person you are calling is no longer available at this number."

No longer available? Olivia had barely started her job at the BIA—where could she be?

Her heart pounding, Lizzy redialed Olivia's cell number—still no answer—and continued redialing it every couple of minutes.

Olivia picked up on the fourth try.

"What's up?" asked Olivia, her voice hovering between irritation and concern. "Are you okay?"

Lizzy could hear what sounded like restaurant noise in the background. "I'm okay. Are *you* okay? I called your office, and the message said it wasn't your number anymore."

"Yeah, I'm not working there anymore. But you called me four times in the last ten minutes. You're saying nothing's wrong at your end?"

Lizzy laughed sheepishly. "Sorry, I sort of panicked when I heard the message. I was just calling to tell you that I'm going to

Baltimore to look for Philip, and I thought I might swing by Bethesda—maybe we could grab lunch."

"You don't need to come to Baltimore," said Olivia. "I'm here." Then she called out, voice aimed away from the phone, "One minute—I'll be right there!"

"You're in Baltimore?" asked Lizzy, surprised. "How long have you been there?"

"About a week. I decided I couldn't just stay in Bethesda waiting for some message from Philip."

Lizzy felt a pang of guilt—wasn't waiting for some message from Philip exactly what she had been doing? "What have you been doing in Baltimore?"

Olivia's voice aimed away from the phone again. "Just one more minute!"

Lizzy heard footsteps on a wood floor, then background noise that suggested Olivia had stepped outside.

"I drove by Billy Chapel's house in Owings Mills a couple of times," said Olivia. "Or, to be more precise, I drove by the property. I looked it up online ... the lot is almost sixteen acres. You can't even see the house from the road. A wall runs along the road, and there's a gate at the driveway. There's always someone at the gate—someone dressed like a gardener, but I suspect it's one of Chapel's goons. There are cameras at the gate, and I think I saw a couple of cameras along the wall as well, so I don't want to drive by it too often. And it wouldn't do any good anyway— there's nothing to see. Unless Chapel assigns Philip as gate guard." She tried for a laugh, but it was clear her heart wasn't in it. She cleared her throat, then continued. "Billy also spends a lot of time at the restaurant he owns in Baltimore—it's called *Charm City Diner*—and at least it's less guarded and more visible." Olivia paused, then continued, "I figured I couldn't just hang around watching who came in and out of the restaurant, so

I got a job at a coffee shop across the street. That's where I am now."

"Doing what?"

"Barista. Server."

"You got a job waiting tables? What about the BIA job?"

"I left it. I figured if I was working that job during the day and spending only a couple of hours in Baltimore in the evenings, it was that much less likely that I'd see Philip."

Olivia had been working at the Bureau of Indian Affairs providing legal support for her fellow Native Americans back in her home state of Arizona. She had said more than once that she felt she had done more good in her short time at the BIA than she had in years back home. "Olivia, that's awful—I know you loved that job."

"I did feel bad leaving them short-handed," Olivia said. Then, with another apparent attempt to lighten the mood, she added, "I waited tables in law school, so at least I'm getting to tap into some past experience."

"I can't believe you've been doing this all on your own! I can help—"

"It's really not necessary. I don't think you coming here is going to make much difference."

Lizzy heard a voice in the background—the speaker must have popped their head out the door—"Olivia, there's a line at the counter."

"Lizzy, I've really got to go," said Olivia. "But the chances that Philip is going to be out and about are almost nil, and we don't need more than one person wasting their time—" Her voice caught, and she cleared her throat. "Also, it wouldn't do Philip any good if Chapel saw you and recognized you from the compound."

"I got my hair cut. I can wear glasses. I can stay out of sight. Plus, if I was there, you could go back to your job."

"That's not an option. It was a temporary assignment. It didn't come with vacation time or leave. And I can't just go back to Arizona without knowing what happened to Philip ... and helping him out if I can."

"Well, I can't stay in Philadelphia for the same reason. I'm coming to Baltimore, and we can decide how I can be most helpful."

Olivia sighed. "Okay, fine. We can talk about a plan when you get here."

5

It was late morning, and Philip lay on his bed, boots off, ankles crossed, fingers interlaced behind his head. His choice was lying on his bed or sitting on it, since the room had no chairs. He shared the room with Donny, the man he had watched beat Lucas, Theo Viklund's head of security, almost to death. Philip assumed the room was not Donny's regular quarters, and that Donny had been put there to keep an eye on him.

When they had first arrived in the room, the only furniture other than the two twin beds was a single dresser.

"You take the bottom drawer, Tonto," Donny said.

Philip couldn't have cared less which drawer he took to store the two changes of clothes he had been issued, but if the dynamics among the men who worked for Chapel were anything like the dynamics of men serving time in prison, he couldn't let that stand. He hoped that the prison rule also applied that whatever happened outside the view of the guards was the business of the inmates, not the warden—the warden in this case being Billy Chapel.

"Like hell," Philip said. "Take the bottom drawer yourself, Donny."

That exchange had resulted in a bruised jaw for Philip and a bloody nose for Donny. It might have escalated further if Billy's lieutenant, Tony, hadn't arrived and told them to knock it the fuck off.

It was the most fun Philip had had since being escorted into Billy Chapel's suite back at the compound.

It was the *only* fun he had had.

Tony made them carry the dresser down to the basement and told them to store their clothes under their beds. With not only no dresser but no phone, no books, no music, no TV—not even a view, because the one window was painted shut and the glass was frosted—Philip passed the time lying on the bed and sorting through his options.

There were always members of Billy's posse around, indoors and out. Having seen what had happened to Lucas, he knew that any escape attempt resulting in him being brought back alive would be worse than him being killed. But even if Philip could figure out how to get away, Billy could take his revenge elsewhere. Billy had encountered Andy McNally at the compound, and as a physician and surgeon, McNally must have an extensive professional presence online. It couldn't be that hard to find out where he lived, and from that find Owen McNally and even Ruby DiMano. Maybe even Lizzy.

No, escape wasn't feasible—at least not without a better plan to protect Lizzy and her allies.

It would be easier to strategize if he had any idea what Billy intended to do with him. He'd love to know if Billy's claim that he was keeping Philip around based on a glowing recommendation from Billy's late business partner, Theo Viklund, was true. He'd give a lot for a dose of Lizzy's mind-reading drug that would work on someone who wasn't the result of Louise Mortensen's experiments. Hell, he'd give even more for a dose of a drug that would give him the squeeze. After seeing what Billy and his men were capable of, he'd be happy to squeeze the whole goddamned lot of them.

Philip heard a heavy tread approaching in the hallway. There was a single sharp rap on the door and, without waiting for a response, Tony stepped in. "Billy wants to see you downstairs." Leaving the door open, he retreated down the hall.

Philip swung his legs off the bed, pulled on his boots, and made his way downstairs to the black-walled command center.

Billy was seated behind the desk, while Donny lounged near a window, striking a pose of studiously casual menace that Philip suspected he practiced in a mirror.

"Phil, I got a little errand for you and Donny," Billy said.

Philip felt a brief flicker of hope. Maybe this would present an opportunity to warn Lizzy and her friends about the danger Billy posed. Any assignment that included Donny was bound to be unpleasant, but while Donny was sadistic, he was also stupid, and Philip couldn't imagine it would be too difficult to slip away from him. And he didn't much care what punishment Chapel meted out to Donny for losing track of his charge.

"Donny," said Billy, "bring one of the 'Slades around back, and I'll send Phil out in a minute."

"Sure thing, Billy," Donny said and left the room.

As if blessed with the ability to read minds himself, Billy said, "You might think this is an opportunity for you to skip town, but just because we don't know where your underage girlfriend Ballard ended up doesn't mean we can't find other people you'd maybe rather not see hurt."

Jesus, did Billy already know about Lizzy, Owen, Andy, and Ruby? Did he know about Olivia, less than an hour away in Bethesda?

"Billy," Philip said, "do you really think it's a smart move to keep doing things that will attract official attention? Every time you do something to keep me in line, you increase the chances that the cops will trace it back to you."

Billy took a few steps toward him, stopping a couple of feet away. "How would they ever track it back to little ol' Billy Chapel in Baltimore?" His tone was teasing, and Philip was unprepared when Billy's hand snapped up and smacked him in the jaw, precisely on the bruise Donny had left. "And don't you ever question a decision I make, Phil."

Forcing his hands to stay at his sides, Philip glared at him.

Billy moved half a foot closer. "Understand?"

"Yeah. I understand."

"And just because I think you could be useful doesn't mean I trust you further than I could throw you. I am always going to find a way to keep you in line. Always."

Philip bit back a retort. "Fine."

Billy stared into Philip's eyes for a moment longer, then turned and strode toward the door. "Shake a leg, Phil," he called back gaily.

Philip followed Billy to the back of the house, then outside, where Donny sat in the driver's seat of an Escalade.

"Keep an eye on Donny for me, will you?" Billy boomed, loud enough to ensure Donny would hear him. "Make sure he doesn't do anything too stupid."

"Nobody's that useful," Philip muttered under his breath.

With a raucous laugh, Billy slapped Philip on the shoulder. "Have fun storming the old folks' home, boys." He turned and disappeared back into the house.

Philip climbed into the passenger seat. "Old folks' home?"

Scowling, Donny turned the key in the ignition. "You'll see."

6

———

Even though Lizzy waited until after the morning rush hour to leave Philadelphia, it still took her two nerve-jangling hours to drive to Baltimore, her mood not improved by the light rain that was falling. She knew she overestimated the ability of any kind of precipitation to make the road slippery, but she couldn't talk herself out of her nervousness.

Her nerves were frayed, and not just by the traffic but by the arguments she had met when she told Owen, Andy, and Ruby her plan to go to Baltimore.

Owen waylaid her in the kitchen. "I should come with you. I could be your chauffeur, we could drive around the city, and you could concentrate on keeping an eye out for Philip. It would be safer than you trying to drive *and* keep an eye out."

"You couldn't spend all your time in the car, and you're too tall to blend into a crowd. Changing your hairstyle and wearing sunglasses isn't going to keep Billy from recognizing you if he sees you."

"Maybe if I lost more weight in a hurry—"

"I said *too tall*. Losing weight isn't going to make you shorter.

Plus, Andy and Ruby need you here. Ruby's focus is on Andy, and they need someone to keep an eye out for Billy."

"And Louise," said Owen.

"You think we still need to worry about Louise? It's not like she has anyone to keep her around here." Lizzy thought with a pang that she herself had killed two of the people who might otherwise have factored into Louise's plans: her husband, Gerard Bonnay, and her enforcer, George Millard. "Maybe once she ran away from the compound she just kept on running."

"Let's hope so." Owen ran his hand over his hair. "I hope Billy Chapel and Louise both have better things to do with their time than pester us."

Ruby waited to make her pitch to Lizzy until that night, whispering from the bed she had made up on the couch next to Lizzy's air mattress. "I could come with you. I know how much you hate highway driving—"

Lizzy smiled. "Uncle Owen already tried that argument on me."

"Billy Chapel doesn't know what I look like. That could be a plus."

"Yes, that *could* be a plus theoretically, but let's not give him a chance to figure out that you're part of Team Lizzy."

"I could stay off his radar. And I'm good in a pinch."

Lizzy laughed softly. "That's for sure. But that's why Andy and Uncle Owen need you here."

She almost expected Andy to make his own pitch to accompany her, but he must have realized that he wasn't in any condition to be of assistance.

When Lizzy arrived at the Baltimore block that was home to both the coffeeshop where Olivia worked, *Chesaperk*, and, directly across the street, Billy Chapel's restaurant, *Charm City*, she found that neither business had a dedicated parking area. The restaurant offered valet parking, but Lizzy would have to park on the street and walk to the coffee shop in full view of anyone watching from the restaurant. She considered the nod she had made toward a disguise: in addition to her recently cut and dyed hair, she was wearing a baseball cap, sunglasses, and a baggy T-shirt and jeans that added a few pounds to her slender frame. It wouldn't stand up to a direct encounter with Billy Chapel, but from a distance it should do. As she hurried from her parking space to the coffee shop, she kept her head down and fiddled with her glasses, further obscuring her face from any observers.

Lizzy entered *Chesaperk* to the cheerful jingle of a bell. Directly ahead of her was the counter, behind which stood the elaborate machinery of gourmet coffee-making. Further back, she could see a rudimentary kitchen. To her left and stretching toward the back of the shop was a room with mismatched chairs and tables where patrons chatted or tapped the keyboards of their laptops in earbud-protected cocoons.

Olivia was behind the counter, her long black hair in a braid, a delicate turquoise pendant at her throat. Lizzy assumed Olivia was near Philip's age—around thirty—but despite her unlined skin and ramrod-straight posture, Lizzy always thought of her as a little older. Olivia and Philip were both equally serious—Lizzy had caught herself wondering if they would have been better suited to partners who were more demonstrative—but Olivia's demeanor was a little more careful, a little more guarded. Certainly Olivia was more of a rule-follower than Philip was. In fact, Lizzy thought with a smile, there were few people who were less of a rule-follower than Philip. Lizzy suspected that Olivia's demeanor was both a result of and an asset in her legal work, and she felt a pang of guilt that she herself was ultimately responsible for the fact that Olivia had felt compelled to leave her job at the BIA to take orders in a coffee shop.

"Hello," Olivia said, "Can I—" She raised her eyebrows and smiled. "A new look, I see."

Lizzy grinned. "It doesn't pay to stick with one look for too long."

Olivia came around the counter and gave Lizzy a hug. "I have to say I'm glad to have someone here I can talk with." She released Lizzy and pointed to an empty table with a hand-lettered *Reserved* sign on. "I saved the table by the window for you. You sit down, and I'll bring you a drink. What do you want?"

"Herbal tea?"

"We have that, but it's just standard stuff. The coffee here is really excellent—you should try that."

"Sure—what do you recommend?"

"How about a latte?"

"Sounds good."

Lizzy sat down while Olivia returned to the counter. Several more customers had come in, and Olivia began taking their orders.

Lizzy looked across the street at Billy's restaurant. It was not at all what she had expected based on the name. *Charm City Diner* arched in metal cursive script between a pair of brick columns, at the foot of which enormous wooden planters over-flowed with red, orange, yellow, and purple petunias. Beyond the entrance was a courtyard roofed with strands of lights and a number of high-top tables occupied by a robust lunchtime crowd.

She was engrossed watching people come and go from *Charm City*, none of whom looked like Billy or one of his men, when she jumped at a voice right beside her.

"Lizzy?"

She looked up to find a woman standing next to her table holding a giant coffee cup.

Lizzy looked nervously over at Olivia, who gave her a thumbs up. "Suki's the owner," she called over from the counter.

Lizzy turned back to the woman. "Yes, that's me."

Suki was wearing a low-cut black tank top that revealed an elaborate bird tattoo stretching across her upper chest with a pattern of feathers running down each arm to her wrists. Her hair was long on top, but shaved over her ears, which were decorated with a half dozen small silver studs. She set the cup down in front of Lizzy. "There you go—the best you'll get in Baltimore."

"Thanks." Lizzy hesitated. "I like your tattoos."

Suki grinned. "I also know the best tattoo artist in Baltimore. You want one?"

Lizzy laughed. "I don't think so."

"Just a little one." Suki struck a contemplative pose and regarded Lizzy. "Maybe a Zuni bear, like your necklace."

Lizzy fingered the pendant—a gift from Owen. "If I ever did get a tattoo, that's the design I'd like."

"Well, you let me know if you change your mind. I'll make sure my guy does a good job for you."

Lizzy looked around the coffee shop. "This is a nice place."

Suki laughed. "Don't say that until you've tried the wares. Want a biscotti? Homemade ... and the first one's on the house."

"Don't pass up that offer," said Olivia.

Lizzy smiled. "Sure, that would be great."

While Suki returned to the counter to get the biscotti, Lizzy sipped the latte. She had never had a latte before—she generally drank tea rather than coffee—but she could imagine developing a taste for it. It was less bitter than the coffee Owen and Andy brewed, and sweet enough, even without any sugar. The biscotti Suki brought over wrapped in a piece of wax paper was just as good.

Lizzy sat back, nibbling on the biscotti, and watched Olivia make a drink that involved a lot of noise and steam from the huge stainless-steel machine behind the counter. Once the steam subsided, the other sounds of the coffee shop reemerged: not only the hum of conversation of other patrons and the click of fingers on keyboards but also an old song she recognized from one of Owen's playlists: Crosby, Stills, Nash, and Young. The walls were decorated with a surprisingly pleasing combination of old Japanese movie posters and antique needlepoint samplers.

She thought she'd enjoy working at a place like *Chesaperk*. But she could never apply for a real job. The ID that showed a false name and reflected her age as twenty-one might get her access to casino poker tables, but it wouldn't pass muster on a job application, especially because it didn't come backed by a social security number. And if she gave a potential employer her real name, it wouldn't be long until her presence hit the radar of law enforcement in Philadelphia.

When Olivia had cleared the line at the counter, she joined Lizzy at the table and looked out the window. "Billy and his men often show up when the lunch or dinner crowd is thinning out," she said, her voice low. "They all drive Escalades. They all look the same to me, but Suki says that the one Billy comes in is the top-of-the line model."

Lizzy glanced toward where Suki stood behind the counter, chatting with a newly arrived customer. "How much does she know about why we're here?"

"Nothing from me. But it seems like everyone on the block keeps a nervous eye on who comes and goes at *Charm City*. I thought today you should just keep an eye out to see if you recognize anyone."

"Okay."

Olivia straightened the sugar packets in their holder. "Do you have a place to stay?"

"I can stay in the Caravan."

"That's silly. I'm renting a motel room nearby—you can stay with me."

"I don't mind sleeping in the Caravan. I've done it a lot."

Olivia raised an eyebrow, and Lizzy realized that she was probably thinking of the fact that Lizzy and Philip traveled from Arizona to the East Coast in the van. "I know you have," Olivia said, "but it can't be that comfortable. You're welcome to stay with me ... or, if you want more privacy, you can get a separate room. The motel is the cheapest one I could find, but it's clean and quiet."

The bell on the door jingled, and Olivia stood up. "I better get back to work. Just give a wave when you need a refill."

"Okay." Lizzy dropped her voice. "How long can I stay at this table before I overstay my welcome?"

"As long as you want. Suki won't mind—I'll bring you another drink every hour or so." She smiled. "And more biscotti."

As Olivia returned to the counter, Lizzy wondered how many lattes and biscotti she could afford before she'd have to find a local casino and "replenish the coffers," as Owen would say.

7

It had taken Philip and Donny a little less than two hours to get from Billy's Owings Mills house to their destination: Letort, Pennsylvania.

Donny had pulled the Escalade off the two-lane state highway into the parking lot of Cedar Grove Care Center. The paint on the sign in front was peeling, the drive was overdue for a repaving, and several of the lights illuminating the small parking lot were out. A fine rain misted the air and speckled the windshield.

"Shit," muttered Donny, stopping with a jerk in front of the building's entrance. He gestured toward a tan Toyota Prius. "Pearson's here."

"Who's Pearson?"

"Wouldn't you like to know," Donny sneered.

Philip rolled his eyes.

That had been almost eight hours earlier. Other than each man taking a break to relieve himself in the neighboring corn-field, they had remained in the Escalade, watching the Cedar Grove entrance from a corner of the parking lot, Donny muttering profanities related to the mysterious Pearson. At least Donny didn't feel the need to engage in conversation.

There was surprisingly little activity: only a handful of people dressed in scrubs came and went during what must have been a shift change, and no one who looked like a visitor arrived.

Shortly after sunset, just as the rain spluttered to a stop and as Philip was weighing the pros and cons of suggesting to Donny that they get something to eat, Donny sat forward.

"About fucking time," he said, his tone excited.

Someone had come out of the facility: a Black man in his mid-sixties, medium height and slender, his head shaved and with a close-cropped mustache and goatee. He headed for the tan Prius, climbed in, and drove away.

Donny removed the key from the ignition, pocketed it, and turned to Philip. "Stay here." He climbed out of the Escalade and jogged across the parking lot to the front door.

When Donny had disappeared inside, Philip popped open the glove compartment—it contained the owner's manual for the Escalade and a jumble of takeout menus from Baltimore-area restaurants—and felt under the front seats—a repository for an empty Red Bull can and a wad of paper towels stained with some reddish-brown substance. He returned the detritus to under the seat and wiped his hands on his jeans. He felt under the dashboard and encountered a clip that he imagined might be used to hold a gun, but it was empty.

He was wondering if he'd have time to check the back of the vehicle when Donny reappeared and strode toward the vehicle, his expression smug.

"Mission accomplished," Donny said as he climbed into the driver's seat.

"I hope I'm not supposed to understand what that means," said Philip.

"I'll tell you what you need to know. You just have to do what I tell you." Donny started up the Escalade and entered another Letort address in the GPS. "Now we just need to go share what I got with the dearly beloved."

Fifteen minutes later, Donny slowed as they passed a tidy brick rancher on a generously sized lot. A porch light illuminated a row of carefully trimmed bushes under a bay window, recently mowed grass, and a freshly blacktopped drive leading to a single-car garage. The house itself was dark. Behind it was a corn field and beyond that, the monotonous monstrosity of an enormous distribution warehouse.

"That's Richard Pearson's house," said Donny.

"And Richard Pearson's the dearly beloved?"

"You know it." Donny scowled. "Looks like nobody's home."

Donny turned into a parking lot a few properties beyond the house—a closed service station—and pulled the Escalade around to the back of the building. He turned off the ignition and swung his door open. "Let's go."

Philip got out and followed Donny to the back of the service station property and then along the edge of the field that backed the intervening lots. Philip kept a close eye on the houses—although the sun had set some time before, there was still some residual light in the sky, and they were far from invisible. When they reached Pearson's lot without attracting any obvious notice, Philip wasn't sure whether to be relieved or disappointed.

The house was as dark from the back as it was from the front, and Donny shook his head. "Damn, where'd he go? I figured he'd head home after visiting wifey." Without waiting for a response, he gestured for Philip to follow him, and they crossed the yard to an enclosed breezeway that connected the garage to the house, a storm door providing access from the backyard.

Donny gestured to the door. "You're the ex-con," he said. "Get us in."

Philip depressed the latch and swung the door open.

Donny flushed. "Only hicks out in the goddamn boonies wouldn't lock their doors."

"Now what?"

Donny's flush was replaced by a grin. "We wait for Professor Pearson to get home." He stepped into the breezeway, scanned the space, and gestured to a couple of webbed lawn chairs collapsed and leaning against the wall of the breezeway. "Set one of those up for me."

Philip unfolded one and set it on the concrete floor. "There you go, champ. If you need help with anything else, just let me know."

Donny glowered at him and dropped into the chair.

Philip leaned against the wall, arms crossed, and looked out across the back yard to the field beyond.

Half a minute ticked by, then Donny said, "Curious about what I did at the old folks' home?"

"I don't think it was an 'old folks' home'—it looked like a rehab facility to me—but, sure, what did you do?"

Donny got out his phone, tapped, and turned the screen toward Philip.

Philip crossed the breezeway and reached for the phone.

"Uh, uh, uh," Donny said, shaking a finger. "No touching."

Philip sighed and bent down to look at the image on the phone.

It was a photo of a sixty-ish Black woman lying in a hospital bed. Her torso and head were elevated and encased in a white plastic brace with a chin cup, all of it held in place by an elaborate web of black straps. Her eyes were closed, her features relaxed.

From the side of the photo, a hand extended, holding a gun an inch from the woman's temple.

Philip straightened and glared at Donny. "What the hell?"

Donny grinned. "Pretty cool, huh?"

"What did you do that for?"

"Why do you think, you dumb fuck? Because Billy said to."

"Billy told you to wait until some woman in a rehab facility was asleep, point a gun at her head, and take a picture?" Philip was pretty certain Donny hadn't actually pulled the trigger. He thought he would have heard a gunshot, even in the parking lot, and someone certainly would have raised an alarm.

"Actually, the plan was for me to take the picture from the hallway, but when I got there, she was asleep, so I figured this would be cooler." He held the phone up again for Philip's benefit.

Philip kept his stony gaze on Donny's face.

Donny shrugged, put the phone in his pocket, and said with exaggerated patience, "Billy wanted the picture because we need some ammunition for our upcoming conversation with Pearson. We need to be able to show him we can get to his wife if he doesn't cooperate."

"You—sorry, you and Billy—think it's smart to walk into a healthcare facility and wave around a firearm?"

Donny shrugged. "No one was there. That place is like a ghost town."

"Maybe she wasn't really asleep. Maybe she was faking and knew exactly what was going on."

Donny crossed his arms. "She wasn't faking." He grinned. "I would know if a woman was faking."

"I doubt that. But even if she wasn't faking, they might have you on security video."

"Did you see that place? Do you really think it has some fancy security set-up?"

"It doesn't have to be fancy—"

"Listen—" Philip could almost hear the terms Donny was ticking through in his mind—he had heard them all—but Donny thought better of using one of them. "—*Phil*, Billy has it all worked out. The place has a system installed but it's been on the fritz for months." Donny got his phone out, tapped, and started scrolling. "Plus, you're here to do what I tell you—not to ask a bunch of dumbass questions."

The light on the phone was turned up high, and Philip thought that when Pearson pulled into the driveway, he might see the glow coming from the breezeway, but Philip wasn't about to point that out to Donny. He returned to his position next to the door leading to the back yard and gazed across the cornfield to the lights of the warehouse.

8

Lizzy watched as the third Escalade of the evening pulled up to the valet station. As with the first two, the windows were tinted, and now that it was dark enough that the streetlights were on, it was impossible to see who was inside. Her stomach tightened as she waited to see who would emerge from the vehicle.

As before, neither occupant was Billy Chapel, although the style of their clothing was similar to his. They headed for the entrance, one slowing as he passed the valet station—evidently to insult the valet, based on the young man's angry flush—then passed through the courtyard and disappeared into the restaurant.

For lack of anything better to do, Lizzy tapped a note about the vehicle's arrival time into her phone.

She had been at *Chesaperk* all day, and the caffeine jitters from three lattes were finally wearing off. She kept expecting Suki to ask her to vacate the table, which was obviously prime real estate, but Suki didn't seem to mind. She had even brought Lizzy dessert on the house, although Lizzy had paid for the turkey and brie sandwich she had for dinner.

Lizzy had expressed surprise that *Chesaperk* stayed open so late, and Suki explained that a lot of *Charm City* diners came to the coffee shop for dessert. But the last patrons had finally left a few minutes earlier, and Suki and Olivia were closing up.

Lizzy had offered to help sweep or wipe down tables, but Suki waved her back to the table. "It will be a cold day in hell when I let my customers help with clean-up."

Lizzy had just looked up from her notetaking when yet another Escalade pulled up. A middle-aged, dark-haired man climbed out of the front passenger seat, waved away the valet, and opened the back passenger door.

Out stepped Billy Chapel.

Her fingers tightened on her phone, and her arm gave a sympathetic throb where Billy had cut her with a broken champagne bottle.

She looked over to where Olivia stood at the register. She must have seen Billy through the store's glass front door, because she hurried over to Lizzy's table, reaching it just as Billy disappeared into the restaurant.

Olivia sat down across from Lizzy and stared out the window. "The guy with Billy is Tony, his ... lieutenant, I guess you might say," she whispered. "You didn't see him at the compound, did you?"

"I don't think so. I saw some of Billy's men after they broke in, but only from a distance."

"Would any of them recognize you?"

"I don't think so. They would only have seen me at a distance, too, with different hair and clothes and no glasses."

Suki emerged from the back of the coffee shop, caught sight of the Escalade, and scowled. "I hope those guys aren't in the mood for dessert." She turned the sign on the door to *Closed* and flipped the lock.

"They never let the valets park the car Billy arrives in," Olivia said, her voice lowered, "and one of his men—usually Tony—always escorts him inside."

"Do they think someone's going to attack him on the sidewalk?" Lizzy asked, skeptical.

"It happened once."

Lizzy's eyebrows rose. "Really? Some competitor?"

"No. The wife of some guy Billy's men had killed. Tony beat her almost to death, and," Olivia continued with a grimace, "because she was carrying a gun, the court ruled that it was self-defense, even though Tony kept beating her after she dropped the gun."

Lizzy turned back to the window and watched as the Escalade glided away. "He does have a lot of guys guarding him."

Olivia squeezed the bridge of her nose. "Always someone with him." She dropped her voice almost to a whisper. "Never Philip." She drew a deep breath and looked out the window. "I don't know if that's a good sign or a bad sign."

"Olivia," Suki called over from the counter, "you guys can get going if you want. I'll finish cashing out."

"Thanks, Suki," Olivia called back, then said to Lizzy, "Once Billy shows up, there's usually not much more to see. We might as well head out."

"Okay."

"I'll just get my stuff out of my locker." Olivia got up and disappeared into the back of the shop.

Lizzy stood, put her hat on, and slipped her sunglasses in her knapsack, since wearing them after dark would be more likely to attract attention than divert it. She was examining one of the antique samplers—an impressive effort signed in silk thread *Eleanor Crew 7*—when she heard the front door rattle and Suki mutter, "Oh for God's sake," then, louder, "We're closed!"

Lizzy moved so she could see who was at the door. It was Tony.

"Billy sent me over," he called through the door. Before Lizzy could duck out of sight, he spotted her in the seating area and gestured toward the doorknob. "Come on, open up. Won't take a minute."

Lizzy cast a panicked glanced toward Suki, whose mouth was pressed in a thin line.

"Fine," Suki yelled, then, lower, to Lizzy, "I'll take care of it."

As Suki unlocked the door, Lizzy tugged the brim of her baseball cap lower. Had Tony been one of the men who stormed the compound? Had he been one of the men firing at the helicopter as she tried to get Andy aboard? It wasn't like she could remember individual faces from among the dozen gunmen.

"Hey, Tony," Suki said, her tone cool, her hand on the partially open door. "What's up?"

Tony pushed past her and stepped inside. "Billy wants a nitro cold brew."

"It'll take a couple of minutes—I'll bring it over when it's ready."

"Nah, I'll wait for it." His eyes drifted idly to Lizzy, and she was relieved that there was no flicker of recognition in them. "You're new."

"I don't work here," Lizzy said. "I was just getting ready to leave. They're closing."

Tony shrugged. "Folks stay open for Billy Chapel."

Olivia appeared from the back room.

Tony stuffed his hands in his pockets. "You're new, too," he said to her. "And you must work here, coming out from the back and all."

"I'll get your cold brew," Suki said to Tony and disappeared into the back room.

"We'll be going," Olivia called after her.

Tony's eyes drifted from Olivia to Lizzy and back. "You guys friends?"

"Yes." Olivia beckoned to Lizzy. "Come on, we'll go out the back."

"Girlfriends?" asked Tony.

"We're *friends*," said Olivia.

Tony held up his hands. "Hey, no offense—just wondered. You know, with—" He jerked his head toward the back where Suki was working. "—just thought she might be inviting more of her 'friends' to come round here. I got no problem with it." He stuffed his hands in his pockets. "You got a boyfriend?"

"That's none of your business," Olivia said briskly. She turned to Lizzy. "Let's go."

Lizzy followed Olivia into the back, where Suki was dispensing a creamy coffee concoction into a takeaway cup.

"Want us to wait around until he goes?" Olivia whispered to Suki.

"No," said Suki, obviously irritated but apparently unworried. "It's fine. You guys head out."

"Okay, thanks. See you tomorrow."

They went out the back door, outside of which were two tiny parking spaces.

Lizzy pointed to the purple Jeep occupying one of the spaces. "Suki's?"

"How did you guess?" Olivia said, with an attempt at a smile. "Mine's the rental Corolla. Where are you parked?"

"Just down the street."

"I'll give you a ride."

They climbed into Olivia's car.

"Why do you think he was asking if you had a boyfriend?" Lizzy asked.

Olivia started up the car. "Who knows. They're like dogs marking their territory."

Lizzy laughed, then subsided when Olivia shot her a look. "Sorry. It was just a funny visual."

When they reached the Caravan, Olivia asked, "You want to follow me to the motel?"

"Sounds good."

"There's an extra bed in my room—more comfortable than the van."

And probably safer, thought Lizzy. "Yeah, I think I'll take you up on that offer."

Lizzy followed the Corolla, grateful but unsurprised that Olivia drove at or below the speed limit—Lizzy always stuck to the speed limit—and grateful that she had offered to share her room. The encounter with Tony, as benign as it has been, had rattled Lizzy. She was quite sure he hadn't recognized her—he had seemed more interested in Olivia—but she couldn't get past the idea that he represented one degree of separation between her and Billy Chapel.

9

———

Full dark had fallen when a car pulled into the driveway of the Letort house, its headlights sweeping through the breezeway's storm door.

Donny jumped to his feet and stuffed his phone in his pocket. "Put the chair back the way it was."

As Philip folded the chair Donny had been sitting in, the garage door rumbled open.

"Stand on that side of the door," Donny said, "back against the wall. I'll tell you what to do."

Philip took up his position, and Donny mirrored him on the other side of the door.

The car door thunked closed, and the garage door rumbled down.

A moment later, Richard Pearson came through the door, a plastic grocery bag in one hand, a ring of keys in the other.

Donny stepped up behind him and looped his arm around Richard's throat.

Richard let out a squawk. He dropped the keys and the bag, sending two oranges rolling across the floor, and tried to pull Donny's arm away from his throat.

"Shut up, old man," growled Donny. "Phil, get the keys and unlock the door."

"Sure, Donny." Philip figured if Donny was throwing his name around in front of Pearson, he'd return the favor. He retrieved the keys from the floor, sorted through them until he found the Kwikset key that matched the door's Kwikset lock, and unlocked the door. He stepped into the kitchen.

Donny followed, steering Richard in front of him.

The kitchen looked like it had been remodeled in the nineties and maintained in perfect condition ever since. White ruffled curtains with cheerful yellow tiebacks framed the over-the-sink window, complementing the yellow laminate countertop and white-and-yellow vinyl flooring. Painted yellow flowers decorated the white porcelain knobs on the cabinets. A tea towel featuring a daisy hung over the handle of the white electric range.

"Where's the basement?" Donny asked Richard.

Richard looked too terrified to realize he had been asked a question, much less to answer it.

Philip pointed to a door opposite the sink. "I'm guessing down there."

"Check it out," said Donny.

"What am I checking it out for?"

"To make sure it's the basement, moron." Donny grinned. "And to see if it's appropriate for what we need to do."

"I have no idea what we need to do—how am I supposed to tell if the basement is appropriate?"

"We just need to have a little conversation with the professor."

Richard stared wide-eyed at Philip, his fingers gripped ineffectually onto Donny's beefy forearm.

Philip opened the door and flipped on a light, illuminating a flight of green shag-carpeted stairs. "Yup. Basement." He turned back to Donny. "Why don't you take your arm off his neck, at least for the trip down the stairs. He's not going anywhere with you behind him."

After a moment, Donny released his hold on Richard's neck and gave him a little shove toward the basement door. "Don't try anything funny, Professor."

Philip hurried down the stairs in front of Richard, wanting to keep some distance just in case the panicked man decided it was a good idea to try to push one of his assailants down the stairs.

A ping pong table stood in the middle of the basement. Along one wall was a neat workbench under a pegboard hung with tools. Another wall held totes arranged on plastic shelving. Dusty exercise equipment occupied one corner. In another, two heavily padded recliners faced an ancient TV.

Donny pointed at one of the chairs. "Sit."

Philip thought that forcing Richard to sit in a recliner wasn't creating the threatening atmosphere Donny probably was going for, but clearly having two men appear in his home and force him into the basement was intimidation enough. Richard hurried to the chair and sat.

Donny stepped to within a foot of him and leaned over, his face inches from Richard's.

"Someone needs you to do a favor for them."

"Who?" Richard looked from Donny to Philip. "Him?"

Donny straightened, looking disgusted. "No, not him. You ever heard of Billy Chapel?"

"The name sounds familiar ..."

"Billy Chapel of Baltimore?"

Richard's eyes widened. "*That* Billy Chapel? What could he want from me?"

Donny looked satisfied that Chapel's name had elicited the desired reaction. "He'll tell you himself. We're going to take you to him now. But the reason I wanted to have this little chat with you first is to let you know that if you aren't completely cooperative, you aren't the only one who will pay the price."

Richard paled, and his eyes darted again from Donny to Philip and back. "What do you mean?"

Donny grinned. "Let me show you." He got out his phone, tapped, and turned the screen toward Richard. "Because I'll use that gun on your wife if you don't cooperate—and the first shot might not be a kill shot."

Richard looked at the photo, and his expression froze. He looked up at Donny, over at Philip, and back to Donny.

Then he launched himself out of his chair and drove his shoulder into Donny's stomach.

Donny, his face a comic mask of surprise, let out a whoosh of air and staggered back into the ping pong table, which slid across the floor and banged into the knotty pine-paneled wall.

There were a few seconds where only Philip stood between Richard and the stairway, and if Richard had tackled him with the same ferocity he had displayed in his attack on Donny, Philip wasn't sure he could have stayed on his feet.

But the man's goal was clearly not to get out of the basement, but to punish Donny for threatening his wife.

As Donny tried to regain his balance, Richard drove a fist into his chin.

Donny grabbed the edge of the ping pong table, pushed himself upright, and drew back his fist, ready to piston it into Richard's face.

By that time, Philip had reached Richard. He grabbed a handful of the back of Richard's shirt and yanked him backwards, causing Donny's fist to miss Richard's cheek by an inch, and once again sending Donny off-balance.

Philip propelled Richard away from Donny. Standing between the two men he barked, "Stop it!"

Both men froze.

Philip turned to Richard. "You think beating Donny up is going to keep him from going back to Cedar Grove and shooting your wife?" He turned to Donny. "And you think Billy wants Pearson to show up in Baltimore beaten and bloody?"

Donny flexed his fingers. "Was just going to teach him a lesson," he said sullenly.

"Billy doesn't need you teaching him a lesson. He needs you to bring him to Baltimore. In one piece." Then, in case Richard misread Philip's position as support, he turned back to him. "And if there *are* any lessons to be taught—to you or your wife— Billy Chapel will do it. And trust me, you don't want that."

Richard's expression of desperate hopefulness morphed into a loathing of Philip matching his loathing of Donny.

Philip turned back to Donny. "What now, Donny?"

Donny made an exaggerated display of shrugging his jacket back into position on his broad shoulders. "We'll take him out back, to the Escalade. And, Professor, if you make a sound ..." Donny put a finger pistol to his temple and jerked the thumb trigger. "Bye-bye, wifey."

10

———————

The next morning, with a pleasant breeze blowing off the harbor and a few fluffy clouds dotting the otherwise clear sky, Lizzy and Olivia returned to *Chesaperk* for Olivia's ten o'clock shift. Lizzy ordered a latte—decaf, this time—and a chocolate croissant at the counter. The coffee shop was busy, and the table at the window was taken, so Lizzy took the only available table, near the back. She wasn't sure what she'd do until *Charm City* opened at noon, and she didn't feel like spending another day watching people other than Philip come and go from the restaurant. At least the coffee shop was a pleasant place to formulate a plan.

While Olivia wiped down a recently vacated table nearby, Lizzy opened her map app. She was examining the area around Billy's Owings Mills home when she heard the jingle of the shop's front door and then, from near the counter in the adjoining room, a drawl that froze her blood.

"You must be Suki—am I right? Glad to finally meet the person behind those great nitro cold brews. Wouldn't mind one right now to get me through the morning."

Olivia shot a look at Lizzy, her eyebrows raised in a question she didn't have to verbalize. *Billy Chapel?*

Lizzy nodded and scanned the space frantically. As long as Billy stayed by the counter, he couldn't see her, but if he wandered into the room where she sat, he couldn't miss her. To get to either the front or back doors, she'd have to walk right by him.

"Thought I'd come over and fetch one myself for a change," Billy said. "Check the place out. Maybe meet some of the staff."

Lizzy jumped up from the table and hurried over to the restrooms at the back of the seating area and tried the door of the women's room. Locked.

"My man Tony was over here last night," Billy continued. "Well, you know—you're the one who let him in—and he told me you have a new waitress."

Lizzy and Olivia exchanged an alarmed look.

"New? I don't know about that," said Suki, clearly irritated.

Olivia gestured urgently toward the men's room door.

Lizzy stepped over to the men's restroom. Also locked.

"Maybe just the first time Tony's seen her," said Billy. "Not a local, was his guess."

"I don't know of anyone like that," said Suki, her voice raised slightly, as if wanting Olivia, in the next room, to hear.

"Well, you won't mind if I just take a look around, do you?"

"It's not necessary ..." began Suki, but Lizzy heard Billy's tread headed toward the seating area.

Olivia dropped the rag on the table and hurried toward the door to the counter area, reaching it just as Billy reached it from the other side. From where Lizzy stood, pressed to the wall next to the restroom doors, she could just see his profile and the swell of his wide chest. She realized she had left her knapsack at her table.

"Hey," Billy said, obviously delighted, "I believe this is the girl Tony told me about!"

A few patrons looked up, either amused by Billy's enthusiasm or annoyed by his use of the word *girl*.

"Hello," said Olivia. Would Billy hear the tremble Lizzy could perceive?

Billy stuck out his hand. "I'm Billy."

Olivia took his hand reluctantly. "Olivia." She took a half step toward him, obviously trying to herd him back toward the counter area. "I'm sure Suki will have your drink ready in just a minute."

He didn't move.

"So, Liv," he said, "been working here long?" Lizzy's stomach clenched at Billy's use of a nickname for Olivia that normally only Philip used. She wished the squeeze was something she could summon on demand rather than a reaction to an imminent threat.

"No, not long," said Olivia.

"I own the place across the street," said Billy. "*Charm City Diner.*"

"Congratulations."

"It's a nice place. You know what 'charm city' is?"

"No."

"Nickname for Baltimore."

"Ah."

Silence again, this time broken by Olivia. "It doesn't look like what I think of as a diner."

"No, that was the marketing guy's idea. What's the phrase he used ...?"

"Under promise and over deliver?"

Billy snorted out a laugh. "That, too, but no. *Elevated nostalgia* is what he called it." He shook his head in mock annoyance. "Those goddamned marketing guys have some fancy term for everything."

"Yes. Would you like to check out the pastries we have available? If you want to come over to the counter—"

"Listen, I'm always looking to upscale my staff. You ever waited tables? Bartended?"

A few disapproving looks from the patrons indicated that they were more surprised than Lizzy that Billy Chapel would try to poach *Chesaperk's* staff right in the middle of the coffee shop.

Lizzy saw Olivia's gaze slide over Billy's shoulder, toward where Suki must be standing. "Yes, to both," she said.

"Stop by the restaurant," he said. "The manager will give you a trial shift or two. Tell him Billy sent you. In fact, if you stop by today, we could give you a shift this evening." He laughed again. "There might be a little added bonus in it for you."

"And what would that be?"

"A little surprise. I love surprises."

Billy's footsteps receded back toward the front of the shop. "Don't bother with that cold brew, Suki," he called. "I got what I wanted." The bell on the door jingled.

Lizzy moved so she could see through the front window but stayed far enough back to avoid notice by anyone outside.

Tony was waiting just outside the coffee shop, and he and Billy crossed the street to *Charm City* and disappeared inside.

Lizzy joined Olivia and Suki at the counter. "What was that all about?" she whispered.

"That's what I was wondering," said Suki, her arms crossed, her features tight.

"I have no idea," said Olivia.

"If you just ignore him," said Suki, "he'll probably forget about it."

"You just said that's the first time he's ever come in," said Olivia.

Suki looked uncomfortable. "Yeah ..."

"So he's not likely to forget about an offer he made a special trip to make," said Olivia.

Suki looked out the glass front door toward the restaurant. "I suppose that's true. What are we going to do?"

"We?" said Olivia.

Suki's gaze returned to Olivia. "We can come up with some cover story—some explanation of why you can't take the job."

Olivia was silent, and Suki's eyes narrowed. "You weren't asking around at *Charm City* about a job, were you?"

"No."

"But you're thinking about his offer."

"It would be ..."

Suki crossed her arms and raised her eyebrows. "Yes?"

"... convenient," said Olivia, looking resigned.

"Was this your plan all along? To hang out at *Chesaperk* until something better came along. Until—" Suki glanced toward the seating area and dropped her voice. "Until Billy fucking Chapel waltzed in here and offered you a job?"

"Suki, how would I possibly—"

"And I notice you've been awfully interested in what was going on over there." Suki's eyes slid to Lizzy and then back to Olivia. "And you've had your little mascot here keeping an eye out, too."

Lizzy's eyebrows rose. "Mascot? What's that supposed to mean?"

The three jumped at the jingle of the front door, but it was just a mother dressed for yoga, a toddler on her hip.

Suki dropped her arms and stepped to the counter. "Good morning!" she said, a little too enthusiastically. "Welcome to *Chesaperk!*"

Suki took the woman's order, and Olivia made the double espresso to go while Lizzy stood awkwardly to one side, wondering if it would be rude to go back to her table, and if she really cared if it was rude, considering Suki had called her a *mascot*.

When the woman had left with her espresso, Suki, her features arranged into polite neutrality, said to Olivia, "Of course, I don't want to lose you, but that's not the only reason I'm saying this: Steer clear of Billy Chapel. You've heard enough of the stories to know why." She disappeared into the back room.

Olivia, her expression grim, gestured Lizzy back into the adjoining room and followed her to the table where, Lizzy was relieved to see, her knapsack was undisturbed.

Lizzy sat down, and Olivia sat across from her.

Lizzy dropped her voice. "Maybe you shouldn't keep working at *Chesaperk* now that Billy knows you're here."

"But what does he really know?" Olivia's features twisted in irritation. "I'm guessing Tony mentioned he had seen an honest-to-God Indian working at *Chesaperk*, and Billy thought I'd be an exotic addition to the waitstaff at *Charm City*."

"Well, whatever the reason, I don't think you should stay here. In fact, maybe if you went back to Bethesda now, you could get your job back."

Olivia crossed her arms and regarded Lizzy. "Are you kidding? I'm pretty much guaranteed a job at the place we're most likely to see Philip, and you think I should just go back to the office?"

"Olivia, you can't take a job at *Charm City*!"

"It's not dangerous—Chapel doesn't even know who I am. And bartending is perfect. The men who work for him hang out at the restaurant, and bartenders, no matter how exotic, eventually become invisible—who knows what I might overhear." She uncrossed her arms and leaned forward. "But you should definitely leave. I never expected Chapel to come into *Chesaperk*, and if I'm working at *Charm City*, there's really no reason for you to hang around." She raised her hand to head off Lizzy's protest. "In fact, right now I'm just an interesting curiosity for his restaurant, but if he or one of his men sees us together and recognizes you, having you around might make it more dangerous for me. You should go back to Philly and keep an eye on Owen and Andy and Ruby."

Lizzy considered and rejected arguments against this plan, but finally sighed and said, "Okay, I'll head out for now. But if you need anything, I'll come right back." She thought of her conversation with Ruby and marshaled a smile. "I can be useful in a pinch."

11

Philip sat in the passenger seat of the Escalade, parked in the alley that ran behind Billy's restaurant. Donny was in the driver's seat, Richard in back.

He, Donny, and Richard had arrived back at the Owings Mills house the previous night. Tony had taken Richard away, ostensibly to a bedroom where Richard could sleep. Philip hoped the actual destination wasn't the concrete-floored and soundproofed basement.

He was relieved when Richard had appeared that morning, looking exhausted but apparently unharmed, to be bundled into the vehicle to which Philip had been summoned.

They had been waiting for almost an hour, Donny scoffing at Philip's suggestion that they shut down the car while they waited, when Billy arrived, trailed by Tony.

"I want to talk to Phil," Billy said to Tony.

Although Philip's window was down, and he could hear Billy perfectly well, he waited for Tony to come to the Escalade.

"The boss wants to talk with you."

Philip climbed out and went to where Billy stood a few dozen feet away, idly kicking a battered recycling container, evidently pleased by the *thump ... thump* his heavy-soled Doc Martens made on the dented plastic.

"Well," Billy said, "Letort sounds like it was a cluster."

"What did you hear?" Philip asked.

"That you were interfering with Donny keeping the professor in line."

"I'm guessing you heard that from Donny."

"What's your side of the story?"

"Do you really care? You got what you wanted—Pearson scared and in Baltimore."

"*Is* he scared?"

"Sure. If I had two guys show up at my house and threaten to hurt me and kill my wife, *I'd* be scared."

"But he wasn't *just* scared. Scared ... and mad as hell. Donny complained about getting a shoulder in the gut." Billy chuckled. "I knew Professor Pearson wasn't the wimp you might think at first."

"You know him?"

"Oh, I know him. I'm curious if he'll know me." Billy looked over Philip's shoulder and nodded.

Philip turned quickly, half expecting Tony to be looming behind him, but Tony was by the Escalade, opening the back door for Richard. He gestured Richard toward where Billy and Philip stood.

When Richard reached them, Billy said, "Hey there, Professor."

After a moment, Richard said, "Hello."

Billy gestured toward Philip. "You know my man, Phil."

Richard glanced at Philip. "Yes."

"But you don't know me?"

Richard returned his gaze to Billy. "Not personally."

"Picture me skinnier ... and as I recall, I was going through my goth phase then."

Richard knit his brow, but after a few moments his look of confusion changed to surprise.

"Bill? Bill Chapelski?"

Philip couldn't keep his eyebrows from rising.

Billy laughed. "That's right. Bill Chapelski from Rush College. How you doin' Prof?"

"What in the world ..." Richard began, then his voice faded away.

Billy switched his attention to Philip. "Phil, you look surprised. Didn't think ol' Billy Chapel had gone to college?"

"Hadn't given it much thought one way or the other."

"Yup, I spent four glorious years at Rush College, and took a couple of Professor Pearson's Signals and Systems classes."

"And now you're ..." said Richard, obviously having trouble getting his mind around his captor's identity as a former student.

Billy dropped his voice dramatically. "Billy Chapel, crime kingpin of Baltimore." He laughed, then added, his voice back to its normal register, "Not the usual career for a Rush alum—right, Prof?"

"Well ... no. Not really."

"And you—you've been on leave for the last semester, I understand."

The look of confusion left Richard's face, replaced with a stony anger. "That's right. My wife had an accident. She needs some specialized help while she recovers."

"So, you think she'll recover?"

Richard drew himself straighter. "Yes, I do."

"Not in that dump, she won't."

Richard's expression darkened. "Are you threatening—?"

Billy waved a hand. "Don't worry about that for a minute. You know where Cedar Grove ranks among facilities in Pennsylvania? Pretty much dead last."

"They're good people there."

"They might be good people, but they're doing shit-all for your wife."

"They're doing the best they can."

"Let's not argue semantics, Prof. Your wife isn't going to get the help she needs there."

"It's—" Richard's voice sounded strangled. "It's what we can afford."

"You help me out, you'll be able to afford better. The best out there."

Richard stared at him. "What do you mean?"

"Jeez, Prof, I always thought of you as a bright guy, but I have to say you're pretty slow on the uptake. Let me lay it out for you. You don't cooperate, there's another gun pointed at Mrs. Pearson's head, and this time the trigger gets pulled."

Richard looked like he might faint.

"You *do* cooperate," Billy continued, "she not only lives, but gets moved to a place where they might actually be able to help her. Might help her walk again." He shrugged. "So there are your choices. A dead wife or a healthy—or at least healthier— one. You pick."

Richard glanced again at Philip.

"Don't look at him," Billy snapped, any trace of good humor gone from his voice. "You think he's your buddy? He's not your buddy." His eyes drifted to Philip. "And if he *is* your buddy, that's not going to help you ... or him either."

Richard, his eyes now glued on Billy, forced the words out. "I'd choose a healthy wife, of course."

Billy's glower relaxed into a smile, and he returned his gaze to Richard. "Good choice, Professor, good choice." He leaned back in the desk chair. "I'm sending you two and Donny—my Three Musketeers—to Philly to look for one of your fellow scientists. Louise Mortensen. Know of her?"

"No," said Richard. After a moment, his panic returning, he added, "Should I?"

"No reason that I know of. I'll give you all the information you need. There's an iPad in the 'Slade. Take a look at the documents on it. See if you can make heads or tails of them. There's an audio file, too—listen to that. When you guys catch up with Mortensen, I want someone there with knowledge of electrical systems. I'm sure Phil and Donny won't have any idea what she's talking about."

"All right," Richard said uncertainly.

Billy jerked his chin toward the Escalade, and Tony took Richard's elbow and led him back to the vehicle.

"So," Billy said to Philip, his tone brisk, like a high school coach issuing orders to his team during practice, "I'm sending you, the professor, and Donny to Philly to look for Mortensen. Check around the post office where she was supposed to pick up her fake ID docs, then check around the Vivantem clinic. If you don't find her at either place, let me know, and I'll send Tony to follow McNally."

"You think she's still hanging around Philly?"

"Probably not, but it'd be stupid not to check the couple of places we can assume she'd go. And to avoid a repeat of whatever happened in Letort, you're going to be Richard's minder. I need him focused on the science stuff, not on whether or not Donny's going to snuff him."

"If Donny's such a loose cannon, why do you keep him around?"

Billy heaved an exaggerated sigh. "Donny's a buddy's cousin. I let Donny work Lucas over because I knew he'd enjoy the assignment—Donny's a sadistic fuck—but I didn't expect to get such juicy info from Lucas. Once I heard what Lucas had to say, I didn't want to get anyone else involved. *Need-to-know basis* is my motto." He smiled wolfishly. "Plus, if Donny gets too big for his britches, he's expendable—buddy's cousin or not." His expression sobered. "But I hate whacking my own guys, so I want you minding Donny as well as Richard."

Philip grimaced. "I can't imagine Donny's going to appreciate that."

Billy shrugged. "Not my problem what Donny does and doesn't appreciate." He grinned. "And if things go smooth, I have a little surprise for you I think you'll like." His grin barely changed but any good humor faded from his eyes. "But if things don't go smooth—if you let Donny fuck up again—I'll have a different surprise for you, one you definitely *won't* like."

12

Lizzy sat in the Caravan just down the street from *Chesaperk*, deciding on next steps. She hated to leave Baltimore with nothing to show for it but a near encounter with Billy Chapel, especially with Olivia evidently contemplating taking a job—or at least a shift—at *Charm City*. She couldn't face retreating to Philly and going back to hiding out in Andy's crowded apartment.

Of course, the only other location she knew of in the Baltimore area where they might find Philip was Billy's house.

Olivia had described perimeter walls and guarded gates, but Olivia clearly wasn't the breaking-and-entering type, it would be like her to downplay the possibility of getting access to the house in an effort to deter Lizzy from making the attempt. Lizzy wanted to see the property for herself.

Plus, she'd seen Billy go into *Charm City*, so at least he wouldn't be at the house.

Lizzy would see what she could scope out about the property in the daylight and, if it seemed worthwhile, would go back after dark. She'd wait to formulate a grand plan until she knew what she was dealing with.

She plugged Billy's address into her GPS and drove.

When she reached Owings Mills, she found the situation to be pretty much as Olivia had described it. There was indeed a man in a T-shirt, jeans, and wide-brimmed hat loitering near the front gate—a man who showed more interest in the passing traffic than the garden. She didn't want to risk making a second pass of the entrance.

Keeping an eye on the map app, she continued along the roads that encircled Billy's property until she reached a house whose property backed up to Billy's. The map's satellite view showed that this house was smaller than Billy's, but it was still enormous, gables and turrets visible above the manicured hedge that ran along the road. She imagined that not all the houses in Owings Mills were as carefully guarded as Billy's, but she was uncomfortable trying to sneak past this house, mainly because it would mean parking the Caravan on the road. The side of the van still sported the long silver scrape that was the memento of Lizzy's first attempt at a highway merge, and it would definitely attract unwanted attention in the upscale neighborhood.

After a few moments of thought, she pulled into the driveway.

She followed the drive to the back of the house, where a nondescript Ford Focus was parked in a paved area near the back door. Lizzy pulled the Caravan up next to it, went to the door, and knocked.

In a moment, a female voice came from a speaker next to the door. "Yes?"

"My dog got out of my van and ran into the woods behind your house. Is it okay if I go after her?"

There was a pause, then the door opened to reveal a middle-aged woman in what Lizzy guessed was the current uniform of a housekeeper—a knee-length black dress and black flats, although with no lacy apron or head covering.

"Into the woods behind the house?" the woman asked with some concern.

"Yes. I think she might have seen a deer."

"That wouldn't surprise me." The woman crossed her arms, more as if she were responding to a chill than any irritation. "We generally don't go back there."

"I'll be careful—I won't damage anything."

The woman shook her head. "It's not that. It's just that ..." She glanced back into the house, then stepped outside and closed the door behind her. "Do you know who Billy Chapel is?"

"No. Is he your neighbor?"

"Yes. Well, he's the owners' neighbor. But he's also ... not a very nice man. He wouldn't like having someone trespassing on his property." She dropped her voice. "He *really* wouldn't like it."

"Would it be clear where his property started?"

She scowled. "Oh, it'll be clear. It's the only chain link fence you'll see in this part of town. Totally against the zoning regulations. Drives the Rayburns crazy—but it's not like they're going to complain."

"I promise not to go onto his property." Lizzy wrung her hands. "And if he's not a very nice man, I'd like to find Peanut before she crosses into his property."

The woman smiled thinly. "Yes, that would be best." She sighed. "Okay, you can go look—but no crossing any fences."

"No, I won't—thanks!"

Lizzy started to turn away, then a thought struck her. She turned back. "Do you know if he has dogs? I'd hate to have Peanut run into some strange dog. She's not very brave."

"No dogs that I know about—at least none that come on our property. As long as you—and Peanut—stay on this side of the fence, you should be fine."

Lizzy nodded with unfeigned relief. "Okay, thanks."

As the woman stepped back inside, Lizzy hurried across a

large and meticulously mowed lawn, toward the woods that surrounded it. "Peanut!" she called. "Come, Peanut!"

The woods immediately behind the Rayburn house appeared almost as well-maintained as the grass, with no fallen branches or the other debris. Some of the understory growth looked like it had been shaped with clippers to provide an attractive backdrop to the lawn.

She reached the chain link fence sooner than she would have expected ... or liked. On the other side of the fence, the woods were dense and wild.

She glanced back toward the Rayburn house, barely visible through the trees.

The fence provided much less of a challenge than the six-foot-high stuccoed wall at the front of the property would have. In fact, in one place it had been squashed flat by a fallen tree. It seemed more geared to marking the property boundary than providing protection, but she couldn't lower her guard—Billy wouldn't have left the woods undefended.

Was it possible to electrify a chain link fence? She did a quick online search on *how to figure out if a fence is electrified*. She listened but heard no buzzing and touched a blade of grass to the fence and could feel no tingle. Laying a careful finger on it was similarly uneventful.

She scrambled over the fence.

Leading away from the fence was a faint path, narrow enough that she thought it had more likely been made by animals than people. However, animal paths could be followed by humans, as she herself was proving, and would be a likely place for Billy to set a trap. She was glad she was reconnoitering during the daytime—it would be easier to see something like a tripwire ... or the covering of a spear-lined pit. She shuddered. For anyone else, it would seem fantastical. For Billy Chapel? She wasn't sure.

She followed the path until she could pick out Billy's house —it was in fact even more enormous than the Rayburns'— through the trees. She stepped off the path, trying to find an angle that would give her a better view. But even once she located a vantage point that gave her a view through a break in the branches, she was too far away to see anything useful. She began to work her way closer to the house.

She stayed low and kept undergrowth or tree trunks between her and the house, but she couldn't help making quite a lot of noise. That, along with the rustle of the breeze through the branches, would make it hard for her to hear anyone approaching. If she got caught, it would be bad for her, but it would be bad for Philip, too. She had no idea if Billy believed Philip's claim back at the compound that he didn't know Lizzy, but he certainly wouldn't if he caught her here. And if one of Billy's men encountered her in the woods? Her experience suggested that the squeeze was only effective within a dozen feet or so and would be no defense if someone decided to shoot her from a distance. And if they tried to grab her? She might be able to get away, but not without adding to her tally of victims.

She gasped at the sound of branches crackling and looked around frantically, expecting to see one of Billy's henchmen aiming a pistol at her head—or maybe a slavering guard dog heading her way.

Instead, she saw a medium-sized buck walking down the path toward Billy's house. The buck was clearly not concerned about making noise. Maybe she could use the buck's sound to cover her own.

When it had moved past her, she began making her way through the undergrowth toward the path. The deer startled and turned toward her but didn't run. She stopped moving, and a few moments later, it resumed its progress down the path. It didn't seem to consider her a threat—she doubted anyone was hunting in the woods of Owings Mills, and it was probably used to grazing on the plantings around the houses.

By pausing whenever the buck showed signs of nervousness, she eventually regained the path and began following the deer's leisurely progress toward Billy's house.

She had just gotten close enough to the house that she thought she'd be able to pick out forms inside—although the view would be better at night if the interior was lit—when the buck froze and raised its head, ears perked forward.

Lizzy froze as well and slowly lowered herself to her knees.

The deer—and Lizzy—remained motionless for half a minute, then it took a tentative step forward, tail flicking.

Lizzy was debating whether or not to follow when the deer stopped again. It gave a forceful snort and stamped a hoof.

Then Lizzy heard what sounded like a couple of balloons popping from the direction of the lawn, and the deer reared up.

"Got him!" a man yelled.

The deer spun on its back legs—there was a starburst of yellow on its chest—and came galloping back down the path toward her.

There was no way she could get off the path in time. She dropped to her stomach and covered her head with her hands.

The deer sailed over her—she could feel the breeze in its wake and the thud of its hoofbeats as it continued its retreat.

"You sure it was you?" a second man said. "I think I hit him."

The voices were coming from beyond a curve in the path, but they couldn't be more than fifty feet away.

"I'm yellow," said the first man. "I got him right in the chest."

The voices were closer—they'd see her any second. Could she crawl off the path without making noise? She didn't think so.

The first man laughed. "There's yours—purple. You missed him by a mile."

"Wish these things had more range—I could hit him for sure if he was in the yard. It's the goddamned trees—"

"Hey, assholes!" a third voice called. It was a little further away but approaching. "Did I not tell you to put away the goddamned paintballs?"

"Aw, Tony, come on," the second man called. "Who's going to care if there's a little paint in the woods?"

Tony had reached the place where the two men stood on the path. "There's paint on the goddamned deer, assuming you managed to hit it—"

"I got him—" began the first man.

"Well, I wish you had missed it, because some do-gooder is going to call the goddamned SPCA and report us for shooting deer."

"It's only a paintball—" the second man began, his tone truculent.

Lizzy heard a slap and a muffled yelp, more of surprise than pain.

"Give me those things," said Tony. "And get back to work. Mickey, you're supposed to be patrolling the yard, for Christ's sake. And Bobby, you're not even supposed to be out here—you want one of the boys to plug you because they don't know you're sneaking through the woods?"

There was some mumbling, then Lizzy heard what she thought were two sets of footfalls retreating up the path toward Billy's house.

She strained her ears, trying to figure out if one of them—probably Tony—was still standing on the path.

A minute ticked by. Then two.

Surely Tony wasn't still standing on the path ... was he?

She was steeling herself to raise her head to look when she almost gasped at a guffaw.

"That's a good one," Tony said, obviously to himself.

A moment later, his footsteps followed the others.

She remained motionless for another minute, then slowly raised her head. Although the place where the men had been standing was hidden from view by the curve in the path, she could see part of the lawn through a break in the trees. Tony was walking toward the house, the two paintball guns in one hand, his phone, which commanded his attention, in the other. Based on a slight shaking of his shoulders, he was still laughing at whatever he saw there.

She turned and, on her hands and knees, retreated down the path toward the Rayburns' house until she reached the fence. Once she had scrambled over the fence, she brushed dirt and twigs from her clothes, face, and hands.

As she crossed the lawn toward the Caravan, the Rayburns' housekeeper came out onto the back porch.

"No luck?" she called.

"I'm afraid not," Lizzy called back. "I'll drive around the neighborhood a bit, see if I can see ..." She had a panicked moment when she couldn't remember what name she had given her fictitious dog. "... Peanut."

"You want something to lure her with? Baloney? Slice of cheese?"

"No, thanks—I've got some treats in the car."

"Okay. Hope you find her." The woman went back into the house.

Lizzy climbed into the Caravan and leaned back in the seat, waiting for her heartbeat to slow. She wouldn't entirely discount the need to return to Billy's house, but she hoped it wasn't necessary. She wasn't surprised that Billy had men patrolling the yard, but experiencing it certainly brought home the danger.

She jumped when her phone rang, and her stomach flipped

with the thought of what would have happened if the call had come in just a few minutes earlier, while she was lying on the path.

She checked the screen, then answered. "Hey, Olivia."

"Hey, Lizzy. Still on your way back to Philly, I guess?"

"Yeah." *Although not directly*, she added to herself.

"Are you okay to talk and drive, or do you want to pull over? Not that it's an emergency," Olivia added hastily.

"That's okay," said Lizzy, suppressing a pang of guilt. "I made a stop—thought I'd break up the drive up a bit."

"Good idea. I wanted to let you know that I'm going to be working a trial shift at *Charm City* later today, and I was told that staff aren't allowed to have their phones with them while on shift, so don't be alarmed if you call and it rings to voicemail."

Lizzy began to consider arguments she would make to talk Olivia out of doing anything that would put her in danger of a run-in with Billy Chapel, but it felt a little hypocritical. "I can't imagine Suki was too thrilled about that."

Olivia sighed. "No, she wasn't. I don't think I'll have *Chesaperk* as an observation post after today."

"She fired you?"

"She said if I was so excited about throwing in my lot with Billy Chapel, I probably wasn't interested in 'slumming' at the coffee shop anymore."

"Well, I hope you don't have to spend too much time at *Charm City*. For that matter, I hope you don't have to spend too much more time in Baltimore."

"Yeah. I hope we can figure out what's going on with Philip ... and get back to normal."

"I second that."

They ended the call, and Lizzy stared through the Caravan's bug-spattered windshield in the direction of Billy's house.

She wouldn't count out another venture onto the property, but she hoped not to have to do it without more evidence that Philip might be there. But that didn't mean she was out of options.

She tapped a destination into the map app.

Things were sure to get less normal before they got more.

13

———

When Philip, Donny, and Richard arrived at the Philadelphia Main Line post office where Louise was to have picked up her fake ID documents, Donny stayed in the car with Richard and sent Philip in to investigate.

Each P.O. box had a small glass window in the front, and Philip could see that Louise's was empty. If he had been looking for her for himself, he might have tried sweet-talking the grumpy-looking woman at the counter into giving him some information about the owner of the box. However, he didn't feel the need to go out of his way to discharge Billy's assignment, and he didn't want to have to explain to Donny the no doubt extensive time it would take to warm up the woman.

He returned to the car. "Nothing in the box."

Donny got out his phone and began tapping.

"What are you doing?" asked Philip.

"I'm going to call around to some hotels in the area, see if they have anyone staying there named Louise Gerard."

"That's not part of the assignment, Don."

"Oh, come on, Phil, show some initiative." Donny put the phone to his ear. "You guys shut up for a minute."

As Philip listened to Donny's side of the calls, he guessed that even if Donny had reached a hotel staffer who was unprofessional enough to consider sharing information about their guests, his overly aggressive tone would have scuttled that option. Sweet talking was obviously not in Donny's repertoire.

Neither was persistence. He gave up after three calls.

"Assholes," Donny muttered as he started up the Escalade. "Okay, Vivantem next."

When they reached the Center City high rise that housed the Vivantem facilities, Donny double-parked in front and once again sent Philip in.

Philip approached the reception desk. "Can you tell me where the Vivantem offices are?"

The guard glanced toward the street. "You delivering flowers?"

Philip raised his eyebrows. "No."

The guard shrugged. "Just wondering, because some guy came by with a delivery for Vivantem a couple days ago, but that place is closed up tighter than a drum."

Philip suppressed a wry smile. He guessed Louise Mortensen had thought of a more clever way to determine the facility's status than they had. He returned to the car and reported the conversation to Donny.

"So she must be in the area!" Donny said, more excited than Philip thought the news merited.

"The guy said it was a couple of days ago. She could be anywhere."

Donny rubbed his hands. "No, I've got a good feeling about this. I think she's nearby."

Philip rolled his eyes.

Richard, in the back seat, looked up from the iPad Billy had given him, which he had been studying throughout the drive. "I hate to say this," he said tentatively, "but if you want someone to decipher the information in here, you'd better find this Louise Gerard. This really isn't in my area of specialization."

"Close enough," said Donny.

"It really isn't," said Richard.

"Well, you better expand your area of specialization pretty fast if you don't want your wife's head blown off."

Richard flushed and returned his attention to the iPad.

Donny tapped a destination—clearly not Billy's address—into the car's GPS.

"Where are we going?" asked Philip.

"Andrew McNally's apartment," said Donny as he pulled into traffic, flipping off the honking motorist he had cut off.

"Donny, Billy's instructions were pretty clear: look for Mortensen near the post office and near the Vivantem offices, and if we didn't see her, go back to Baltimore."

"So that Tony can find her and get all the credit."

"It's not a matter of who gets the credit. It's a matter of following Billy's instructions."

"Tony's a moron."

"Regardless, looking for Mortensen is his job now."

Donny shot him a sidelong glance. "Just as I suspected—no initiative." He returned his eyes to the road. "We go to McNally's apartment, break in, and force him to tell us whatever he knows about Mortensen."

"Donny, I'm telling you—"

"Shut up, Phil. It's not your job to tell me anything."

Philip clamped his lips shut and turned to look out the passenger window. Since Billy had assigned him as Donny's minder, he could argue that it *was* his job to tell Donny some things, but he doubted that argument would carry much weight. Donny's "initiative" was going to piss off Billy, thereby jeopardizing not only their safety but Richard's wife's as well. Just as bad, Lizzy might be holing up at Andy's apartment, and even with Lizzy armed with the squeeze, there were all sorts of ways Donny's plan might end badly for her, Andy, Owen, and Ruby.

Fifteen minutes later, Donny pulled up in front of a modern, multi-story apartment building with a tasteful but prominent sign next to the entrance: *Protected by GuardianSafe Security*.

"That's where McNally lives," Donny said, then added with a sneer, "Fancy."

A dozen yards ahead, a car pulled out of a space, and Donny pulled in. "I'm going to check it out."

Philip's patience was fraying. "You're just going to walk in and ask to be buzzed up to McNally's apartment?"

"No, Einstein. I'm going to pretend I'm there to do some work."

Philip eyed Donny's clothes: the same cheaper and gaudier style of Billy Chapel's usual outfit as Philip himself was wearing. "What kind of work are you going to claim to be there to do?"

"Handyman to the bored and horny housewives of Philly." He laughed. "Don't worry—I come prepared. There are always coveralls and a toolbox in the trunk." Donny grinned, and Philip suppressed a shudder at its malevolence. "I've been on a couple of jobs where it was handy to have tools—and a way to keep splatter off my clothes."

Philip glanced back at Richard. He looked like he might be sick, and Philip didn't feel much better. He hoped that *Guardian-Safe* was as good as Andy had bragged it was. He turned back to Donny. "Go get 'em, champ."

Donny pocketed the keys and got out. Tossing his jacket into the back of the Escalade, he got out the toolbox and a coverall, which he slipped on.

"You guys wait here," he said to Philip and Richard. "And

don't forget ..." He mimed a bullet to the temple. He slammed the door shut and headed for the apartment building.

"This really isn't my area of expertise" Richard said despairingly. "There are notes on this iPad about someone ..." He swallowed. "... someone reanimating a severed hand using electricity."

"The electricity angle is why Billy got you involved."

"But that kind of work isn't just about electrical systems—you'd need medical knowledge to do that. And all this talk in the recording about enabling people to create strokes in other people or to read minds ... I don't even know what branch of science that would involve. Certainly not Signals and Systems."

"Do your best."

"You don't seem as if you like Donny much."

"I don't."

"Do you think you and I—" Richard began hesitantly.

"No. Don't even think about it—unless you don't care if Billy Chapel has your wife killed."

Richard, his expression a heart-rending mixture of fear and fury, returned his attention to the iPad.

Philip watched as pedestrians passed the vehicle, both dreading and hoping that he might see Andy or Lizzy. Andy's height and reddish hair would make him easy to pick out, but Philip didn't doubt that Lizzy would have changed her hair cut and color after escaping from the compound, so his heart clenched at the sight of any slender young white woman.

Donny was back at the car less than five minutes later. He tore off the coverall and threw it and the toolbox into the back of the Escalade. He climbed into the driver's seat and slammed the door behind him.

"Fucker at the security desk wouldn't even let me past the lobby."

"So, back to Baltimore?" asked Philip.

Donny started up the vehicle. "It's going to take more than that to keep me from laying eyes on McNally. We'll figure out where the tenants park and see what we can see."

They found the entrance to an underground garage, but it was blocked by a gate and monitored by at least two cameras that Philip could see.

Donny parked on the street—not, as far as Philip could tell, necessarily out of range of the cameras—and they settled down to wait.

14

P hilip was dreading another marathon stakeout like the one at Cedar Grove—this one with the added annoyance of Richard's nervous shifting in the back seat—but after a little less than an hour, the parking garage gate lifted, and an SUV pulled out.

Donny sat up, excited. "That's McNally in the passenger seat! Who's the old lady driving?"

Philip knew it was Ruby DiMano, but he wasn't about to volunteer that information.

Fortunately, Donny didn't seem to expect an answer. He started up the Escalade and followed the other SUV.

Donny was better at tailing a vehicle than he was at sweet talking information out of people, keeping the SUV in sight, but with a few cars between them.

They soon reached a more suburban setting, and the SUV pulled into a campus of medical buildings and stopped at the entrance to one of them.

By the time Donny had backed the Escalade into a spot where it was partially hidden by a dumpster but from which they could still see the SUV, Andy had climbed out of the vehicle and was walking stiffly to the building's entrance. Philip could tell by the way he moved that he must still be in some pain from his gunshot wound.

"The old lady must be going to park the car," Donny said, tapping the steering wheel.

However, rather than parking in one of the open spaces near the door, Ruby chose a space along the lot's perimeter. She got out and crossed a narrow strip of grass that separated the campus parking lot from the Starbucks on the adjoining lot.

It was the best chance Philip was going to have to get a message to Lizzy and her allies.

"Well, what are you waiting for?" he asked Donny.

Donny shot him a look. "What?"

"You're going to follow McNally, right? He might be meeting Mortensen. She's a doc—maybe she's using a colleague's office as a meeting place." Philip wasn't happy about instigating a situation that might result in Donny encountering Andy, but he couldn't pass up the opportunity to try to talk to Ruby.

Donny turned back toward the medical building's entrance and twisted his hands on the wheel. "You think?"

"It's more likely you'll find her in a medical building than hanging around a post office. And you should take Richard. If McNally *is* meeting with Mortensen, you two might be able to get close enough to hear what they're saying, and Richard could help translate."

"I don't have any medical—" Richard began but subsided under Philip's glare.

"Yeah," sneered Donny, "send us inside so you can take off."

"Don, I know this is hard for you to understand, but I actually don't want to be responsible for you killing Richard's wife." He glanced back at Richard, whose panicked expression suggested that he was even less sure that Philip wouldn't run than Donny was. "Plus," Philip added, turning back to Donny, "you'll have the keys."

Donny still looked uncertain.

"Initiative!" said Philip.

Donny roused himself. "Yeah, it's at least better than sitting in the car staring at the building." He turned off the vehicle and pocketed the keys. "Come on, Pearson." He and Richard climbed out and headed for the entrance.

As soon as they were inside, Philip jumped out of the Escalade and sprinted for the Starbucks.

He found Ruby standing with a few other customers waiting to pick up their orders.

He stepped up beside her. "Ruby, it's Philip Castillo."

Ruby's head snapped around, her eyes wide. Philip had never met Ruby DiMano in person, but from the affectionate stories Lizzy had told him, he felt as if he knew her well. And he knew that he'd pick the scrawny seventy-year-old over Donny as his wingman any day.

"I only have a minute," he said. "I have a couple of messages for you and Lizzy. And Andy and Owen, of course."

Ruby glanced around the café, probably confirming that Philip was alone, then returned her flustered gaze to him. "All right."

"Billy Chapel has an audiotape of Lizzy mediating a conversation between Mortensen and Edmund Rinnert about using electricity to create clairvoyance and the squeeze," he said, low and fast, "so based on the fact that Lizzy was conveying to Louise things Rinnert wasn't saying out loud, he knows that she can read minds."

Ruby paled. "That's not good."

"No. But I think Chapel thinks she can only do it if the other person is drugged."

Ruby nodded.

"As far as I know, he doesn't know about the squeeze."

"That's good."

"Now Chapel is pursuing the electricity angle, and he has kidnapped a professor from his alma mater to try to help him, although it sounds like the professor doesn't actually have the knowledge to do what Chapel wants him to do."

"That's good, too."

"Yes. The professor and one of Chapel's goons followed Andy into the medical building."

Ruby's posture stiffened. "Why?"

"I convinced Donny that Andy might be meeting up with Mortensen there."

Ruby looked alarmed. "But Doctor McNally—"

"I just needed to get away from them long enough to talk with you."

She glanced around the café again. "Okay. But ... are you working for Chapel now?"

"No—but I'm having to pretend that I am. If I don't cooperate, Chapel's going to kill the professor's wife. And he could come after you guys as well. Are you all staying in Andy's apartment?"

Ruby examined him, her distrust clear in her expression.

He held up a hand. "You don't have to tell me. Just be aware that Chapel and his men know where Andy lives, so be extra careful."

"We're always extra careful."

"I know you and Owen are, but Andy ... and Lizzy ..."

"I'll make sure we *all* are."

The barista called out, "Pistachio Frappuccino for Ruby!"

Philip raised his eyebrows and suppressed a smile. "I didn't take you for a Pistachio Frappuccino type, Ruby."

"I'm hardly in the mood for it anymore," Ruby muttered. She

retrieved the cup from the counter and turned to a teenager waiting for his order. "You can have it."

"No kidding?" said the young man, taking the cup. "Thanks!"

Ruby turned back to Philip. "Anything else we should know?" she asked, her voice low.

"Those are the most important things, and I want to get back to the car before Donny does. I don't have access to a phone now, but as soon as I can get another message to all of you, I will. Will you give me your phone number?"

Ruby recited a number, then repeated it twice more at Philip's request.

"Can you tell me Lizzy's cell number?"

Ruby hesitated for only a moment, then nodded.

Philip dreaded having to wait through Ruby getting out her phone, opening the Contacts app, finding Lizzy's number, and reading it out to him—how long could Donny actually spend in the building? But Ruby immediately recited a number and again repeated it for him.

"Thanks, Ruby."

Philip hurried out of the Starbucks ... and his stomach twisted when he saw Donny standing next to the Escalade, scanning the parking lot, his face red with fury.

Richard stood next to Donny, wringing his hands. When he saw Philip jogging across the parking lot toward them, his face collapsed in relief. He said something to Donny and pointed toward Philip.

"What the fuck?" Donny spluttered when Philip reached them.

"I had to use the bathroom," said Philip. "My stomach is bothering me. I figured the Starbucks was a good option. How did you guys do?"

"McNally went into some hand doctor's office. No sign of Mortensen."

"That's too bad—but, you know, checking it out showed real initiative. Ready to go back to Baltimore?"

"Sure. Just one thing I need to do first." Donny gestured to the space between the Escalade and the dumpster. "Over here. I'll show you."

Philip was pretty sure he knew the one thing Donny had to do, and he wasn't surprised when, as soon as they were hidden from view of the building's entrance and windows, Donny shoved him against the dumpster and buried his fist in Philip's midsection. Philip had tightened his stomach muscles before the blow landed, but it doubled him over, nonetheless.

"Stomach still bothering you?" Donny sneered.

"Not anymore," Philip gasped.

Donny leaned over so that his mouth was an inch from Philip's ear. "Don't you ever—and I mean *ever*—jerk me around again. Understand?"

Philip, still trying to get his breath back, didn't respond.

Donny pulled Philip upright and drove his fist into Philip's stomach again.

Philip was grateful that he hadn't eaten anything since breakfast, since it definitely would have come up.

"I said, *understand?*"

"Yeah," Philip ground out. "I understand."

Donny shoved him toward the passenger door. "Get in." He brushed past a wide-eyed Richard on the way to the driver's side. "You, too, Pearson."

Philip, one hand pressed to his stomach, fumbled with the door handle, and Richard reached around him and opened the door for him, then eased it shut once Philip had climbed in.

Almost before Richard had gotten his own door closed behind him, Donny peeled out of the parking space and headed for the exit. Just before they turned onto the road, Philip glanced back toward the Starbucks.

Ruby was standing outside, her arms crossed even though the day was warm. He realized that, from that position, she would have been able to see what had happened behind the dumpster.

As the Escalade turned into the road, she raised her hand to her face, as if to adjust her glasses, but at the last minute curled her fingers into a fist.

Despite the pain still throbbing up from his stomach, Philip allowed himself a mental smile. A fist bump had been his and Lizzy's departing gesture, and he had given Lizzy a disguised version of it as the helicopter on which she and McNally rode lifted off the helipad back at the compound. It had been his signal to Lizzy that he was still on her side.

He had Donny to thank for providing some evidence for Ruby that Philip was on her side as well.

15

———

Lizzy turned off Interstate 70 and headed north on Maryland Route 15, her phone propped on the Caravan's dashboard with the GPS app open. The four lanes were separated by a wide grass median down which a line of telephone poles ran. Fenced pastures and scatterings of woods stretched away on either side.

Her phone rang, and she glanced at the caller ID: Ruby. She put on the blinker and, another quarter of a mile on, carefully turned into the parking lot of a closed restaurant.

By the time she had stopped, the call had gone to voicemail, but she called Ruby back without waiting to hear the message.

When Ruby answered, Lizzy said, "Hey, Ruby. I saw you called."

"I just saw Philip," Ruby said, an uncharacteristic tremble in her voice.

Lizzy's fingers tightened on the phone. "Where? What happened?"

"I dropped the younger Doctor McNally off to get his hand checked, and I walked over to the Starbucks next door to get a coffee. I was waiting for my order when I heard my name, and Philip was standing right next to me."

Ruby relayed the information Philip had given her, and the fact that Ruby had given him Lizzy's cell phone number. "I hope that's all right."

"Of course," said Lizzy. "How did he seem?"

"He seemed fine … when I talked to him."

Lizzy knit her brow. "*When you talked to him*? What does that mean?"

Ruby sighed. "When Philip got back to his car, Chapel's goon was already there. He … roughed up Philip a little bit."

Lizzy's throat clamped shut. "How much is 'a little bit'?"

"He punched Philip a couple of times in the stomach."

Lizzy closed her eyes. "Oh, no."

"I don't think Philip was badly injured. He got back into the car on his own."

The idea that Philip had felt he had no choice but to get into a car with the man who had just beaten him brought tears to Lizzy's eyes. "He had to go with him because of me."

"He had to go with him because of *all* of us," Ruby said, some of her usual briskness returning, "and because he couldn't put the professor's wife at risk."

"Did he say who this professor was?" Lizzy asked.

"No, just that he was from the college Chapel went to."

Man, even Billy Chapel went to college, she thought, a twinge of jealousy sneaking past her alarm. "And you had dropped Andy off for his check-up? Where is he now?"

"He's still in the doctor's office," said Ruby. "He should be out soon."

"How about Uncle Owen?"

"He's at the apartment—I'll call him next." Ruby sighed. "Sounds like you might be better off in Baltimore than here."

"Actually …" Lizzy's voice trailed off.

"Actually ... what?" Ruby asked sharply.

"I'm not in Baltimore anymore. Billy showed up at the coffee shop where Olivia is working—*was* working—and she and I decided maybe it wasn't a good idea for me to be hanging around near his restaurant."

"So you're on your way back to Philly?"

"Well ..."

"Lizzy!"

"I'm on my way to the compound."

"*What?* Why?"

"It was the only place other than Baltimore that I thought Philip might be."

"But now we know he's not there."

"Well, we know he's not there *right now*, but we don't know that he's not headed there." Then she added, with sudden excitement, "In fact, you said Philip told you that Billy has kidnapped some guy to help him figure out how to use electricity to squeeze brains and read minds. He might be using the lab at the compound to do it! Billy might even be planning to take over the compound for his own use, and since Billy knows that Philip was there when Theo was alive, he might have thought Philip was the person best equipped to make the best use of whatever Theo had left behind."

Or, she thought with a shiver, *maybe Billy just wanted someone to clean up the mess—there had been bodies everywhere.*

"It's not enough just to know Philip is alive," she continued. "If Billy's forcing his cooperation, we need to help him get away. Olivia has Baltimore covered. I'm going to check the compound."

"Do you need any help? I could come with you."

Lizzy had to smile at the idea of Ruby sneaking through the Western Maryland woods in one of her shirtwaist dresses and her slip-on sneakers, her purse hanging from her arm. "No, I appreciate the offer, but I think it will be better if I go by myself."

"Does the older Doctor McNally know you're going to the compound?"

"No." On top of everything else that was happening, she just couldn't face a conversation with Owen, who would be even more upset about her plan than Ruby was. "Could you tell him?" she asked sheepishly.

Ruby sighed. "Okay."

"If anything looks fishy, I'll leave right away." Before Ruby could mount more arguments against her plan, Lizzy hurried on. "I better call Olivia and let her know about Philip."

She ended the call with Ruby with a promise to stay in touch, then called Olivia.

The call went to voicemail—Olivia must already be at *Charm City*. After the beep, Lizzy said, "Olivia, it's Lizzy. Ruby saw Philip—he's all right. He was with one of Billy's guys and is having to pretend he's joined Billy's side." She considered what else she might want to include in the message but decided that the rest would be better to tell Olivia directly. She also didn't see any reason to worry Olivia with the news that she was headed for the compound. "I'll call you back later."

She ended the call, then reopened the GPS app, set to her best guess of the general location of the compound. Lizzy had travelled to and from the compound by helicopter, and the landmarks she remembered—the large pond, the concrete square of the helipad—would have to be visible on the app's satellite view. Philip had told her it was situated to the east of Hagerstown, Maryland, where Theo had put Philip on a private plane to Arizona to kill a man. But that still left a huge area to reconnoiter. Who knew how long it would take her to locate the compound?

But, she thought as she pulled back onto the road, as long as Philip wasn't in immediate danger, she didn't necessarily mind the extra time to try to formulate a plan.

16

L ouise pulled off the two-lane highway into a strip mall parking lot. The stores included a pizzeria, a pet salon, a tag and title service, a vacuum cleaner repair shop, and, at the end, her destination: a pawn shop. A neon *Open* sign flashed in the window.

She parked the Lincoln Navigator she had rented—she would have preferred something smaller, but she didn't know if her plans would require a more robust vehicle than a sedan—and went inside.

A buzzer sounded, and a moment later, a man lumbered out from the back room. She could almost see his mental calculator running as he assessed her appearance: salon haircut, finely tailored dress, low-heeled Christian Louboutin pumps, and Louis Vuitton handbag. "Help you?"

She recognized him from her earlier visit, but she wasn't surprised he didn't recognize her. She hadn't been so expensively dressed last time she had been there, and her haircut had been self-inflicted.

She took a receipt out of her bag and handed it to him. "I'd like to redeem a wedding ring I pawned recently."

He took the receipt in fingers stained either by cigarettes or tarnished silver, then looked back up at her. "I remember you now." He smiled—not unpleasantly. "I guess things are looking up for you."

"Yes, I believe they are."

He got out his phone, tapped in some numbers, and jotted the result on the receipt. He turned the receipt so she could read the number. "There's your total."

As she got out her wallet and counted out the needed cash, he disappeared into the back of the store and returned a minute later with a small resealable plastic bag. "Nice ring," he said, as he slid the ring—a plain but heavy gold band—out of the bag. "People generally go for something flashier these days."

"Flashy isn't really my style."

He grinned. "I can see that."

He handed her the ring, and she slipped it on. The wedding rings she and Gerard had chosen—his had been the same—had a lovely heft, the ring's rounded edges pleasant against her finger.

When Gerard had proposed to her, he had presented her with an engagement ring—a huge diamond flanked by two only slightly smaller rubies—but after some internal debate, she had asked that they return it. Her medical and scientific work required frequent hand washing, and the ring felt unhygienic. The jeweler had given them credit. Louise realized that, despite the fact that they had used the balance not only for the wedding rings but also for a gold necklace and a pair of emerald earrings she had worn to a charity event she and Gerard had attended, there must still be a considerable credit on their account. Despite the millions available to her in her offshore accounts, she couldn't help feeling some irritation that the credit would now go unused—she couldn't very well go into the jeweler and identify herself as the woman wanted for questioning by a variety of law enforcement agencies.

She handed the plastic bag back to the proprietor. "Thank you."

"Nice doing business with you," he said. His eyes flicked to her watch—a Jura Bernois—and to her earrings—small diamond studs. "You have any other jewelry you'd like to trade for cash, you let me know."

"You're looking at all the jewelry I have," she said, amused. "I doubt I'll be back."

He raised a hand in mock surrender. "Can't blame a guy for trying."

17

———

Donny pulled the Escalade up to the back door of Billy's house, where another of Billy's men stood. He turned his head toward Richard in the back seat. "Go with him," he said, jerking his head toward the man.

Richard and Philip both opened their doors.

"Not you," Donny said to Philip. "You're coming with me."

Philip pulled his door shut as Richard climbed out, then Donny pulled away.

They retraced the route they had taken earlier that day to their meeting with Billy in the alley behind his restaurant, but this time they went to the entrance, marked by a gate over which the words *Charm City Diner* were worked in metal script. They climbed out of the vehicle, and Donny handed the keys to the valet. "Is Billy here already?"

"Yes, sir," said the valet.

Donny's smug expression suggested he liked the *sir*.

Philip followed Donny through the courtyard, which was furnished with high-top tables and occupied by twenty- and thirty-somethings who looked like they had come straight from their corporate jobs. Philip had heard the name of the restaurant from Donny, and he had expected it to be a true diner. If he hadn't known the name, he would have expected any restaurant owned by Billy Chapel to have an interior heavy on leather and a menu heavy on steak. But the vibe was much more high-end farm-to-table.

The dining room was fairly empty—it was early for the main dinner crowd—but there was a robust crowd at the bar. Donny leaned between two of the patrons.

"Hey, Ricky, where's Billy?" he asked the bartender.

"Upstairs."

Philip followed Donny as he wended his way through tables toward the back of the restaurant, then climbed a flight of stairs.

They passed a few rooms visible behind glass-paned doors —private event rooms or maybe for overflow from the restaurant —then reached a black door at the end of the hallway labeled *Private*.

"You let me do the talking," said Donny.

"Sure thing." Philip had been worried that Donny would make Philip explain what had happened in Philly, and he was only too happy to let Donny take the lead. He followed Donny into the room.

This room was more what Philip would have expected—a few deep chairs grouped around a huge, tufted leather ottoman, a light illuminating the immaculate green felt of a pool table.

Billy was standing in the middle of the room. Rather than his usual leather jacket, black jeans, and heavy boots, he was wearing an expertly cut light gray suit, an open-necked salmon shirt, and silvery alligator-skin boots. He raised a glass of what looked like whiskey or bourbon. "Welcome home, boys." He took a sip. "I should have told you guys to stop by the house long enough to get cleaned up first." He laughed. "Fortunately, I know the owner." He turned to a young man standing near a door on the other side of the room, dressed almost as fashionably as Chapel. "Johnny, send in the drink tray. And then grab yourself dinner in the kitchen."

Johnny nodded and stepped out of the room.

"So, Billy—" Donny began.

Billy held up a hand. "Just shut up for a minute, would you, Donny? I want everyone to have drinks in hand when I get the update, like civilized people."

Donny flushed. "Sure, Billy."

A moment later, Johnny reappeared and held the door open. Accompanied by the rattle of bottles and glasses, a woman backed into the room, pulling a drink cart.

Philip would have recognized that long black braid anywhere, and it gave him a second to compose his features as Olivia finished pulling the cart into position near the door and turned to face the room.

When she saw Philip, her eyes widened almost comically.

He shot a look toward Billy, trying to come up with possible explanations he could give for Olivia's response. He was relieved to see that Billy was looking at him, grinning. "So, Phil, what do you think of our new bartender?"

Philip looked back at Olivia. She had gotten her initial shock under control, and now her lips were pressed in a thin, angry line. "She looks very competent."

"Competent?" Billy laughed. "Don't be such a cold fish, Phil." He waved his glass toward the cart. "You guys get yourself drinks."

Donny ambled over to the cart and ordered a Woodford on the rocks, which, Philip guessed, was what Billy was drinking. He hoped Billy didn't notice the clacking of the ice cubes when Olivia held the drink out in a trembling hand to Donny.

"Go on," Billy said to Philip, an edge of irritation creeping into his voice. He dropped his voice, although not low enough to keep anyone in the room from hearing it. "I lined her up special for you. Thought you two might hit it off."

Philip bit back the obvious response—*Why, because we're both Indians?*—and approached the cart.

Olivia turned from him and reached for a bottle of Philip's usual drink: Knob Creek.

"They're drinking Woodford," he said sharply.

It took her only a second to realize her mistake. "Of course," she said, her voice cold as the ice in the silver bucket. "My mistake."

Billy had joined him at the cart. "You don't have to order based on what I'm drinking, Phil." He shot an amused glance at Donny. "That's not the way to suck up to the boss."

Donny, who had been about to take a sip of his drink, scowled and lowered his glass.

Billy reached over to the cart and pulled out a pretty blue and white bottle. "You like tequila? Try this."

"I prefer bourbon," he said.

"Oh, come on, Phil, you're ruining my buzz." He handed the bottle to Olivia. "Give him two fingers of that neat, sweetheart."

Olivia poured the drink, her hands now steadier, and handed it to Philip.

"Phil is the newest member of my team," Billy said to Olivia. "He came highly recommended by a good friend."

Olivia busied herself returning the bottle to its place on the cart. "I'm sure."

"He looks all holier-than-thou, but he can get his hands dirty if he has to."

She shot a glance at Philip. "I'll bet."

"A regular Frank Castle." Billy guffawed. "Hey, *Castle ... Castillo.* I didn't even plan that!"

"Who's Frank Castle, Billy?" Donny asked. "Have I met him?"

"No you haven't met him, you moron—he's a Marvel character. The Punisher." Billy handed his glass to Olivia. "Top me up with Woodford, sweetheart." As Olivia transferred a few cubes from the ice bucket into Billy's glass, he asked her, "Where you from?"

"Arizona," she said.

"No kidding! Phil's from Arizona, too. Maybe you guys know some of the same people."

"Arizona's a big state, Mr. Chapel."

Billy threw up his hands. "Okay, okay, so my little matchmaking effort isn't going to be successful. Just thought you're all the way out here, so far from home, you might both like a little company. Can't blame a guy for trying."

Olivia handed Billy his refilled glass without a word.

He gestured to the cart. "We can help ourselves. You go help out at the bar."

Flushed a deep red, and without meeting Philip's gaze, Olivia crossed the room and stepped through the door.

"Jesus, not much bedside manner there. I told her I'd give her a shift as a test run, but I don't think I want her serving people at my bar—*ice princess* is not really the vibe I'm going for." Billy took a sip of his drink. "So," he continued, shifting his stance to include Donny in the conversation, "how'd it go in Philly?"

Philip looked expectantly toward Donny.

Apparently deciding that at the moment, Philip held more social credit with Billy than he himself did, Donny said sullenly, "Why don't you tell him, Phil."

With an internal groan, Philip relayed the facts of the trip to Philadelphia, trying to keep his tone neutral but being sure to "credit" Donny with the idea of following Andy.

Billy's expression darkened minute by minute.

"So while Donny and Richard followed Andy into the building," Philip concluded, "I went next door to the Starbucks to use the restroom."

"Why didn't you just go in the building?" asked Billy.

"I didn't want to risk running into McNally. He might have seen me at the compound, and I didn't want him recognizing me and knowing that someone associated with you or with Viklund was following him."

"If I thought you were telling me the whole story," Billy said, his hand white-knuckled on his heavy glass tumbler, "I'd say that makes sense. So then what?"

"I met up with Donny and Richard at the car." He glanced toward Donny, wondering if Donny would describe the punishment he had meted out. Philip could almost see him weighing the pros and cons, but Donny must have decided the less he said, the better. It was the first smart thing Philip had seen him do.

Billy drained the rest of his drink and put the glass down with a thud. "Well, that sounds like a complete clusterfuck."

Philip decided to follow Donny's lead and stay silent.

Billy stepped to within a foot of Donny. "And, dumbass, when I give you instructions, you follow them, got it?"

Donny, apparently feeling that he was getting off easy, said, "Sure thing, Billy."

Billy put his finger to his lips. "Shhhhh ..."

Donny looked from Billy to Philip and back. "What—"

Billy brought his foot up and smashed the heel of his boot down on the top of Donny's foot.

Donny let out a muffled yelp. His glass dropped to the floor and shattered.

Billy pointed to the floor. "Clean that up, Donny." He turned toward Philip. "And, Phil, I thought you were going to keep this moron in line. I'm very disappointed." He strolled over to Philip and stopped a couple of feet away.

Philip wondered if it would be better or worse for him to try to keep his feet out from under Billy's boot heel.

"I'm willing to overlook the fact that I hired Pocahontas specifically because I thought you might like her," said Billy, his tone conversational, even friendly. "But, hey, maybe she's not your type. Maybe *women* aren't your type. I know you have some guy friends, Phil. Are guys more your speed?"

While Philip racked his brain for which guys Billy might have in mind—Theo Viklund? Andy McNally?—he tried to judge whether Billy actually expected an answer.

But Billy shrugged with exaggerated indifference. "Guy friends or girlfriends, I don't care. Either way, I'm guessing that in your case, you remembering that their well-being depends on your performance is more effective for keeping you in line than a boot heel to the ol' metatarsal."

Billy turned away from him, toward where Donny was squatted down, picking up shards of glass and placing them gingerly into his open hand, and straightened his jacket. "You guys—and Pearson—need to find out if Mortensen had more documentation about what she was working on than what we got from Lucas."

Donny stood, scanning the room for a place to deposit the broken glass. "And how will we do that, Billy?"

Billy tossed back the Woodford. "Go to the only place we haven't looked yet. Viklund's compound."

18

———

L ouise arrived in the vicinity of the compound just after sunset but while the sky was still light—she didn't want to be stumbling around the grounds in the dark. She wasn't sure that even in the daylight she would be able to find where she had slipped under the perimeter fence when she had been Theo Viklund's prisoner, but it didn't seem worth trying. Not only was she sure that Theo would have had the hole fixed—the hole to which he had intentionally guided her as a test of her loyalty or, perhaps more accurately, of her compliance —but there was really no need: Louise was much better equipped now than she had been then.

She drove by the front gate, which was padlocked. From the road, there was no sign of the violence that had taken place inside. She followed the roads that encircled the property until she was about half a mile from the entrance.

Checking both ways for any other traffic—the road was clear, as it has been for most of the drive as she neared the compound—she pulled the Navigator off the road. She bumped across the uneven ground to a stand of trees that hid the vehicle from the road and climbed out.

She had swapped her usual dress, pumps, and handbag for the more appropriate clothing she had picked up at a sporting goods store: pants, a jacket, and a baseball cap in camouflage patterns as well as heavy hiking boots. She gave her ring a little twist, a sad smile tugging her lips as she thought of how Gerard would have teased her about her uncharacteristic wardrobe.

She removed her Louise Gerard driver's license from her purse and slipped it under the carpet in the trunk. Into a camouflage knapsack, another of her recent purchases, she put tissues, lip balm, and bug spray. She was more interested in using the knapsack to carry items *out* of the compound than to carry them in. She removed a pair of bolt cutters from the trunk and closed it with a soft thunk. Making her way across the wooded ground, she soon came to the chain link fence that surrounded the property.

She followed the fence for a bit—in case someone happened upon the Navigator, she wanted some space between it and where she entered the property—then dropped the knapsack and knelt by the fence.

She cut an opening, then she covered the bolt cutters with a few branches and an armful of leaves. She pulled back the fencing like a door, pushed the knapsack through, climbed after it, then bent the fence back into an approximation of its original position. She slung the knapsack over her shoulders and started in the direction in which she thought the main house lay.

Her sense of direction proved to be correct when she recognized the topography of the land around the house, and soon the house itself came into view, its burnished metal and glass making it almost disappear into the rolling hills. She lowered herself behind a bush, hoping that between her own camouflage and the fading light, she would be invisible to anyone who might be keeping watch.

She scanned the area for several minutes. Seeing no movement, she began moving slowly toward the house and the lab beyond.

She had almost reached the house when she saw—and smelled—the first person, although he clearly didn't present a threat. The body of a man lay on the ground, the skin greenish-black and beginning to peel away from the head, revealing that part of the skull was gone. Louise supposed it could be the work of a fox or coyote, but she suspected the more likely explanation was an execution shot to the back of the head. She had no wish to look closer to confirm her theory—maggots wriggled in the exposed tissue, and the odor was stomach-turning. Although it was difficult to tell, she thought the hair was blond—most likely one of Lucas's men.

As she continued through the woods and toward the lab, she saw the body of another blond man on one of the paths that snaked through the property. She wondered what had happened to the bodies of Chapel's men—they couldn't all have survived their attack on the compound. Perhaps Chapel had had them removed.

As she neared the lab, she knelt down behind the understory growth and scanned the area for signs of life. The side of the building facing the house had no windows, and, she realized, she didn't recall seeing windows in either of the apartments in the lab annex. To confirm this, she circled the building at a distance. It was true—there was no way she would be able to tell if anyone was inside, other than staking out the entrance or risking a trip inside.

She waited until full dark had fallen before approaching the building. As she reached the door, another possible issue occurred to her—what if it was locked?

She carefully turned the metal knob. It was unlocked, which was a relief, but also suggested that someone might be inside. She eased the door open.

The interior was dark, and Louise grimaced at the odor that rolled out the door. She pulled the neck of her shirt up over her nose and mouth.

She stepped inside, groped along the wall, and flipped the light switch, grateful when the fluorescent lights flickered to life. It would have been difficult to do her work without electricity.

The lab was largely as she had last seen it. The shards of glass from the broken champagne bottle Billy Chapel had used as a weapon still sparkled on the polished concrete floor. She could see a sneakered foot protruding from behind one of the lab tables, and she stepped over to see Edmund Rinnert's body stretched out on the ground, surrounded by a stain of blackened blood. The decomposition was as advanced as with the men outside, but she noticed that there was no insect activity. Perhaps there was some filtration system in the lab's air circulation system that had kept them out. A bit beyond Edmund's body was another streak of old blood, probably Andrew McNally's.

With a shudder, she let the shirt drop from her face, knowing that it was providing more psychological than olfactory benefit in combating the smell of decaying flesh. But the smell seemed to be too strong to be explained by one decomposing body.

Then she noticed that the lid of the lab's chest freezer was propped open.

She carefully crossed the blood-smeared and glass-covered floor and peered in.

Theo Viklund's body—minus his left hand—lay as it had when she and Lucas had stowed it there, wrapped in a fragment of bedspread but now seeming to puddle in the bottom of the freezer. The body had been frozen solid, and so even with the lid of the freezer propped open, the decomposition was less advanced than with Edmund. The freezer was possibly large enough for two bodies. Could she manage to get Edmund's into it? Could she stomach the process? Even her medical background hadn't prepared her for such a gruesome task.

As she lowered the lid, thinking with revulsion through the logistics of that operation, she realized there had been no waft of cold air coming out of the open freezer. The lights were on, so it wasn't that the electricity was out. Had the freezer been unplugged?

She peered behind the freezer and saw that it had not just been unplugged—the electrical cord had been cut.

A wave of anger at Billy Chapel washed over her, because who besides him would have done that? It wasn't enough to leave Theo and Edmund's bodies behind. He had ensured that they suffered the final indignity of becoming like a car-hit deer's carcass by the side of the road, except without even the benefit of vultures to clean up the scene.

She turned from the freezer and leaned back against it, steadying herself against a wave of dizziness and nausea. She couldn't work like this. With the lid now closed, the odor from Theo's body might eventually dissipate, but she'd have to do something about Edmund's body. Getting it into the freezer was out of the question, she decided.

And before she dealt with that issue, she had to ensure she wouldn't be surprised by other visitors.

She went to the door and looked for a lock, but there was no way to lock it from the inside. Evidently, she thought sourly, Theo had been more worried about people getting out than getting in.

But despite her fear of an encounter, despite the horror of what she had found, she felt calmer than she had in weeks. She was back in a lab, where she had always felt most comfortable, most herself—and where she was most likely to be able to do the work she needed to do.

She didn't want to stay at the compound longer than was absolutely necessary. She needed to narrow her focus. She was better equipped to pursue a pharmaceutical rather than electrical solution to creating clairvoyance and what Ballard referred to as "the squeeze" in normal adults, and she needed to pick the ability that would be of most immediate use to her.

Once she had developed a drug for that, she'd be able to bring this situation with Billy Chapel and Lizzy Ballard to a head.

19

─────────

Lizzy took her eyes off the road long enough to glance at the clock on the Caravan's dashboard: eight o'clock. Not only was it starting to get dark, but she desperately needed to detach her cramped fingers from the steering wheel and, ideally, find a bathroom other than the camp toilet in the back of the van. And, she realized, get something to eat. She was starving.

She saw a strip mall and pulled off. Most of the stores—a pet salon, a tag and title service, a vacuum cleaner repair shop, and a pawn shop—were closed, but a pizzeria was open.

She went inside, used the restroom, bought two slices and a Coke, and returned to the Caravan. She climbed into the cargo area and settled down on its tiny couch/mattress combo.

She had no better idea of where the compound was than she had that morning. Much of the land east of Hagerstown was forested, dotted with small bodies of water but with no helipads that she could see on the satellite view. The twists and turns of the wooded roads scrambled her sense of direction, and several times she spotted landmarks she recalled having passed miles or even minutes earlier.

When she finished her pizza, she tried calling Olivia again, but again the call went to voicemail. Lizzy hoped the reason was no more serious than that Olivia was still working her test shift at *Charm City*.

She considered calling Owen. She knew that Ruby had told him about Lizzy's plan to go to the compound—she had already gotten three voicemails and four texts from him, all of which she had responded to via text, letting him know she was fine and, in fact, couldn't even find the compound. She still wasn't quite up to a conversation that would require her to justify her plan again.

And what was her plan? If the compound was deserted, or if she could confirm that Philip wasn't there, maybe she'd go back to Baltimore but steer clear of Olivia and *Charm City*. And if Philip *was* at the compound ... she just didn't know enough to make a plan. She'd have to play it by ear once she got there.

She had eaten only one of the two pieces of pizza, but she had lost her appetite. She shoved the second slice back in the bag and wiped her fingers on a wad of paper napkins.

Full darkness had now fallen, and if she couldn't find the compound in the daylight, she wasn't likely to find it after dark. She had noticed three cars parked at one end of the parking lot with *For Sale* signs in the windows. She'd park next to them—carrying a *For Sale* sign in the Caravan for just such situations might be a good idea—unfold the mattress, and hunker down until daylight.

20

———

Lizzy awoke in the back of the Caravan to find someone peering in the window.

She wasn't sure which one of them was more startled.

Bleary-eyed and with her heart still pounding, she climbed out of the van to find a young man in a University of Maryland T-shirt standing next to it, hands up as if he was surrendering to her.

"Sorry," he stammered. "My cousin has been looking for a van like this for his delivery business—I thought it was for sale."

She laughed shakily and ran her fingers through her hair. "That's the effect I was going for—I just didn't realize I'd be so successful."

He laughed as well, then sobered. "You okay?" He stuffed his hands in his pockets. "Are you living out of your van?"

She waved a hand. "No—I'm on my way to see ... friends. Just got tired last night and didn't want to keep driving. I don't like driving during the day, but I *really* don't like driving at night. What time is it, anyway?" She pulled her phone out of her pocket: past nine o'clock. "Jeez, I didn't realize it was so late. I better get going. Sorry to have scared you."

"Sorry to have scared *you*," he said. "Safe travels."

She climbed into the driver's seat and searched her map app for a gas station. She didn't really need gas, but she'd put a couple of gallons in the tank in order to use the restroom.

The station had a well-stocked convenience store, and she got a bottle of orange juice and a breakfast sandwich. She ate in the back of the Caravan, scanning the map app for clues about where the compound might be.

After almost half an hour of scanning, tapping, and zooming, she spotted what she had been looking for: a wooded area marked by a pond and a square of pavement that she hoped was Theo Viklund's helipad, although it didn't bear the big H she had seen on other, less covert pads. The compound was further north than she had expected.

She dropped the rest of the breakfast sandwich back into the bag and disposed of it and the remains of her pizza dinner in one of the convenience store trash cans.

Then she climbed back into the Caravan and headed for the compound.

21

Donny turned off the road and pulled the Escalade up to the gate of the entrance to the compound. Philip could see that the gate was slightly bent—a result of Billy Chapel's men forcing their way inside—but not so bent that it would be noticeable at a casual glance.

Donny took a key out of his pocket and handed it to Philip. "Unlock it. And relock it once I'm through."

Philip climbed out of the SUV and went to the gate. The built-in lock no longer engaged, but the gate was held closed with a short length of chain and a padlock. He unlocked the padlock and swung the gate open, then closed and relocked the gate after the Escalade had passed through.

He climbed back in and handed the key back to Donny. Richard, who was in the back seat, was scanning the wooded grounds with a combination of curiosity and trepidation.

"Where's the house?" asked Donny.

"Just follow the drive," said Philip.

They were about half-way along the quarter-mile long drive when Philip spotted a body a dozen feet off the road. He didn't see any reason to point it out, but Donny coasted the Escalade to a stop.

A gasp from the back seat indicated that Richard had seen it, too.

"Billy just left them where they lay?" Philip asked, not bothering to hide his disgust.

"Only Viklund's men," said Donny. As he pulled away, he added with a note of vicarious pride, "Billy took care of his own."

Philip spotted the house before anyone else did, since he knew to look out for the camouflaged structure nestled into one of the property's rolling hills.

Donny pulled up in front of the flagstone terrace at the entrance and turned to Philip. "So, what now?" He clearly didn't like having to rely on Philip for instructions, but, as Billy had pointed out to them before they left, Philip was familiar with the compound, and Donny wasn't.

"Let's start with the house and then start checking the other building and the grounds," said Philip. He was quite sure that if Louise was at the compound, which seemed more likely the more he thought about it, she would be in the lab. However, he had no reason to want her to fall into Billy's hands—the only thing worse than Louise's grotesque experiments would be having her knowledge at Chapel's disposal. If she was in the lab, she might notice their presence at the house and slip away.

"Fine," Donny said, then turned toward where Richard sat in the back seat. "You, too, Pearson. And bring the iPad in case we find Mortensen."

The three men climbed out of the SUV, and Philip led them to the front door.

Donny drew his gun, then motioned for Philip to enter.

"You have the gun," said Philip, "but want me to go through first?"

Donny grinned. "That's right."

Philip didn't really picture Mortensen as the type to carry a gun, but he hoped she hadn't enlisted replacements for the men —now dead—she had previously used as her muscle. He turned the doorknob, almost disappointed to find it unlocked, and eased the door open. He slipped inside, grimacing at the stench that hit him, and stepped to one side so that he wouldn't be backlit against the bright morning light. He scanned the space. There weren't many places a person could hide in the sparsely furnished entrance hall. "Clear so far," he called softly out the door.

Richard and Donny stepped inside, their footsteps echoing disconcertingly in the cavernous space.

Donny's features twisted. "Holy fuck, what's that stench?"

Philip pointed to a form sprawled at the base of the far wall. "Another one of Viklund's men, I'm guessing."

Richard buried his nose in his elbow and peered wide-eyed over the top of his arm.

"Let's move," Donny said. "Where to?"

"There are suites at the end of each of these halls." Philip kept his voice low, since he assumed Donny wouldn't want them telegraphing their presence to anyone in the house. "Let's check those first."

They checked the suites, one where Louise had housed Philip and Lizzy, the other where he, and later Lizzy, had first met Chapel. They were both empty and seemingly unoccupied. Then they followed the main hallway toward the back of the house. As they went, they checked rooms and off-shoot corridors, including one that led to the overgrown conservatory.

Much to Philip's relief, the spaces were empty, even of bodies, which jibed with what Philip had seen during the gun battle between Viklund's men and Chapel's—he believed most of the casualties would be outside.

On a lower level, they located the staff quarters: a short corridor of bedrooms accessed from a break room equipped for ping pong, pool, and darts.

"You take the rooms on the right," Donny whispered to Philip, "and I'll take the ones on the left." He turned to Richard. "And you stay out of the way."

Philip reached the last bedroom on the right and had almost turned back to tell Donny it was clear on his side when he noticed a camouflage-patterned baseball cap lying on the floor, almost under the bed. It caught his eye because of its position, and because it was so out of character with the rest of the prettily decorated, pastel-colored room.

He suspected that someone other than the room's usual tenant had spent the night here. And if it was someone Philip knew, he hoped it was Mortensen and not Lizzy.

He turned back to Donny. "Nothing here."

Donny emerged from the last bedroom on his side and ran his hand through his hair. "Shit. We're supposed to check in with Billy by mid-afternoon, and when we do, I want to tell him we found Mortensen." He pulled his phone of his pocket and glanced at the screen. "I can't believe there's no cell service here."

"I thought we were supposed to be looking for a lab," said Richard.

Donny dropped his phone back into his pocket. "A lab?"

"Yes. Chapel told me the woman you're looking for might have come here to use the lab."

Donny turned a glare to Philip. "You knew about this?"

Philip shrugged. "I thought we were supposed to search the whole compound."

Donny's glare turned into a scowl. "Like hell you did. You know where this lab is?"

Philip gave an internal sigh. "It must be in the building where they had locked Billy up."

Donny swept his hand out. "Lead the way, Phil."

22

Lizzy rolled slowly past the front gate of the compound. She could see that it was damaged and was now secured by a length of padlocked chain. She doubted she could find a way to unfasten the padlock, and in case anyone was in the compound monitoring security cameras, she didn't want to linger at the gate.

She drove as close to the perimeter fence as the roads allowed until she found a place where she could pull the Caravan far enough off the road to not be seen by the drivers of the few vehicles she saw in the area.

She changed out of the clothes she had been wearing since the previous morning and into something more appropriate for bushwhacking across Viklund's property: jeans, a long-sleeved T-shirt, and sneakers. She slipped a bottle of water and the case containing a vial of the juice and a few syringes into a small knapsack. Then she set off to explore options for entry on foot.

23

———

The three men left the house by the back entrance, and Philip led Donny and Richard up the path toward the lab that Theo Viklund had built for Louise Mortensen. It was a utilitarian concrete block building with a single door and no windows in its unwelcoming facade. Philip guessed Viklund had built it that way to prevent curious compound staff from peering in at whatever Mortensen was doing in there, but it also had the disadvantage to anyone inside of not allowing them to see anyone approaching.

As they neared the door, Donny, gun still in hand, said to Philip, his voice low, "Open the door."

Having anticipated this command, Philip stepped up to the door, turned the handle, and pushed the door open, stepping back as he did so—and giving anyone inside a clear shot at Donny.

Donny's eyes widened in surprise, but he recovered quickly and stepped forward, sweeping the space with his gun.

Philip was sorry to see the gun halt mid-sweep. Obviously, someone was in the lab.

"And what have we here?" Donny said, his voice a caricature

of self-satisfaction. "Dr. Mortensen, I presume." He turned his head slightly to call back over his shoulder. "Come on in, you chickenshits."

Philip and Richard stepped into the lab.

Mortensen sat at one of the lab tables, her hand on the adjustment knob of a microscope, her expression a mixture of alarm and resignation.

Donny waggled his gun at Louise. "Move back from that thing."

"What do you think she's going to do," said Philip, "bludgeon you with the microscope?"

Donny shot him an angry look. "You shut up. I want her away from everything." He turned back to Louise. "Move your stool into the middle of the room."

Louise stood, moved her stool, and sat.

Donny grimaced. "Where the hell is that stink coming from? You hiding bodies in here?"

Louise's eyes flickered to the corner of the room, and Philip followed her gaze to the chest freezer.

Donny looked at the freezer and laughed. "You storing someone in there?" His smile dimmed in the face of Louise's stony expression. He crossed to the freezer and reached for the lid.

"I wouldn't if I were you," she said. "If you think the odor is bad now ..."

Donny took a beat to consider, then stepped away from the freezer. He turned to Richard. "Pearson, look around the lab and see what you can find."

Richard looked around the space in confusion. "This is a medical lab."

"No shit."

"I'm not a doctor," said Richard, his voice cracking with frustration. "I keep telling you people—I'm a Signals and Systems professor."

"Okay, so look for Signals and Systems stuff."

Richard cast a panicked look at Louise.

She crossed her arms and stared back at him, expressionless.

Richard began to circle the room tentatively. "Well, that's a spectrophotometer. That's a centrifuge."

"What would she use them for?" asked Donny.

"The spectrophotometer shines light of different wavelengths through a sample and measures how much light gets absorbed at each color, which indicates the properties and concentration of the substances in the sample. And a centrifuge is used to separate components of a mixture based on their densities."

"But what would *she* use them for?"

Richard wrung his hands. "I have no idea." His eyes scanned the room, desperate, and landed on another machine. "That's a spectrum analyzer!" He launched into a detailed description of the machine's uses.

Donny stared, brow furrowed, at Richard, but Louise's gaze was on Philip. He wished he had a dose of Lizzy's juice—one that would work on a person who was not a product of Louise's Vivantem experiments—to tell what Louise was thinking. Or, he thought, he wished that Mortensen had a dose of the juice that would enable her to read his thoughts, or at least some of them. He lifted his shoulders in a minute shrug, the best he could think to do to telegraph that he was not cooperating willingly with Donny.

Richard had started in on a biography of the inventor of the spectrum analyzer when Donny cut him off. "Stow it, Professor." He waved to the iPad in Richard's hand. "Ask her to explain what's on there."

No doubt relieved that the attention was going to shift from him to Louise, Richard tapped the iPad, and after a moment, Louise's voice came through the speaker.

"I'll ask questions, and you'll relay to me what you can gather about his answers. Don't say anything unless it's to convey what he's thinking. In the course of our conversation, I may mention the work we did at Vivantem, but he won't remember any of what we discuss. Your friend Philip could confirm that for you."

As the recording played, Louise's features tightened into a combination of fury and fear. It was clear that she was as concerned as Philip was about what Billy might do with the information. "Where did you get that?"

Richard stopped the playback and looked between Donny and Philip.

"That's none of your business," Donny said to Louise.

"It's more my business than yours," she shot back.

"Should I keep playing it?" Richard asked tentatively.

"Donny," said Philip, "I doubt Billy wants me to hear whatever's on that recording, and Mortensen doesn't need to be told what was said—she said it. How is this doing us any good? Actually, let me rephrase. How is this doing *Billy* any good? We should have Richard search the lab for anything he thinks might be important, and then we should bring Mortensen and whatever Richard has found back to Baltimore. We can always come back to the compound if we find out we missed something. And you said we need to check in with Billy, and we can't do that from inside the compound—cell signals are blocked."

Donny pulled his phone out of his pocket, tapped, and examined the screen. "Shit." He shoved the phone back in his pocket and turned to Louise. "Where should Pearson be looking?"

She raised her eyebrows. "For what?"

He reversed the gun in his hand so that he was holding the barrel, took a step toward her, and drew back his hand.

Richard gasped, and Louise jumped to her feet, sending the stool clattering to the floor.

"Donny!" Philip said, his voice sharp. "If she's going to get hurt, I'm guessing Billy wants to be the one to do it."

After a moment, Donny lowered the gun and flipped it back to its normal position. He scanned the lab. "We can't bring everything in this place back with us. We need her to tell us what we need to bring." He turned to Louise. "What are you working on?"

Louise surprised Philip by answering. "A pharmaceutical approach to what Chapel wants information on." She narrowed her eyes at Donny. "How much do you know about why Chapel wants to see me?"

"That's none of your business."

Louise was silent.

If she was weighing her options, Donny didn't give her much time. He pointed the gun at her knee. "I'm guessing Billy won't mind too much if you're missing a kneecap."

The blood drained from her face, and she held up her hands. "Fine. If Chapel didn't intend for you to know, then it's not my fault you forced me to tell you."

Donny lowered the gun.

Louise smoothed the fabric of her camo pants ... or maybe she was wiping sweat off her palms. "When I worked at the Vivantem fertility clinic, I developed a process that resulted in special abilities—*dangerous* abilities—in subjects, and I imagine Chapel wants to find out how to reproduce it in others."

"And you're doing more of that here?" asked Donny.

"No, I'm working on an associated project. The subjects of my earlier experiments couldn't control their abilities. I'm working on a drug that would render those abilities temporarily ineffective. I call it neuroinhibitol."

Donny knit his brow. "Why would you do that?"

"Because if I—or Chapel—wanted to work with these subjects, we wouldn't want to risk becoming a victim of their abilities. You wouldn't build a race car without making sure you could apply the brakes, would you?"

"And that's it? You're building a race car and now you're working on the brakes before you take it out for a spin?"

"That's all I'm willing to say ... until I can speak with Chapel."

Donny groaned. "Fine. We'll take you back to Baltimore, see what Billy can get you to say, then we can come back here and get what we need from this place." He gestured toward the door with his gun. "Let's go."

24

Lizzy had been following the chain link fence—battling her way through trees, bushes, and undergrowth for almost twenty minutes—and was considering coming back with a ladder when she came to a breach. But it was not the result of a maintenance lapse or a fallen tree, as she had expected. It was a neatly cut person-sized flap of fence, probably made with bolt cutters. She thought with a sigh that she should have thought of that herself.

She scanned the surrounding woods. Confirming that she was alone, at least as far as she could tell, she returned her attention to the fence. The interior of the cut metal was not rusty, so the cut must have been made fairly recently, but what was "recently"? How quickly would the metal rust—over days? Weeks? The grass around the opening was a little matted, but animals as well as humans might have been using the opening as a passage, although the flap had been pushed back into place, so currently only squirrels or chipmunks or maybe a fox could get through.

She sat back on her haunches and considered. Who would want to break out of Theo Viklund's compound? Billy Chapel could be using the compound to hold people against their will, just as Theo Viklund had held Louise and Philip. Maybe one of them had found a pair of bolt cutters and escaped. Lizzy doubted that Louise could be Chapel's prisoner, since all indications were that she had escaped from the compound by helicopter. And Billy obviously wasn't holding Philip there as a prisoner, at least, not as of Ruby's interaction with him in Philly.

Another possibility was that someone had broken *in* rather than out. That could be something as harmless as curious local teenagers, but it could also be someone coming back to look for something at the compound. Louise or Lucas might have left something behind when they fled.

Was there anything in the compound Philip would have come back for? When Louise had summoned Lizzy and Philip to the compound, she had made him turn over his wallet, and the wallet contained his fake Philip Riva ID, but she couldn't imagine him risking a trip back here for that.

But Philip was working for Chapel now, or at least pretending to. If Chapel's men had put the padlock on the front gate when they left after the gun battle, as seemed likely, why would Philip have to sneak in?

After another minute of thinking, she decided that the most likely explanation was casual curiosity-seekers. She pulled back the wire and stepped through the hole. She'd go to the house, assuming she could locate it on the enormous property, and see what she could find. There were plenty of places there for her to hide if she found it was occupied.

And, after all, she'd have the element of surprise.

25

"Line up, guys," Donny said, gesturing with the barrel of his gun toward the door. "Pearson, Castillo, Mortensen, then me. I'll be in back keeping an eye— and my gun—on you."

Richard stepped to the door, and Philip, Louise, and Donny fell into line behind him.

"Okay, Pearson, lead the way," said Donny.

Richard opened the door and stepped outside—and stopped so suddenly that Philip almost walked into him.

Richard's gaze was fixed on the woods near the house, and Philip's heart clenched when he saw a figure moving stealthily among the trees. It was clearly a woman, and based on her size and the way she moved, it could only be Lizzy. Her attention was focused on the house's back entrance and surrounding woods, and she obviously didn't see the four of them.

Behind him, Louise drew in a quick breath.

In what Philip guessed was an attempt to distract Donny's attention from the woman in the woods, Richard dropped to one knee, put the iPad on the ground, and began fiddling with his shoelace. It was a gutsy move, considering how eager Donny was to do some damage to someone.

But Donny had apparently seen Lizzy as well, because he stepped round Louise and Philip, grabbed Richard's arm, and hauled him to his feet. He herded them back inside and closed the door behind them.

"Who's that?" Donny barked. When no one answered, he turned to Louise. "Do you know who that is?"

"No."

"Me either," said Richard, unprompted.

Donny turned to Philip. "You?"

Philip realized the story he had given Billy could work to his advantage. "I didn't get a good look, but it might be the girl I ran into at the compound when I was here before. I understood she was Theo Viklund's niece. In fact, she and I hooked up—" He sensed a surprised start from Louise. "—and if I went down to the house, I might be able to grab her and bring her back here. No muss, no fuss."

He had no intention of bringing Lizzy back to the lab, either to turn her over to Donny or to put her in the same room with Mortensen, which could end badly for Mortensen if Lizzy was driven to squeeze her. Philip was almost as interested as Billy in finding out what Mortensen was up to, but equally interested in making sure Billy wasn't the one who could capitalize on it. And a trip to the house alone would give him a few minutes to try to figure out how to deal with the evolving situation.

"Are you fucking kidding me?" said Donny with exaggerated disbelief. "You think I'm going to let you have all the glory? I'll go. You stay here with these two."

"And I'm supposed to keep them in line with the power of my personality?" said Philip.

Donny bent and pulled one of his pants legs up, revealing a knife in a calf holster. He took it out and slid it across the concrete floor toward Philip, who picked it up. Donny turned to Richard. "Don't forget what will happen to your friends and family if things go tits up—" He turned to Louise. "And don't you try to run. We found you once—we'd find you again. And when I get back," this directed at Philip, "I'll have the girl in front of me, so don't get any ideas about jumping the first person through the door." He slipped outside.

When the door closed behind him, Philip met Richard's gaze —hopeful—and Louise's—calculating—then went to the door and cracked it open.

Donny was jogging down the path toward the house. Then he disappeared through the back entrance, where Lizzy had likely gone just a minute earlier.

Philip turned back to the room, reversed the knife so he was holding it by the blade, and extended it handle-first to Richard. "You keep an eye on Mortensen. And remember what Donny said about friends and family—it won't go well for Marjorie if I get back here and one or both of you are gone."

Without waiting for a response, he stepped outside and sprinted down the path to the house.

26

Lizzy stood just inside the back entrance of the house, shifting her knapsack into a more comfortable position on her shoulders and listening for anything that would suggest she wasn't alone. She couldn't hear anything other than the shush of a breeze through the trees and the cry of a hawk far above.

She had spent barely a day in the house on her earlier visit, and during her walks through it, she had been distracted—by uncertainty about whether she could use the squeeze if needed, by excitement at the idea of being reunited with the kidnapped Andy, or by terror when she was dragged by Billy Chapel through its corridors in search of Louise. If she had ever expected to return to Theo Viklund's compound, she would have spent some time after that visit trying to sketch out her memories of the layout of the house.

The suite where she and Philip had briefly been housed would be easy enough to find: straight down the wide central hallway toward the entrance hall, then along the upward sloping corridor. The suite where she had been taken to meet with Billy, and where she had been shocked to find Philip with him, was at the end of the downward sloping corridor on the other side of the entrance hall. But what was she likely to find there? If someone was in the house and wanted to keep their presence a secret, would they really be staying in one of the suites? And if someone had settled into one of the suites, did she really want to encounter them on their home turf?

She'd check the other parts of the house first.

She had just reached the central hallway when she noticed another corridor branching off to the side, at the end of which was what looked like a conservatory. She turned down the corridor to investigate.

It *was* a conservatory, although not a particularly well-maintained one. In the center was a small circular area paved in brick, on which stood a metal cafe table and two chairs. A couple of brick paths littered with yellowed leaves wound out of sight among the bushes and small trees. She couldn't get a good sense of how big the room was—at least two or three times the footprint of Owen's house, she guessed. She peered in from the doorway. She had been nervous about entering the suites in case someone was hiding there, but the conservatory offered even more hiding places.

She'd save the conservatory for last—assuming she didn't find anything or anyone in the rest of the house.

She turned back toward the main hallway—and almost screamed at the sight of a backlit figure at the end of the corridor.

Her first thought was a combination of terror and hopefulness: Could it be Philip?

But the figure was beefier than Philip.

Her second thought was that perhaps whoever it was hadn't seen her ... but she would be even more clearly backlit by the bright light in the conservatory than he was.

Any doubt on that score was eliminated when the figure

called, with a grin in his voice, "What are you doing playing all alone in this big ol' house, little girl?"

She jumped back into the conservatory and slammed the glass-paned door closed behind her. One of the panes shattered, sending a shower of shards onto the floor of the corridor. She ran across the brick-paved area, intentionally upending one of the two chairs—maybe it would slow him down if he followed her—and sprinted down the path furthest from the door.

The space was smaller than she had imagined—the path was only a couple dozen feet long. It ended at another glass-paned door leading outside. She ran to the door, grabbed the lever handle, and tried to wrench it open.

Locked.

The man's voice drifted through the conservatory—he must have been standing near the door to the corridor. "Come out, come out, wherever you are, sweetheart ... or I'm coming to get you."

Lizzy tried to quiet her gasps of panicked breath. There were several paths leading away from the brick-paved area. Maybe he would explore one of the other ones and she could get past him and out of the conservatory. If he caught up with her, she could squeeze him.

If he had a gun and shot her from a distance, there wasn't much she could do about that.

She heard the screech of metal on brick—he must have picked up the chair she had knocked over. A chair that would point him to the path she had taken.

She pressed her back to the locked door that stood between her and the relative safety of outdoors.

Then she heard another voice.

"Did you find her?"

Philip.

27

Philip had just started down the hallway toward the front of the house when he heard Donny's voice coming from the direction of the conservatory.

"Come out, come out, wherever you are, sweetheart ... or I'm coming to get you."

Shit.

When Philip stepped into the conservatory, Donny was setting one of the metal cafe chairs on its feet.

"Did you find her?" he asked.

Donny spun, bringing the gun up.

Philip raised his hands. "Don't shoot. I'm here to help."

"I told you to stay in the lab," Donny snarled. "What the fuck are you doing here?"

"Hey, just showing some initiative, like you suggested. Mortensen had some suggestions for where we could look."

"I don't need Mortensen's suggestions." Donny waved his gun toward one of the paths. "The girl's down there."

"Really? Did you see her?"

"Of course I saw her, you moron—that's how I know she's in here."

Philip glanced around the conservatory. "That specific path? There are a bunch of them."

Donny gestured to the chair. "She pulled that over when she ran, so she was going in that direction. She's down there. And I'm going to go get her. Stay out of my way."

"Billy's going to want her unharmed."

Donny let the gun arm fall to his side and took a step toward Philip. "Based on what you said back at the lab, I think *you're* the one who wants her unharmed. Looking for some more action before we leave for Baltimore?"

"I'm getting all the action I need, thanks. What I'm hoping for is to be unharmed myself—by you or by Billy if we show up back in Baltimore with Mortensen or the girl in bad shape."

"You know, Castillo," sneered Donny, "based on what I saw you do, I didn't figure you for the squeamish type."

Philip's peripheral vision caught a flicker of movement among the bushes behind Donny. "I'm trying to keep *you* out of trouble, Donny. You haven't been covering yourself with glory lately. I don't think you want to piss Billy off any more than he's already pissed off."

The flicker was moving closer.

Donny took another step toward him. "You know what's going to piss Billy off? When I tell him that you interfered with me trying to grab the girl."

The flicker had almost reached the mouth of the path.

"As I recall," said Philip, "Billy sent me along with you so you wouldn't screw up this assignment like you screwed up the last one."

Donny drew back the gun to backhand Philip with it, and just as Philip juked to the side to evade the swing, Lizzy stepped out of the path.

"Stop it!" she yelled.

Donny, with an impressive display of agility, continued his turn, now swinging the gun toward Lizzy.

She ducked, and Philip managed to change his own trajectory enough to plow into Donny's back.

The gun discharged, and Philip was vaguely aware of the sound of breaking glass.

The two men hit the floor, Philip on top, but Donny jerked his elbow back, catching Philip in the ribs. Donny twisted, throwing Philip off his back, and brought the gun back up toward Lizzy.

But Lizzy had closed the space, and she kicked out, catching Donny's arm.

Another shot rang out. Another pane of glass shattered.

Donny had kept hold of the gun and his arm was too far away for Philip to grab, but Philip threw himself on top of Donny again and locked his left arm around Donny's neck, his head over Donny's right shoulder, his right hand levering his forearm deeper into Donny's throat.

Donny swung his gun arm back and down, and the barrel cracked into Philip's knee.

Pain sizzled up Philip's leg. He levered his arm harder into Donny's neck.

Then Donny reached his right arm around, pointed the gun over his left shoulder, and fired.

Philip jerked as the bullet grazed his left bicep.

Philip could sense Lizzy dancing around them, probably looking for an opening for landing a kick to Donny's head that wouldn't be just as likely to land on his own.

"Run!" he yelled.

Donny made another attempt to throw Philip off, but unlike earlier, his movements seemed uncoordinated.

Lizzy still stood over them, but she had scuttled to one side so that she was behind Donny.

Donny swung the gun in her general direction and fired another shot, but Philip could tell it had missed her by at least several feet. He gritted his teeth against the pain in his bicep and tightened his arm even further around Donny's neck.

Donny brought the gun back again, toward his right shoulder ... and toward Philip's face.

"No!" screamed Lizzy.

Donny's body convulsed, another bullet whining over Philip's right shoulder, then he sprawled flat on the floor under Philip.

Philip didn't loosen his grip. "Lizzy, are you okay?" he rasped, hoarse from adrenaline.

He heard Lizzy's breathless voice above him. "Yes."

"Was what happened to him because of you or me?"

"Me, I think."

"Can you tell if it's safe for me to let go of him?"

"I think it is."

"Just to be on the safe side, take his gun."

Lizzy nudged the gun out from under Donny's slack fingers and out of reach.

Philip slowly released the pressure on Donny's neck, extracted his arm from underneath the motionless form, and climbed to his feet.

Lizzy stood a few feet away, eyes wide, arms wrapped around herself.

"Are you okay?" he asked.

"Yes. Are you?" Her eyes widened further. "You're bleeding!"

He glanced at his arm. "It's not serious," he said, although the pain in his arm was singing. He picked up the gun, then bent and checked Donny's neck for a pulse but found nothing. Gun at the ready, he rolled Donny onto his back.

His eyes were open, and the whites of his eyes were blood red.

"Yup, I think it was you," Philip said.

Lizzy burst into tears.

28

Lizzy felt herself sway, and Philip took her arm and led her down the path to one of the chairs at the cafe table.

"I'm sorry," he said. "I didn't mean to upset you."

"I hate doing that," she sobbed, dropping onto the chair.

"He didn't give you much choice."

"I hate *having* to do it!"

"I know you do." He pulled the other chair closer to hers, sat down, and took her hand. "I know it doesn't help much, but he was not a good person. The world is better without him."

"I wish someone else had taken care of him."

"I wish that, too."

She wiped her eyes with the back of her free hand, then wiped her nose on the sleeve of her T-shirt. "Where have you been? What happened to you? You're not working for Billy Chapel ..."

She managed to keep from adding ... *are you?*

"No. He thinks I am, but I'm not. I'll explain everything to you, but right now we have some planning to do." He released her hand and fell back in the chair. "As you may have guessed,

Donny works for Chapel, and Chapel sent us here to look for Mortensen. We found her in the lab."

Lizzy's eyes widened. "Really? Did Donny—"

"Donny didn't do anything to her. She's still in the lab with a guy Chapel forced to cooperate with him—Richard. He's supposed to make sure she doesn't leave the lab. But he isn't much of a guard—he's actually a college professor—and I don't want to leave him alone with Louise for too long. I need to get back there."

Lizzy was struggling to process the information. "Is Louise working for Billy?"

"No—and we need to make sure she doesn't fall into his hands. She has plenty of information and expertise related to the squeeze and clairvoyance that he'd love to get his hands on, and he wouldn't stop at much to force it out of her." He was silent for a few moments, then continued. "Here's what I propose: I'm going to go back to the lab to keep an eye on Mortensen, and I'm going to send Richard back here to move Donny's body into the car we came in."

Lizzy was grateful that Philip hadn't suggested she accompany him back to the lab to help deal with Louise. She couldn't guess what might happen in that situation. On one hand, she had more reason to want Louise Mortensen dead than she did the man whose body lay on the floor. On the other, it was unlikely she would be able to squeeze Louise unless Louise posed an imminent threat, and Philip certainly wouldn't let that happen. She'd be happy if she never saw Louise Mortensen again.

But she didn't want to leave it all up to Philip to deal with the situation. "Do you want me to take some of the juice and see if I can find out what she's thinking?"

"You have some with you?"

"Yes."

Philip considered for a moment. "I know there are some people whose thoughts are more difficult for you to read. Do you think you could read Mortensen's thoughts?"

She sighed. "I don't think so." She summoned a wan smile. "She's almost as guarded a person as you are. But I'd be willing to try."

He scrubbed his hands down his face. "Mortensen would have every reason to throw up mental barriers. Let's hold off for now but keep it in mind as an option."

"Okay," she said, somewhat relieved. Eavesdropping on people's thoughts was never a comfortable experience. It made her feel like a mental Peeping Tom, and people's thoughts were usually cruder than what they'd say out loud. Louise's thoughts might not be crude, but she had no doubt they would be disturbing. She gestured toward Donny's body. "What are you going to do with him once Richard gets him into the car?"

"I'm not sure yet." Philip smiled ruefully. "I'm making this up on the fly. But if it's in the car, we can remove it if we want to, and if we decide it's better to leave it, it will be a clear connection to Chapel."

Lizzy nodded. "Okay. I can help Richard with—" She waved toward the body.

"Actually, I think it's better if he doesn't see you. The less he knows, the safer for him. You should hide while he's here."

After a moment, she nodded. "Okay."

"Do you know of a good hiding place? How about the dispensary? Can you find that?"

"Yes, I think so." She sighed. "I'm getting the easy end of the bargain."

"Lizzy, you took care of Donny. There's no way that was *the easy end.*"

She nodded again.

"Once I know Louise is secured," he continued, "I'll meet up with you in the dispensary and we can decide on next steps."

"Should we go there now?" She gestured toward his arm. "Find something to treat that?"

"We can do that once we've taken care of this other stuff." He glanced at the bloodstain on his shoulder. "It really is just a graze—I don't think it's even bleeding anymore."

"It must hurt, though." She swallowed down a lump in her throat. "I'm sorry I couldn't squeeze him faster."

"I'm sorry you had to do it at all ... but you did great." He stood. "I'll get the keys to the Escalade and to the padlock on the front gate off him. I think I'll leave his phone on him, since I imagine Billy might be able to track it once it's out of the compound."

"Makes sense."

He extended his hand, and she grasped it and pulled herself to her feet.

"Are you okay?" he asked. "Relatively okay?"

"Yes. Are *you* okay?"

"Yes." They stood in silence for a moment, then he said, smiling, "But I'll need my hand back."

She blushed and released his hand, stuffing hers in her pockets. "I'm just so glad to see you."

He squeezed her shoulder. "I'm glad to see you, too."

29

After Philip had left to follow Donny to the house, Louise assessed the man he had left in charge. He wasn't much taller than she was and, despite the fact that she was slender, probably didn't weigh much more.

On the other hand, the knife looked like it could do some damage: a four-inch blade with a wicked curve, ending in a needle-sharp point. Pearson might be as likely to stab himself as her if she tried to overpower him, but she wouldn't get away unscathed. He stood between her and the door, so she couldn't hope to outrun him.

Before she could consider other options, he said, "I know I look like a bookworm, but I've done plenty of hunting in my life, and I've gutted a lot of deer. I wouldn't kill you, because Chapel wants you alive, but I could hurt you enough that you couldn't run."

She suppressed a shudder and crossed her arms. "Why?"

"Because I believe the alternative is that Chapel would kill my wife."

"That's the woman Castillo mentioned? Marjorie?"

He nodded.

"Chapel is holding her hostage?"

"As good as. She's in a care home." When he continued, he couldn't hide the tremble in his voice. "He had Donny take a picture of her asleep in bed with a gun pointed at her head."

"I'm sorry to hear that. I'm Louise, by the way."

"Richard. Pleased to—" He stopped. "Maybe not so pleased."

"No. Is it all right if I sit at one of the lab tables?"

"Yes, that's okay."

She moved the stool, and Richard moved another stool to a location between her and the door. He sat, the knife resting on his thigh.

She hoped Castillo came back soon, ideally without the odious Donny.

She wasn't sure whether she hoped Ballard was with him or not.

LOUISE TRIED to engage Richard in conversation a few times, first to see if she could find out any information about what Billy Chapel was up to, and then to see if she could establish some rapport by asking him about his wife. He refused to be drawn out.

Louise jumped when the door handle rattled, and Richard leapt to his feet and raised the knife.

They both relaxed when Philip stepped into the lab. In one hand was the iPad that Richard had dropped outside. In the other was a gun.

"How did it go?" she asked, eyebrow cocked at the blood-stained arm of his jacket, marked with what looked like a bullet hole.

"So far, so good." he said.

"Are you okay?" Richard asked, gesturing toward his arm.

"I'm fine."

"Where's Donny?" Richard asked.

"Back in the house. Dead."

"Where's Ballard?" asked Louise.

"Ran away while I was busy disarming Donny."

Louise cocked a skeptical eyebrow at him.

Richard lowered his arm, the knife dangling by his side, his face creased with worry. "Does Billy know about Donny?"

"Nope."

"But Billy expects a call from him," said Richard, his voice thready with fear. "He'll find out eventually, and what's he going to do when he finds out Donny's dead? I'll tell you what he'll do." His voice became harder as he spoke. "He's going to send another one of his goons back to Letort and ..." He swallowed. "... hurt Marjorie. For all we know, he might have someone there right now."

"We're going to make sure that doesn't happen," said Philip. "First, we need to get Donny's body back in the SUV—"

"Why? Are we going to take it back to Baltimore?" Richard's voice jumped in register. "Are we going to drive back to Baltimore with a body in the car?"

"I don't know where we'll take it yet, or if we'll take it anywhere. I just want to keep our options open."

Richard opened his mouth, but Philip raised a hand to silence him.

"Then we'll get out of here, and once we can get a cell signal, I'll call some friends who can go to Letort and keep an eye on Marjorie."

"There must be a jammer in the compound," said Richard, "although it must be awfully powerful to cover the whole area. If we could find it—or even find a master switch to shut off power —you could make the call from here."

"Where would we look?" said Philip. "The house is enormous, and it might not even be in the house. Theo Viklund would have been sure to put it somewhere that wasn't easily accessible. We'd waste more time than we'd gain."

Richard looked toward Louise. "Do you know where the blocker is?"

She shook her head.

After a moment, Richard, his tone reluctant, said, "Okay, fine. We'll wait until we're away from the compound to make the call."

"Do you remember where the conservatory is?" Philip asked him.

"Yes, I remember it from when we were searching the house —near the back of the building, off that big hallway."

"That's where Donny is. If you can drag him to the back entrance, there's a golf cart there we can use to move him to the Escalade. If you can't get him onto the cart, I'll be there in a few minutes, and I can help."

"What are you going to be doing?"

"I want to search the lab."

"For what?"

"I'm not sure yet—I figure I'll know it when I see it."

"I thought that's what Billy wanted *me* to do."

"I've spent time here before—I know the places to look."

"But—"

"Richard," Philip said sharply, "we're wasting time. I want to get out of here and make that call to my friends as soon as possible so they can get to Letort. I thought you wanted that too."

"Yes, of course, of course." Richard hurried to the door of the lab, then turned back. "You're sure he's dead?"

"Very sure. And Richard," Philip said as Richard opened the door.

Richard turned around.

"If you run, when I get out of the compound, I'll call Billy and tell him *you're* the one who killed Donny."

Richard glared at him. "I won't run." He stepped outside and closed the door behind him.

Philip turned to face Louise.

She crossed her arms. "You're really going to search the lab?"

"Is there anything here worth searching for? And think carefully, because I don't plan to leave anything behind for anyone else—including you—to find."

Louise had been careful to take the important research records when she fled—although most of those had fallen into Lucas's hands. "No, I don't believe there is anything worth searching for. Are you really going to take that man's body away from the compound?"

"Probably not—but I needed to send Richard on an errand."

"And why is that?"

Philip sat down on the stool Richard had vacated. "Because you and I need to talk."

"And why can't we talk in the house? At least it doesn't smell of decomposing bodies." Before he could answer—she doubted he would in any case—she asked, "Ballard didn't really run away, did she. She's still at the house."

Philip was silent.

She sighed. "Fine. What do we need to talk about?"

He held up the iPad. "This contains the records that Lucas took from you when you left the compound, including, as you heard, the recording of Lizzy mediating a conversation with you and Edmund Rinnert about using electricity to create the squeeze or clairvoyance."

She scowled. "How did he come to have that information? Lucas took those records from me. Did he give them to Chapel?"

"In a manner of speaking."

She shook her head. "I never expected Lucas to—"

"Chapel caught up with Lucas before he could get out of the country, interrogated him, and then had him killed."

Louise felt the blood drain from her face.

Philip continued. "The reason Chapel kidnapped Richard is because he hoped Richard could help him interpret the information on here, but it's not really in Richard's area of expertise."

Her eyes drifted to the iPad, then back to Philip. "And what do you plan to do with it?"

"I plan to give it back to you—if you cooperate."

She narrowed her eyes. "All right."

"What you told Donny about what you're doing here—that you found a way to render the squeeze temporarily ineffective— is it true?"

She regarded him for a few moments. "Yes. Obviously, I haven't had a chance to test the inhibitol on a human subject. There's only one candidate that I'm aware of, and I haven't had any access to her."

"And is that *all* you've been doing?"

She weighed her options. Her impulse was to deny working on anything else. However, after hearing Richard play the recording of her Ballard-mediated conversation with Edmund Rinnert, she doubted Castillo would believe her. If he had killed Donny—and she had no doubt that Donny was dead, although she suspected Castillo might not have been the killer—it was unlikely he was cooperating willingly with Chapel. And if she had to make a choice about forming an alliance of her own, Castillo was a far more attractive option than Chapel.

She noticed that her fingers were drifting toward her wedding ring. What would Ballard's fellow poker players call it —her *tell*? It wouldn't do to have Castillo think Louise was looking for psychic support from her dead husband. She relaxed her hands in her lap. "No, it's not all I've been doing."

"Tell me everything—and do it fast."

30

Twenty minutes later, Philip jogged down the path from the lab to the back entrance of the house. The knapsack he carried, which he had taken from Louise, contained the iPad. Donny's gun was tucked into the waistband of his pants.

He found Richard next to the golf cart, arms hooked under Donny's armpits, struggling to heave the body onto the cart.

"Can you get his feet?" Richard puffed.

"Don't worry about it," said Philip. "Change of plans." Then he added, "But I wouldn't mind getting his shoulder holster."

As they worked Donny's jacket and holster off, Richard said, "I thought there'd be a bullet hole. How did he die?"

"Hit his head on the floor in the conservatory." Before Richard could question that, Philip continued. "Mortensen has some work she needs to finish," he said as he slipped on the holster and adjusted the fit, "but she obviously can't use the lab here because eventually Billy's going to send someone to see what's happened. Is there a lab at your college she could use?"

"There's a lab, but I don't know that it would suit her needs, especially if she's doing medical research."

Philip jammed the gun into the holster. "Richard, don't make me keep reminding you that Marjorie's well-being depends on your cooperation."

Richard's fists closed, then opened deliberately. "I'll find a lab she can use. But if Billy sends someone to the compound and doesn't find us, Letort is the next obvious place for him to look. Philip, I need to understand what's going on—at least some of it—otherwise how can I be sure Marjorie will be safe?"

Philip tamped down his frustration—if he were in Richard's place, he'd be asking the same questions. "Fair enough." He dropped onto one of the golf cart's front seats. "As far as I know, the only people who knew about you and Marjorie were Billy, Donny, and me, and now Louise. Billy captured a man who used to work with Louise and tortured him to get information—or, to be more accurate, *Donny* tortured him, under Billy's direction."

Richard's face paled, and he sank down on one of the cart's back seats.

Philip continued. "When this man was being questioned, Donny heard some information that Chapel would rather he hadn't heard. You've been around Donny long enough to know it's possible that Donny didn't realize how important what he had heard was. But if he *did* realize, Billy didn't mind getting rid of him."

"Billy told you that?"

"Yes."

"You two are pretty close."

"Richard, *you're* doing some pretty questionable stuff in order to save Marjorie. *I* want to save someone, too—me—and I'm doing things that I wouldn't otherwise do, including pretending I'm on Billy's side."

"You're saving yourself ... but you're saving that girl we saw going into the house, too, I'm guessing."

Philip nodded.

"And others?"

"Yes. But we can swap stories about that over beers when all this is settled."

"But how is it going to be settled? Donny may be dead, but what about Billy?"

"I'm going to take care of Billy."

"*Take care of* how?"

"I'm going to kill him."

Richard jumped up. "And how do you plan to do that? Just walk up to him, point that gun at him, and pull the trigger? It looks to me like he always has an armed entourage around him—you'd be dead the minute your hand went under your jacket!"

"I agree. But I believe there's an alternative, and we need Louise's help to make it work."

Richard ran a hand across his head. "Even if Chapel is dead, what's to keep some other guy from his organization from coming after us?"

"With Donny dead, and once Billy's dead, there won't be anyone other than me and Louise who know about you and Marjorie, and neither of us has any incentive to cause trouble for you."

Richard regarded Philip. "I guess I believe that about you, but what about her? Why wouldn't she go to the authorities and tell them everything that has happened here?"

"Because she has her own reasons for staying under the radar. She's wanted by the Pennsylvania Attorney General's office."

"What—" Richard stopped, then held up a hand. "I don't want to know." He sank back onto the golf cart seat. "And I guess it doesn't matter, as long as you're sure we can trust her."

"I don't know about *trusting* her, but I feel certain she won't cause you and Marjorie any problems."

"If she wants to stay away from the authorities, what makes

you think she won't run once we leave the compound? I can try to guard her, but I can't keep my guard up all the time."

"I have something she wants: the iPad. I told her I'd return it to her if she cooperates."

"And will you?"

"Let's just see how things pan out."

Richard heaved a sigh. "Okay. What do we need to do?"

Philip stood, and Richard followed suit. "Mortensen has a car parked outside the compound. Meet up with her at the lab, get to her car, then the two of you go somewhere near Letort— let's say Harrisburg—and wait for word from me."

"And you'll call your friends to guard Marjorie until Billy is dead?"

"Yes."

"They'll stay with her at Cedar Grove?"

"Yes ... unless there's a way to move her to some other, more secure location ...?"

"Not without an ambulance."

Philip shook his head. "Too complicated. They'll stay with her at Cedar Grove. Can you remember a phone number?"

"Yes."

He repeated the digits three times, then had Richard repeat them as well. "Don't write it down, okay? That's a friend of mine, Olivia, and I don't want anything that would tie what we're doing to her. When you can get cell service, call her and tell her that Philip wants her to find a couple of guys—big guys who don't mind cracking some heads—who can keep an eye on Marjorie."

Richard's eyes widened. "Who is this Olivia that she'd know these types of guys?"

"She's a defense lawyer, and those will be a couple of her clients who owe her a favor." Philip thought this sounded less alarming than that they'd no doubt be ex-cons who had served time with Olivia's father, Oscar Riva, and Philip.

"Well, if they can keep Marjorie safe from scum like Billy Chapel, I'll shake their hands and buy them the best meals of their lives when this is over."

Philip smiled, and Richard returned the smile, if a bit weakly.

"I'll be in touch as soon as I can," said Philip.

Richard turned and jogged up the hill toward the lab.

Philip dragged Donny's body behind the golf cart—he didn't want Lizzy to have to see it if they came out the back entrance—then he entered the house to give Lizzy the all-clear ... and try to explain to her what the hell he was doing.

31

―――――

Lizzy found the dispensary without too much trouble and went through the cabinets looking for supplies to treat Philip's bullet wound. When she was done, he still hadn't arrived, so she went through all the cabinets again, but found nothing to add to her collection of supplies. She went to the door to the corridor and listened but could hear nothing other than the normal ticks and whispers of any building.

Had Philip run into trouble?

Should she go to the lab and see if he needed help?

She could think of all kinds of ways things could go wrong with that plan—her unexpected appearance would be as likely to be disastrous as helpful—so she decided to explore further down the corridor. Maybe she'd find something that would be of use to them.

A few dozen feet beyond the dispensary, the corridor jogged to the right, and at the end of that hallway was a heavy metal door propped open by what looked like someone's arm. She approached the door, steeling herself for the sight of a body, but saw that it was actually a wadded-up leather jacket of a gaudy orange. It and the floor around it were stained reddish-brown with blood.

She peered through the crack into the room. She could see a desk, a large metal case with a keyhole and combination dial on the front, and the corner of what looked like a bank of monitors.

She jumped when she heard Philip's voice. "Lizzy?"

"I'm here," she called, and hurried back to where the corridors intersected.

"You were supposed to stay in the dispensary," he said with uncharacteristic frustration.

"I got bored and did a little exploring—come look what I found." She beckoned him around the corner. "I think it's the security center," she said as he followed her. "Or a control room." She pointed to the jacket. "What do you suppose happened there?"

"That looks like something one of Chapel's guys would have worn. Donny told me that Chapel had the bodies of his men removed from the compound. I'm guessing the guy got shot trying to get into the room, and when they removed his body, they used his jacket to keep the door open in case they needed to get back in. If it really is a control room, it might lock when it shuts. Have you been inside yet?"

"I didn't have a chance before I heard you calling."

"Let me go first," he said, pulling the gun out of the holster.

"I found it," she said. "I'll go first."

Before he could protest, she pulled the door open and stepped over the jacket and into the room. There was no one there, and nowhere someone could be hiding. "All clear."

Philip stepped into the room behind her. "Would you please let the guy with the gun go first?" he said irritably. Leaving the jacket in place to keep the door from closing, he crossed the room to the metal case and tugged on the handle.

"What do you suppose is in there?" Lizzy asked.

"Guns is my guess." He scanned the room, then stepped over to a pegboard on which hung dozens of keys, each neatly tagged and labeled. "I can't imagine they wouldn't have activated the combination lock, but it can't hurt to see if one of these keys will open it."

"What's with the knapsack?" she asked, gesturing to the bag slung over his shoulders.

"I got it from Louise. It looks like normal stuff—bug spray, tissues—but I didn't feel like taking the time or the brain cells to figure out if there was anything in it we wouldn't want her to have."

As Philip scanned the assortment of keys, Lizzy stepped over to a door next to the board.

"Where are you going now?" he asked, exasperated.

"I'm going to see what's in here."

"Can you just wait one minute?"

She sighed and stepped back, and he pulled the gun out of the holster, opened the door, and peered around the frame. After a moment, he reholstered the gun. "I don't see anyone. But stay by the door because there are a lot of places someone could be hiding."

Lizzy stepped around him and looked out across the space: a garage with half a dozen bays, the two closest to the door housing a limo and a white van with a magnetic sign for *AJ's Auto Repair* on the side.

"Hey," said Lizzy, "I see Uncle Owen's old SUV!"

She went to the pegboard and scanned the keys, then grabbed a key whose fob was a frayed plastic canvas needlepoint pumpkin. "And here's his keyring—I made this for him when I was little! When Louise left Pocopson, she was driving his car— she must have driven it here." She unhooked another key hanging nearby. "This key is for a Lexus ... and it has an RFID tag for Mercy Hospital—this must be Andy's, from when they kidnapped him."

She stepped back into the garage, ignoring Philip's resigned "Lizzy ..."

"The Lexus is here, too!" she called.

"We'll have to find a way to get them out of the compound," he called back.

Lizzy returned to the control room, where Philip was now standing at the gun safe. "Any luck?"

He sighed. "No. I found the right key, but the combination lock is set." He tossed the key onto the desk. "Although I don't know that it makes much difference. I'm already armed, and I'm guessing you don't want a gun."

"Not really."

He went to the desk and began rifling through the drawers. He pulled out a phone and held it up. "Here's mine." He gestured toward the open drawer. "Any of these yours?"

She joined him at the desk as he began looking through other drawers. "This one's mine." She pulled it out and tried to power it up. "Dead." She slipped it into her pocket and opened one of the drawers on the other side of the desk. "Hey, isn't this your wallet?" she asked, holding it up.

Philip took it from her. "Yes, it is." He flipped it open. "My Philip Riva ID is still in it." He peered into a small interior pocket. Lizzy knew he was checking for what was probably the only item he would have regretted losing: a photo of his prison mentor, Oscar Riva.

"Everything in order?" she asked, although his look of relief told her that it was.

"Yup," he said, flipping the wallet closed and slipping it into his pocket. "They didn't even bother taking the money." He glanced around the room. "I wonder if this is where they have whatever they're using to block cell signals."

"What would it look like?" Lizzy said, also scanning the room.

"I haven't any idea. Let's not worry about it."

At that moment, a chime sounded, and a red light illuminated next to one of the security monitors. It showed two people —a man and a woman—making their way through a wooded section of the property.

Lizzy hurried across the room to the bank of monitors. "There's someone else in the compound!"

"Lizzy—" said Philip.

"Philip, there's someone out there." She bent to peer closer.

"Lizzy—"

"I think it's Louise! And she has someone with her!"

"Lizzy—"

She whirled from the monitor. "We have to find them ..." Her voice faltered as she saw he was still standing by the desk. "... don't we?"

"No, we don't. I let her go."

Lizzy's eyebrows shot up. "What? Why??"

He pulled the desk chair out and moved it toward her. "Lizzy, sit down for a minute—"

Her hands closed into fists. "No!"

He sighed. "Okay." He sat down on the desk. "I let her go because she's working on a drug that she thinks would make the squeeze ineffective for a time. She calls it neuroinhibitol. That's why she came back to the compound—it was the only place she had access to that had the facilities she needs."

"She told you that she was working on something that would make the squeeze *ineffective*?" She could hear her voice spinning up. "Why would she do that?"

"Lizzy, think of all the things Louise couldn't do with you because she was afraid of the squeeze. You had—you *have*—

more power than she does. It makes sense that she'd want a way to control that."

"You know how she controlled that when she was holding me hostage in Pocopson?" She was fighting not to cry. "Practically drugged me into a coma!"

He raised his hands. "I know—"

"She ordered my father's death! And I might have been the person who killed my mother—"

"Lizzy—"

"—but Louise is the one who made me into the freak that could do such a thing!"

He stood, his face a mask of pain. "Lizzy ..."

"You know who I *should* have killed instead of my mother? Instead of my mother and about half a dozen other people? Louise Mortensen!" She flung a hand toward the monitors, that now showed only empty woods. "And you're letting her get away so that she can develop something that will take away the one advantage I have over her?"

"Only if we ever let her near you ... but Lizzy, think how much better your life could be if you didn't have to hide away because you were afraid some random person would make you mad and you would squeeze them."

"The juice makes it so I can't squeeze anyone ..." She could hear her voice becoming wobbly with tears.

"But then you have to hear what everyone around you is thinking. I can't imagine that's much fun. And it's a steroid drug. Olivia's right to be concerned about a young woman taking a steroid drug. You shouldn't be taking *any* of it, much less taking it all the time."

"It's not for Olivia or you or Uncle Owen or anyone else to decide for me what I'm going to do!" she yelled. "And it sure as hell isn't up to you to decide to let Louise Mortensen go!"

He was silent for a long moment. "I know. I'm not thrilled

about that either." He sank back onto the desk. "I want to get this new drug she's testing for you, but also I couldn't think of a practical way to hold her prisoner, or to turn her over to the authorities without putting you and Owen and Andy and Ruby in jeopardy. We have Louise over a barrel because we could tell the authorities where they could find her. But she has us over a barrel because, if she did fall into the hands of the police or the attorney general's office, there would be no reason for her not to tell them about you, and about what Andy and Owen and Ruby have done to help you."

Lizzy felt her anger ebbing away. She hated the situation he described, but she couldn't disagree with his assessment of it.

After a beat, her tone straining for a truculence she no longer felt, she said, "And you. She would tell them about what you've done to help me."

"And me. But it would be a lot easier for me to drop off the radar than it would be for them. They have lives—" He stopped and pressed his lips together.

"You have a life," she said, her voice less forceful than she would have wanted.

He raised an eyebrow, trying for a wry expression.

"You do!" she protested. "What about Olivia?"

"Do you know that I saw Olivia at Chapel's restaurant?"

"What? No! When?"

"Last night. Donny and I went there to talk with Billy. Olivia was bartending."

"She didn't let me know she'd seen you!"

"She probably didn't want to encourage you to come back to Baltimore and try to check out *Charm City* yourself."

Lizzy tried to tame the chaos of thoughts swirling through her mind. "So what are we supposed to do?"

"I'm going to go to Baltimore and kill Billy."

Her eyes snapped wide. "Philip, no! You might get caught—

you might go back to prison! You told me once you'd rather die than go back to prison—"

"I won't get caught."

She threw up her hands. "It's not something you can just decide one way or the other. Plus, it might seem like a good idea now, but in the long term you'll regret it—"

"I doubt it—"

"You will! I know that that guy in the conservatory probably wasn't a good guy, but I still feel bad that I killed him ... and I'll feel bad that I killed him for the rest of my life!" Tears were threatening again, and she clamped her lips together to hold them back.

"Lizzy, you shouldn't feel guilty for killing Donny—he was scum. I saw him torture a man almost to death, and Billy Chapel was the man who told him to do it."

Her eyes widened and she twisted her fingers together.

Philip continued. "And Chapel wouldn't hesitate to send someone just like that guy to do exactly the same thing to Owen or Andy or Ruby or you."

"Or you."

"Or me—if he finds me. We need Chapel out of the way. We need him dead."

They were both silent for several long seconds, then Lizzy dropped onto the desk chair. "Okay." Her own voice sounded so small—not nearly as brave as she would have liked. "So what now?"

"Richard's going to keep an eye on Louise in Harrisburg until we know Chapel is out of the way, and then he's going to take her to his college, where she can use the facilities to finish testing the inhibitol. I'll go to Baltimore, and I think you should go to Philly and keep an eye on Owen and Andy and Ruby until I'm done there."

After a moment, she gave a single nod and pushed herself to

her feet. "Okay, but first let's take care of your arm. I have every-thing ready to go—it won't take a minute."

He stood. "That's a deal."

She turned toward the door, then turned back to him. "That man Donny tortured. You said it was 'almost to death.' Did he survive?"

Philip was silent for a long moment. Then he said, "No, he didn't. But that's a story for another day."

32

―――――

Lizzy and Philip went to the dispensary, and she pointed to a chair. "Take off your jacket and sit down there so I can take a look at your arm."

She noticed his wince as he unslung his knapsack from his shoulders. He shrugged out of his jacket, flinching again as he pulled the bloodstained fabric away from his arm.

He sat, and she pulled the sleeve of his T-shirt up over his shoulder. She was relieved to see that although the wound was bloody, it wasn't deep. The bullet had sliced across the tattoo that stretched the length of Philip's bicep: an elaborate castle. She knew that the letters *OR* were worked into the castle's ornately rendered doors, although at the moment they were hidden by the congealing blood. Anyone else might assume that the tattoo was in honor of Olivia Riva, but Lizzy knew it was in memory of Olivia's father and Philip's prison mentor, Oscar.

She poured some hydrogen peroxide onto a large cotton ball and began dabbing at the wound. "Tell me if it hurts."

"Will do." After a moment, he said, "I think we need to destroy the lab. The authorities are going to show up at the compound at some point—maybe not for months or even years, knowing what a secluded life Viklund led—but they *will* show up eventually. I'm afraid there's too much at the lab that could tie it to Mortensen, and from her to us. And until the authorities find it, I want to remove any temptation Mortensen might have to come back here and continue her work."

Lizzy discarded the soiled cotton ball in a trash can and soaked another one. "How are we going to destroy the lab?"

"Probably fire or an explosion. Depends on what we can find to use."

She thought for a moment, then said, "There were some propane tanks in the garage."

He smiled. "Perfect."

"But won't that attract attention? The property is big, but it's not so big that no one would notice an explosion."

"That could work to our advantage. We don't want the authorities to tie the lab to Mortensen—at least not yet, because it's too likely that would lead to us—but it might be beneficial for us if they found clues that pointed them to Chapel, and then to whatever activities he was engaged in with Viklund. Based on what I heard, the cops have never been able to pin anything on Chapel because they can't find witnesses. A search of the compound might give them what they need."

"Sounds like a good idea. What clues will there be?"

"We can leave Donny and the Escalade behind."

"Unless you plan to blow up Donny, if they do an autopsy, they'll be able to tell he died of a stroke."

"True ... but I don't think that will be a problem. There's not a pattern of that in this area."

Not, she thought, *like the trail of victims she had left in Philadelphia.*

"I'll make sure to wipe any prints from me and Richard off it," Philip continued. "We'll need to do a sweep through the rest of the house and see if there's anything else that might tie back to the two of us. Or to Andy, since he was here, too. Your prints won't be on file, and I suspect Andy's aren't either, so that's probably not an issue, although no harm in being overly thorough. But if the cops do dust for prints and find mine, it wouldn't take them long to make a match in the Arizona Department of Corrections database."

"Or your blood," she said, holding up another blood-crusted cotton ball.

"Good catch."

She stepped back and examined his arm critically. The details of the tattoo were visible now, and she saw that the bullet had sliced right across the letters, turning them into just another decoration on the castle doors. "I think that's as clean as I can get it."

He glanced down. "Looks good." He raised an eyebrow. "Although I don't think the guy who did the tattoo would appreciate the effect."

"Let me put a bandage on it, then we can start wiping surfaces, cleaning up blood, and looking for explosives."

Philip laughed.

Lizzy smiled, confused. "What?"

"You sound so badass."

She blushed and laughed. "How much time do we have to do all that?"

"We'll need to work as fast as we can. It won't be long before Billy will start to wonder why he hasn't heard back from Donny yet, and if he decides to send another one of his men to see what's happening, it's only a little over an hour and a half from Baltimore to the compound."

When Philip had worked himself gingerly back into the jacket and knapsack, they donned latex gloves they found in one of the dispensary cabinets. They used paper towels from a roll over the sink to wipe down the surfaces in that room, and pulled the plastic liner from the trash can where Lizzy had thrown the cotton balls. They returned to the control center and wiped the surfaces there as well. Then they moved through the house, wiping down anything they remembered touching and scrubbing up a few drops of Philip's blood from the floor of the conservatory.

They went to the staff quarters, and Philip wiped the door handles on the side of the corridor he had searched with Donny. In the closet of one of the rooms, he also found a navy sport coat he swapped for his bloodstained leather jacket, stuffing the jacket into his knapsack.

"A sport coat really isn't your style," said Lizzy with an amused smile.

"Nothing I'm wearing is really my style," he said ruefully.

When they were done inside, they went outside, and Philip wiped down the Escalade.

"Okay," he said, stuffing the towels into his knapsack. "Now let's get the cars out of the garage."

They re-entered the house and returned to the garage, where they found six full propane canisters neatly stacked against the wall.

"Let's swap Owen and Andy's license plates for the ones from Viklund's limo and van," Philip said, "and then we can swap them back when we're away from the area. One less way to trace the vehicles back to Owen and Andy if they show up on someone's doorbell cam or on some cop's plate recognition system."

They found a well-stocked tool bench at the back of the garage, and while Lizzy unscrewed the license plates, Philip loaded the propane tanks into Owen's old SUV.

Then with Philip driving the SUV and Lizzy following in the Lexus, they headed for the lab, first on a narrow service road that led from the garage and then on the walking paths that crisscrossed the grounds. The path leading to the lab was too narrow for the vehicles, so they lugged the tanks across the last dozen yards to the door.

"What now?" Lizzy asked, flexing her fingers.

Philip described his plan to Lizzy.

She raised her eyebrows. "Are you sure that's going to work? And be safe?"

He smiled grimly. "Pretty sure. But it will be better if we're not all scrambling for the exit at once. Why don't you take the Lexus to the front entrance, and after I've set things up here, I'll follow you in the SUV." He knit his brow. "Actually, how did you get to the compound?"

"I drove the Caravan."

"Where is it?"

"Parked off the property."

"Hidden?"

"Yup."

"Okay, we can come back for that later."

"All right. But I have two objections to your plan."

"Oh?"

"First of all, I don't really feel comfortable driving Andy's Lexus. I'd be better off with Owen's SUV—it's more like what I'm used to driving. Why don't you take the Lexus."

He smiled. "I won't object to that. What's the second objection."

"I don't want to leave you to have to set up the explosion by yourself."

"It's not like it's very complicated—"

"But—"

He raised his hand. "*And* if you hang around until I've set up the explosion, it means you're going to have to drive like a bat out of hell for the front gate."

"How long until the explosion happens?"

"I'm not sure—"

"Philip!"

"But plenty of time for me to get away—assuming I only have to worry about *me* getting away. I know you don't like to drive in the best circumstances, and that is definitely not the best circumstances. Do you agree?"

She sighed. "All right. We'll meet up outside the gate?"

"I think it makes sense for us to drive away separately. The compound is remote enough that it will probably take a while for first responders to arrive, but if I'm wrong, it's best that it looks like we're not together. We just have to think of a place to meet up, without the benefit of a map app."

"How about that airport you left from when Theo flew you to Arizona? You said that was pretty close."

"That's perfect. Hagerstown Airport. It's not a big place. If you park in the parking lot by the terminal, I'll find you." He arched an eyebrow. "Or you can find me, because I'll be driving the flashier car."

She rolled her eyes. "Okay."

"I do have a favor to ask you. When I left the compound with Billy, he made one of his bodyguards give me his clothes—Billy was afraid I was wearing a wire, which I was—and they threw my old clothes into a drainage ditch a couple dozen yards to the right of the entrance as you're leaving. In fact, that's the same direction you'd turn to get to the airport, so you won't have to backtrack. I'd rather not leave them behind for someone to find. If you can look for them, that would be helpful—but don't spend more than a minute or two on it."

"Actually," said Lizzy, looking alarmed, "the bloody clothes I wore to the compound the first time must still be here."

"Any idea where they ended up?"

"No idea."

He considered for a moment, then said, "I don't think we can afford to take the time to look for them. And, just like with the fingerprints, even if someone finds them, there isn't any DNA in any system—at least no *official* system—that they could match it to." He took a key out of his pocket and handed it to her. "This is the key to the padlock on the front gate. Once you're outside, leave the gate open so I can get through."

"Be careful, Philip."

She raised her hand in a fist, and Philip bumped it with his own.

33

A fter the SUV had disappeared around a curve in the drive, Philip stepped back into the lab.

The smell of decomposing bodies seemed even stronger than it had just a couple of hours earlier, and he wondered if Louise or Richard had for some reason opened the freezer containing Theo's body.

He found exactly what he had been hoping for at one of the lab tables: a Bunsen burner. After checking to make sure it would light, he turned it off and stepped outside again.

He ferried the propane tanks, two at a time, into the building and staged them by the door to the lab annex, where the odor seemed even stronger than in the rest of the lab.

When he opened the door to take them into the two apartments that opened off the vestibule, the smell was stronger still, and by the time he opened the door to the apartment that had been Edmund Rinnert's, he wasn't too surprised when the sickly odor rolled out of the room and almost drove him back to the lab. He had forgotten to account for Rinnert's body, which was what he guessed was the disturbingly flattened shape under a bedspread in the center of the room.

Moving as quickly as safety and his eagerness not to trip on Edmund's body allowed, he put three of the propane tanks in the bathroom of Edmund's apartment and the other three in the bathroom of the dreary matching apartment across the vestibule that Theo Viklund had intended for Louise. Putting the tanks as far from the Bunsen burner as possible would give him the most time to make his escape.

As he worked, the blocky red digits on an old-fashioned digital alarm clock on the bedside table caught his eye: past four o'clock. Billy must be getting seriously pissed about the lack of updates from Donny. He'd no doubt be thinking about sending out reinforcements to see what was going on, if he hadn't done so already. Philip hoped that Billy didn't have associates more local to the compound to send to investigate.

Tanks in place, he confirmed that the key to the Lexus was still in his pocket. Then he moved from tank to tank, first in one apartment and then in the other, opening the valves, the propane adding the stink of rotten eggs to the stench of decomposing bodies. In each apartment, he left the bathroom door open only a crack and did the same for the doors from the apartments to the vestibule and from the vestibule to the lab.

Heart pounding, he hurried back to the table where the Bunsen burner was. He was grateful that the burner had a built-in igniter, avoiding the need to deal with a match or a spark lighter, but a few precious seconds ticked by as he tried to get the flame to ignite—seconds during which he could imagine tendrils of propane, like the questing arms of an octopus, making their way across the apartment floors and toward the lab.

At last, the igniter caught, and a cheerful flame leapt merrily up from the burner.

Philip ran for the door.

34

Lizzy climbed out of the SUV, parked just down the road from the now-open front gate, and walked along the shoulder, looking for the drainage ditch. She realized she should have asked Philip which side of the road it was on, but maybe he didn't know—it sounded like he had been busy changing into some other guy's clothes. She thought of the type of clothes he, and for that matter Donny, had been wearing —as if Billy Chapel wanted all his men to mimic his own look of a leather jacket, even in June, black jeans, and heavy boots, but didn't want to risk anyone mistaking one of them for the man in charge. She supposed that making his men look like cheap versions of himself was just one of the less dangerous mind games he liked to play.

She found the clothes fairly easily, although the mud that covered them made them almost unrecognizable as Philip's more usual outfit: a cotton button-front shirt, the sleeves still rolled up a few turns, blue jeans, and finely stitched cowboy boots. She was also surprised—almost shocked—to find socks, a white T-shirt, and a pair of briefs in the pile. If Billy had made

Philip change his clothes to make sure he wasn't wearing a wire, he had certainly been thorough.

She gathered up the clothes, trying with only partial success to keep the mud off her own clothes, tossed them in the back of the SUV, and climbed back into the driver's seat. She got out her phone and checked the reception: it was fluctuating between one bar and *No Service*. She tried putting the call in to Olivia, but it dropped immediately. She started up the SUV and, with a glance back at the gate—how long would it take Philip to set up the explosion?—began rolling down the road.

She periodically glanced down at her phone, and after almost a mile, with the gate long since lost to view behind her, a second bar appeared. Checking that no one was coming up behind her, she rolled to a stop and tapped *Hagerstown airport* into the map app.

She had just propped the phone, displaying the route, on the dashboard and started down the road when a thunderous boom cracked the air, followed almost immediately by a second, and the ground shook as if a giant had smashed his fist into it.

The surprise made her jam the brake pedal hard to the floor, and she jerked forward into the shoulder belt. Heart pounding, she shut down the vehicle and scrambled out. Thick black smoke was billowing over the treetops.

Had Philip really intended for the explosion to be that big?

But if the goal had been to destroy any evidence in the lab and to keep Louise from using it again ... mission accomplished.

She was staring, open-mouthed, as smoke continued to billow up from behind the trees, when she jumped again at the whoop of a siren and looked up to see a police cruiser heading toward her, lights strobing.

She was on a fairly straight stretch of road, and the vehicle must have had her in sight for at least several seconds before turning on its sirens—in response to the explosion, she hoped.

Her heart rate kicked up a notch, and she barely had time to decide what to do when the vehicle—Lizzy saw that it was a Maryland State Trooper cruiser—pulled up alongside her.

The siren cut off, the driver's window buzzed down, and a thirty-ish woman wearing aviator sunglasses and a khaki shirt asked, "Everything all right, miss?"

"Yes—I was just driving along, and then *boom!*" She waved toward the smoke. "What happened?"

"We're checking it out now. Please move your vehicle to the side of the road to allow emergency vehicles to pass." The trooper began to buzz her window up.

Lizzy was about to breathe a sigh of relief that this was the extent of the interaction she would have to have with law enforcement, when she realized that Philip would be driving out of the compound gate, or even appearing around the curve in the road, at any minute.

The trooper's vehicle was already accelerating away from her.

Lizzy ran after the car. "Hey!" She yelled. "Ma'am!"

The car stopped and the window buzzed down again.

"Yes, Miss?"

"An SUV passed me really fast a couple of minutes ago—maybe they had something to do with the explosion!"

The trooper considered Lizzy for a moment, shifted her gaze to the black smoke still drifting over the trees, then said, "Please pull over to the shoulder and put your emergency blinkers on. I'll be with you in just a minute."

"Sure thing."

Lizzy jogged back to Owen's SUV—an SUV that now carried the license plate of one of the cars in Theo Viklund's garage—wondering if her impulse had been brilliant or disastrous.

The trooper pulled to the side of the road. With both vehicles' windows open, Lizzy could hear the woman speaking, probably on the radio, but couldn't pick out any of the words. She did notice the trooper glance toward the SUV a few times and realized that she was probably running the plates.

Lizzy was beginning to fear that the impulse had, in fact, been disastrous.

Then her fears took a different turn as she saw Andy's red Lexus appear from around a bend in the road.

When she had come up with the idea of making up the presence of a speeding SUV, she had hoped that the trooper would go looking for it. Instead Lizzy had manufactured a virtual roadblock for Philip.

The trooper must also have seen the Lexus, because she got out of her vehicle, donning a Smokey Bear hat and adjusting the tool-laden black belt at her waist.

Lizzy held her breath, waiting to see what Philip would do.

The Lexus slowed, maintaining its low speed as it approached the two vehicles.

The trooper raised her hand in a *stop* motion, her other hand resting on the gun in her belt.

The Lexus came to a halt next to the cruiser, and the trooper stepped up to the driver's window. "Good afternoon, sir. I'm Trooper Grabill with the Maryland State Police. We've had an incident in the area—a large explosion nearby. Can you tell me where you're headed and if you saw or heard anything unusual?"

Over the crackle of radio chatter emanating from the open window of the cruiser, Lizzy could hear an indistinct response from Philip.

"May I see your driver's license and registration, please?"

Lizzy's heart dropped. Now that he had his wallet back, Philip could give her his fake Philip Riva ID, although it would render it useless. The bigger problem for him was with the registration. What would Grabill do if faced with a driver's license claiming the driver as Philip Riva, a registration in Andrew McNally's name, and plates showing the car belonged to Theo Viklund?

A few moments passed, then Philip handed something to the trooper.

"Thank you," said Grabill. "Registration as well, please."

She could see Philip leaning toward the passenger side, probably pretending to search through the glove compartment, and Grabill's hand moving a little more intentionally to the butt of her gun. Lizzy heard some apologetic comment from Philip.

She also heard the distant wail of approaching sirens.

Grabill looked up, to where Lizzy could now see the flicker of lights through the trees.

"Sir," said Grabill, "we're going to need to clear the road for the emergency vehicles. Please pull over behind that SUV—" she gestured to where Lizzy was parked, "—and I'll have a few questions for you. And see if you can find that registration."

Grabill stepped back, and the Lexus coasted onto the shoulder.

When the first emergency vehicle—a fire truck—reached them, it pulled to a stop. While Grabill consulted with the driver, another fire truck and another cruiser arrived. Grabill stepped back as the fire trucks continued on toward the entrance to the compound and the second trooper vehicle pulled in behind Grabill's. A young man who looked barely older than Lizzy climbed out.

He and Grabill had a brief conversation—based on his jittery shifting from foot to foot, Lizzy guessed this might be his first emergency—then Grabill climbed into her vehicle, turned on the siren, and sped away down the road after the fire trucks.

Lizzy saw in her rearview mirror that Philip had gotten out of the Lexus and was propped casually against the door, arms crossed, so she did the same.

The young trooper waited for another emergency vehicle to pass, then jogged across the street to Philip. "Thank you for waiting, sir," he said in a voice that sounded like a pre-pubescent boy's. "I'm Trooper Studenroth. I understand Trooper Grabill took your driver's license information. Did she get your phone number?"

Philip quoted a number as Studenroth drew a notepad and pen from his pocket. Lizzy recognized the Arizona area code but nothing else.

"Thank you, sir," said the trooper. "We'll be in touch if we need any other information."

Lizzy thought Studenroth was too amped up to notice Philip's minuscule hesitation.

Then Philip pushed himself off the Lexus. "Thank you, Trooper." He climbed into the Lexus, started it up, and coasted past Lizzy, his hand closed in a fist over the steering wheel. She watched as the Lexus disappeared around a curve.

She jumped at a squeaky voice at her shoulder. "Hello, miss."

Studenroth stood beside her, notepad and pen in hand. "I'm Trooper Studenroth. I understand you saw a vehicle speeding away from the scene of the explosion?"

"Yes. It passed me going really fast just a couple of minutes before the explosion."

"Can you describe the vehicle for me?"

"It was an SUV—a big one. Black." She thought back to the Escalades she had seen coming and going from *Charm City*. "I think the windows were tinted."

Studenroth jotted a note, then nodded encouragingly. "Anything else?"

"No, I'm afraid not."

"No license plate number, I guess."

"No."

"Did you notice the state? Most Maryland plates have a white background with a yellow, black, and red design."

She shook her head. "No. Sorry."

He looked disappointed. "That's okay. Understandable. Did my colleague get your phone number?"

She gave him a made-up number with a Pennsylvania area code, then held her breath. Would she be as lucky as Philip? And if she wasn't, would Junior Trooper Studenroth pay the price of running afoul of Lizzy Ballard?

He tucked the notebook and pen back in his pocket, then nodded toward her torso. "What happened there?"

Alarmed, she looked down ... at the smears of mud that the retrieval of Philip's clothes from the ditch had left on her shirt and jeans. She forced a laugh. "Oh, that's embarrassing."

"What happened?"

"Well ..." Her mind was a complete blank.

His smile faded a fraction.

As her brain cranked through possible explanations, she thought that she should memorize a set of stories that might come in handy for situations like this. If she had them memorized, she wouldn't trip over details or names—

"Peanut!" she said.

He raised his eyebrows. "Peanut?"

"My sister's boyfriend just got a puppy named Peanut, and Peanut got into a mud puddle in their back yard, and I picked her up not realizing ..." She gestured helplessly at her clothing.

He smiled. "That's not embarrassing. Inconvenient, maybe, but not embarrassing."

She returned his smile a little more enthusiastically than the moment required. "That's nice of you to say."

His stance relaxed a bit. "I love dogs."

Oh, God. Was she going to have to have an entire conversation with Trooper Studenroth, wondering the entire time whether or not he was going to ask her for her registration—a registration that would point the authorities right to Uncle Owen?

"Me, too. In fact, I work at a vet, and I'm going to be late as it is. Do you have any other questions for me?"

He sighed. "No, thank you, miss," he said. "I think Trooper Grabill has what she needs." He glanced down at the paper on which he had jotted her number, then gave her a hopeful smile. "But I'll be in touch if I think of anything else."

35

Philip pulled off the highway into a thicket of bushes and winced at the screech of branches on the sides of the Lexus as he worked his way deep enough into the woods for the cherry-red vehicle to be invisible from the road.

Even hidden as he was, it was a risk to stop, but he couldn't drive away with Lizzy still being questioned by Trooper Studenroth. At least the stop gave him an opportunity to swap the Theo Viklund license plate, which was no doubt now logged in a Maryland law enforcement database, for the car's actual plates.

He had just flipped the Viklund plate into the undergrowth when an SUV that must be Owen McNally's passed on the road.

He smiled. However it had happened, it appeared that Lizzy had gotten away from the frighteningly young trooper.

He got back in the Lexus and tapped *Hagerstown airport* into the map app on his phone, which was now plugged into the charger he had noticed in the glove compartment. When there was a break in the traffic, mostly emergency vehicles headed for the compound, he pulled out and followed the path of the SUV.

Then he opened his contacts list and tapped a number, the call playing over the car's sound system.

Olivia's voice was uncertain when she answered. "Philip?"

"Yup." He could hear road sounds in the background. "Are you driving? Do you want to pull over?"

"Are you okay?"

"Yes, I'm fine."

"Are *you* driving?"

"Yes, but I can't pull over right now."

He heard her sigh. "Okay. Give me one minute." The road noises changed, then faded a bit. After half a minute, she said, "I'm parked." He heard her draw a deep breath. "What the hell, Philip?"

The last time Philip had spoken to Olivia—not counting the fraught encounter at *Charm City*—had been when he told her he had to make a quick trip to help out an ex-con buddy. In reality, as Olivia now knew, he had actually gone with Lizzy to Theo Viklund's compound to rescue Andy McNally.

"Liv, I have way more to explain—and way more to apologize for—than I can do in a quick phone call, but right now I need to make sure a man named Richard has gotten in touch with you and passed on a message from me."

"Yes, he got in touch with me." When she continued, her voice hovered between anger and strained amusement. "Interesting that the first message I get from you was someone asking me to find *a couple of big guys who don't mind cracking heads.*"

"I'm sorry, Liv—I didn't know who else to call."

"Well, most of the head-crackers I know from Williams are in the Southwest, but I thought of one or two who might be in this area. While I was trying to figure out how to get in touch with them, I thought I should check to see if Cedar Grove would let in non-relatives. When I called, they told me that there were already 'two tall red-haired men and a petite older woman' with Marjorie."

Philip's eyebrows rose. "The McNallys and Ruby DiMano?"

"That's right."

"How did they get there?"

"When you talked to Ruby in Philadelphia," Philip didn't miss the edge in Olivia's voice, no doubt in response to Philip seeking out Lizzy's family's former housekeeper rather than his girlfriend, "you told her enough about this guy Richard that they were able to figure out who he was, and then where his wife was. I'm on my way there now."

"Olivia, you don't need to do that. If the three of them are there, I'm sure—"

"Philip, I am *not* going to be left out of this—and left in the dark about what's going on—anymore."

He flipped on his signal and pulled around a slow-moving pickup truck. "Liv, I'm really sorry. I did what I did because I thought it was for the best—or, later, because I had no choice—but I don't blame you for being angry. When I see you, I'll explain what I did, but I won't try to excuse it."

She was silent.

"And you've hardly been left out of this," he said, trying to lighten the tone. "As your father would have said, you could have knocked me over with a feather when I saw you come into the room at *Charm City* wheeling a drink cart."

He heard a brief snort of laughter. "'They're drinking Woodford,'" she said in a close approximation of Philip's voice, then, in her normal voice, "Obviously undercover work isn't my forte."

"We have plenty to catch up on when we see each other."

"Is Lizzy with you?"

"Not at the moment, but I ran into her at Viklund's compound. We're both out of the compound now, but we left separately, and I need to catch up with her. And I need to get in touch with Owen and let him know what's going on. Can I call you back once we've done that?"

"I'll be in Letort soon. He can tell me what you discuss. I better get going. You and Lizzy be careful."

She ended the call.

~

When Philip reached the Hagerstown airport, he spotted the SUV right away, Lizzy leaning against the driver's door. He pulled up beside her and climbed out of the Lexus.

"Let's hear it for youthful inexperience and administrative confusion," he said. "If Studenroth hadn't thought Grabill had already gotten our documentation, we would have been in trouble."

"That's for sure." Her eyes widened at the sight of the damage to the Lexus. "What happened?"

"Just hiding in some bushes." He smiled. "It'll buff out."

She gave a relieved laugh. "You better buff it out before Andy sees it."

With Lizzy shielding his activity under the guise of sorting through non-existent luggage in the back of the SUV, Philip changed the plate back to Owen's and stuffed the Viklund plate into a dumpster next to the small terminal building. Then they both got into the SUV, and he filled her in on what Olivia had told him.

Lizzy ran her fingers through her hair. "Owen and Andy and Ruby are with Richard's wife?" She got out her phone. "Let's call Uncle Owen and find out what's going on." She tapped his name in her phone's Favorites list and put the call on speaker.

Owen answered. "Pumpkin! Are you all right? We have so much to update you on—where have you been? We couldn't get in touch with you, but we figured it was because the blocker at the compound was jamming the signal—"

Philip suspected that Owen might have continued in this

vein for a bit, but Lizzy interrupted him. "I'm fine. I'm with Philip and he's fine, too. I have you on speaker."

"Philip? Are you okay? Of course you are—Lizzy just said. We've been so worried."

"Yes, I'm fine," said Philip. "It's good to talk to you Owen."

Lizzy brought Owen up to speed on what had happened since they had last spoken. "I was planning to meet up with you guys in Philly," she concluded, "before we got the news from Olivia about you going to Letort. Where is that, anyway?"

"It's near Harrisburg," said Owen. "When we got here, we went to Rush College first. That's how we were able to find out where Marjorie Pearson was. I saw their facilities. You said that Louise expects to use them to complete her testing of this neuroinhibitol, but I don't think she'll be able to do what she needs to do there. She needs a better equipped lab."

Philip rubbed his eyes. "I don't know what our options are."

"William Penn University," Owen said promptly. "That's where I formulate the juice for you, Pumpkin. I could get Louise in there."

Lizzy sat up. "Uncle Owen, you can't start escorting Louise Mortensen around—she tried to kill you!"

"It might have been her idea," said Owen, "but she relied on her henchman to actually make the attempt. Other than Richard Pearson, who sounds like an unwilling participant, it sounds like she doesn't have any staff to call on to do her dirty work these days. If she doesn't know until I meet up with her that I'm going to be involved, she won't have a chance to make any arrangements."

"But she's still wanted in the Philly area," said Lizzy. "Isn't there a risk that someone at William Penn will recognize her and maybe call the police? I guess we don't want that to happen ..." Her eyes drifted to Philip. "... right?"

"If we want her to finish testing this drug," said Owen, "we don't want them to catch up with her—at least not yet. There isn't much activity in the lab right now—we're between semesters—so I think we can avoid any unwanted attention. And there's rarely anyone around overnight, even during busy periods. That's when I do my own off-the-books work." He paused, then continued. "It would be wonderful for you to have a drug like what she says she's working on, Pumpkin. It would mean you wouldn't have to live such an isolated life."

"Uncle Owen, couldn't you work on something like that for me?"

"Oh, sweetie," said Owen, his sadness clear in his voice, "I've been working on that ever since we found out you had the squeeze—ever since you were a little girl."

Lizzy's throat tightened, and she swiped a hand across her eyes. Owen had been trying to get her the life she wanted for herself even longer than Philip had.

Philip reached over and squeezed her arm. "Can I make a suggestion?"

"Of course," said Owen.

Lizzy nodded.

"Here's what I propose," said Philip. "The three of us meet up in Harrisburg and go to where Louise and Richard are holed up. Richard is desperate to get back to Letort to be with his wife, so Lizzy and Richard can go to Letort to help keep an eye on Marjorie and I'll go with Owen and Louise to Philly. That will give me a chance to get a plan in place for taking care of Chapel."

The three were silent for a few moments, each weighing the pros and cons of this approach against their own criteria, then Lizzy sighed. "Yeah, let's do that."

"It does seem like the best option," said Owen.

They decided on a meet-up location near Harrisburg then ended the call.

"I think that covers everyone who's involved," said Philip. "Owen and I will keep an eye on Mortensen—and an eye out for each other—and you, Richard, Andy, Ruby, and Olivia can keep an eye on Marjorie." He wiped a hand down his face. "Am I forgetting anyone? Anyone else who has been helping us out?"

They sat in silence for a few moments, then Lizzy said, "He's a long way away, but he did help us out ... how about Eddie?"

Philip sat forward. "Eddie—*shit!* I should have thought of that. Billy made some comment about my 'guy friends,' and I thought he meant Viklund or Andy. But it wouldn't be hard for him to find out where I lived in Sedona, and he wouldn't have to dig too deep to find out that Eddie was my landlord, and that he and I were friends. He could have even found out about Eddie from Mortensen."

"Should we call him? Tell him to be careful?"

"Yeah." He grimaced. "I'd rather talk to him myself, but since I'm a 'person of interest,' he'd have to tell the Sedona police. I want to make sure he has plausible deniability. Can you call him?"

"Sure." She gave him a wan smile. "I always like talking to Eddie—just wish it was in happier circumstances."

He gave her Eddie's number, and she put the call on speaker.

"HEL-lo!" came Eddie's booming voice over the phone.

Philip dropped his head back against the headrest. Other than Lizzy and her allies—and Olivia, of course—Eddie was the only person he would count as a friend. Ex-cop or not, Eddie had been willing to rent the casita behind his own home to an ex-con who had just finished doing his time for murder and didn't have a job or a penny to his name.

Lizzy shot him a sympathetic look. "Hey, Eddie. It's Lizzy. Philip's friend."

"Lizzy! How's it going?" Under Eddie's normal cheerful tone, she would sense an undercurrent of alarm—after all, there weren't many happy reasons for Lizzy to be in touch with him.

She didn't think it was likely that anyone would ever hear this conversation, but experience had taught her not to take anything for granted. "I was reading in the papers that there's danger of an increase in crime in Sedona. Have you seen anything like that?"

She raised her eyebrows to Philip, and he gave her a thumbs up.

"Can't say that I have," said Eddie, "but I'll keep my eyes peeled. Any specific kind of crime you've been hearing about?"

"Not sure. Just crime in general. It's always good to be careful."

"That's for sure. I'll be extra careful." After a pause, he asked, "And how about you? Any increase in crime in your area? Are *you* being extra careful?"

Lizzy marshaled a rueful laugh. "There always seems to be increased crime wherever I am. And I always try to be extra careful."

"And your friends? They're all being careful, too?"

"Yup. All my friends are being super careful. *All* of them."

"I'm glad to hear that, Lizzy, friend of Philip. You give my best to your friends. All of them."

She smiled. "Will do, Eddie."

After she ended the call, Philip sighed. "I wish we could be more specific about what he needs to watch out for."

"Maybe it's nothing. Maybe Billy doesn't even know about Eddie. But better safe than sorry, right?"

"Yup."

She slipped her phone into her pocket. "Convoy to Harrisburg?"

"Sounds good. You still want to drive the SUV?"

"Yes." She smiled. "And you still want to drive the Lexus?"

"Absolutely."

With a laugh, she raised her hand for a fist bump. "Just don't enjoy the Lexus *too* much."

36

Billy sat in the black room at his house, the only room he really felt comfortable in. The other rooms had been done by some limp-wristed Baltimore decorator, and although they got compliments from his infrequent guests, it was like living in a photo shoot for fucking *Architectural Digest*.

But when the decorator started describing the soft leather and modern furnishings he planned for the room he had called *the library*, Billy interrupted him. "I want it black. All black. Shiny black."

And all shiny black is what he had gotten.

He loved it.

He was standing at one of the windows, looking out across the lawn toward where one of his men was scanning the surrounding woods with a pair of binoculars, when there was a knock on the door.

He took a swallow of Woodford, then bellowed, "Come!"

Tony entered, his expression troubled. "Boss, stuff's happening at the Viklund place."

Billy turned away from the window. "What stuff?"

"An explosion. Fire. Cops and firetrucks everywhere, news helicopter flying over."

Billy's eyebrows shot up. "Are you fucking kidding me?"

"'Fraid not. I texted you a link to the news report."

Billy got out his phone and opened the link.

In the news helicopter's video, it was possible to pick out the house, as long as you knew where to look. It was much easier to pick out the still-smoldering remains of a building at the center of a ring of charred trees. Lights from what looked like two dozen emergency vehicles strobed across the scene.

He swore. "That's the lab. That's what the Three Stooges were supposed to be checking out." He tossed his phone onto the table. "Maybe Mortensen was there and torched the place to keep anyone from seeing what she had going on there." He scowled. "Or Castillo did it for his own reasons. I wonder if anyone was in the lab when it went up."

Tony was looking at the video on his phone as well. He turned it toward Billy, video stopped. "There by the house—that looks like it could be the Escalade Donny took."

Billy snatched the phone out of Tony's hand and zoomed the image, then began zooming in on other parts of the image. After half a minute, his fingers tightened on the phone. "Shit," he hissed, then slammed Tony's phone down on the giant, black lacquered desk. "And what do you think that is behind the house?" he asked, his voice dripping with disgust.

Tony picked up the phone and peered at the screen. After a moment, he said, his voice tight, "Donny."

"I told you we should have had that thing registered in Donny's name. That's going to come right back to me."

"I can have the registrations of the other 'Slades switched over to the boys."

"Little fucking late now, isn't it?

Tony eased back half a step. "Yes, boss."

Billy crossed to the drink cart in the corner. He dropped an ice cube from the silver bucket into his glass, then sloshed in a generous portion of Woodford. "Send Mickey to Letort—see if you can track down Pearson, at least. Check Rush and the old folks' home."

"How about Mortensen?"

"I'm hoping she's with Pearson."

"How about Castillo?"

"I'm hoping he was in that building when it exploded." He downed a swallow of bourbon. "And if we do find him, he'll wish he had been."

37

"Richard!" Louise snapped as the Navigator drifted toward the shoulder.

Richard started awake, gasped, and overcorrected into the opposing lane, and Louise had a moment to think it would be ironic if this whole sordid situation ended with her dying in a wreck caused by a sleep-deprived college professor. Her reaction would have been less sanguine if there had been a car in the oncoming lane.

Richard maneuvered the vehicle back into his lane. "Sorry about that," he muttered.

"Don't you think it would be safer if I drove?" As badly as she had slept in the staff quarters room she had selected at the compound, one ear out for the sounds of other intruders, she suspected that Richard, as an unwilling guest at Billy Chapel's home, had slept even worse. It would be getting dark soon, and if Richard was having this much trouble staying awake now, it wouldn't get any better after sunset.

"I'm fine—I'm fine," said Richard. After a moment, he added, "Maybe we can stop at a Sheetz for a Red Bull."

"Richard, we're nearly to Harrisburg, which is where Philip

said he'd meet us. Let's just go there. Then you can take a nap, and you won't need the Red Bull." She shuddered.

"I don't want a nap," he snapped. "And I was kind of hoping we could stop in Letort—"

"No, we cannot stop in Letort. It's the first place Chapel would look for us, and you'd be more likely to jeopardize Marjorie than to help her by going there. Plus, that person you called is sending people to keep an eye on her, right?"

Richard had called someone named Olivia, asking her to find a few men to act as bodyguards for his wife. Louise wondered what Olivia's relationship was to Philip Castillo, whose name Richard had used during the call.

Richard groaned. "I just wish I could be there myself."

They were approaching a cluster of fast-food chains anchored by a tired-looking motel. "There," Louise said, pointing. "That looks fine. We're close enough to Harrisburg. Stop there."

"Fine," Richard muttered.

He pulled off into the motel parking lot and went in to register, taking the keys to the Navigator with him. As she waited for him to come back, Louise decided she would assess what resources she had available to her. She climbed out of the vehicle and opened the back.

She had checked out of the hotel in Wayne and had all her possessions with her. It didn't amount to much—mainly just the few changes of clothes she had purchased in a shop near her hotel. She didn't need any of it to strike out on her own—her most important resources were in her head. But she wasn't likely to get far on foot.

Richard appeared at her side, holding a key.

"What are you doing?" he asked, worried.

"Taking inventory. What floor is our room on?"

"Second."

She cast a sour glance toward the building. "I'm guessing they don't have bellhops." With a sigh, she opened her luggage and began moving items from one bag to another. "I'll make up an overnight bag so I don't have to carry the suitcase up the stairs."

When she had packed the bag, they trudged up the outdoor staircase to the second floor, then followed the walkway to a room with two double beds and a rattling air conditioner.

Richard threw the lock and then jammed the desk chair under the doorknob.

"I need to lie down for a couple of minutes," he said blearily.

"That's fine."

"I'll hear you if you move the chair."

"I'm sure you would."

He lay down on one of the beds ... and was snoring a few minutes later.

Louise suspected she could not only have moved the chair but could have danced on it without Richard being any the wiser. But she had no incentive to leave. Where would she go?

She brought the overnight bag into the bathroom, took a shower, and changed from her camo clothes to her more usual uniform: a tailored linen dress, belted at the waist, and a pair of low-heeled pumps.

When she came out, Richard was still sleeping. She set her phone on the bedside table and lay down on the other bed, but she was too keyed up to rest. She got up, went to the closed curtains, parted them a crack, and gazed out over the motel parking and the few fast-food joints that lined the road.

Half an hour had passed, and the sun was almost at the horizon when her phone buzzed. Richard's eyes opened sluggishly, then widened with alarm. He struggled upright. "How long have I been asleep?"

"Not long," she said as she crossed the room, picked up the phone, and hit *Accept.* "Yes?"

"It's Philip. Is Richard with you?"

"Yes."

"Put the phone on speaker."

Louise switched to speaker. "All right."

"Richard, how are you doing?"

"Fine. But I fell asleep," he added sheepishly.

"Understandable," said Philip. "I can meet up with you two now. Where are you?"

Louise gave him the name and location of the motel, and their room number. "How did things go at the compound?"

"Good. I'm not far away—I'll be there soon."

Less than ten minutes later, there was a knock on the door. Richard crossed the room and peered through the peephole, then removed the chair from under the knob and opened the door to reveal Philip.

"Hello, Philip," said Richard, clearly relieved.

"Hello, Richard," said Philip, stepping into the room. "I brought a friend."

Owen McNally followed him in.

Louise started. "What's he doing here?"

"I'm going to take you to William Penn University to use the lab there," said Owen, his tone coldly formal. "I saw the facilities at Rush—they won't be sufficient to make the inhibitol."

Louise's gaze shifted from Owen to Philip. "And I assume the lab at the compound is no longer an option?"

"Not anymore," said Philip. "I blew it up." He turned to Richard. "And we've got a ride for you back to Letort."

Richard's eyes widened. "To Marjorie?"

"Yes, to Marjorie. Go with Owen—he'll introduce you to your driver."

Owen had to hustle to keep up with Richard's dash for the door.

Louise raised an eyebrow. "And who might the driver be?"

"No one you need to worry about," said Philip.

HALF AN HOUR LATER, Louise found herself in a cherry-red Lexus sports coupe headed east on the Pennsylvania Turnpike toward Philadelphia. Owen McNally was at the wheel, Philip Castillo in the front passenger seat. She herself was in the minuscule back seat with so little legroom that she had to sit sideways. McNally and Castillo had briefly discussed tying her hands and decided it was unlikely she would try anything while she was in the car with them. If she somehow caused McNally to lose control of the vehicle, she couldn't possibly extricate herself from the wreckage.

In fact, she thought sourly, she suspected she'd have some trouble extricating herself even assuming they arrived at William Penn University in one piece.

38

Lizzy sat in Owen's old SUV in the parking lot of the Harrisburg motel, anxiously waiting for Owen or Philip to emerge from the room where they were meeting with Richard Pearson and Louise. She knew Philip wouldn't intentionally lead Owen into a dangerous situation, and that he would be careful of his own safety as well, but Louise had surprised them so often in the past ... Lizzy hoped Louise didn't have an unpleasant surprise in store for them now.

She tensed when she saw the door open. A Black man she guessed to be about sixty emerged, followed by Owen. As they descended the steps, Lizzy climbed out of the SUV.

"Lizzy," Owen said as the men approached, "I'd like to introduce you to Richard Pearson. Richard, this is Lizzy."

Lizzy shook Richard's hand. "Hi, Richard."

"Pleased to meet you, Lizzy."

"Lizzy's going to go with you to Letort," Owen said to Richard. "She can help keep an eye on Marjorie, along with the other people who are there."

Richard cast a skeptical eye toward Lizzy.

"Don't underestimate her, Richard," said Owen. "You'll be glad she's with you if trouble comes your way."

Richard smiled sheepishly. "Didn't mean to suggest otherwise." He nodded at Lizzy. "I'm grateful for any help I can get."

As Owen headed back up to the motel room, Lizzy asked Richard, "Do you mind driving?"

"No, not at all."

She handed over the key, and they climbed into the SUV.

As they headed for Letort, Lizzy called Andy to let them know they were on their way, then glanced again at the speedometer. "Richard! You actually want to get to Letort in one piece, don't you? I know I do."

Richard blushed. "Yes, certainly." The speedometer dropped back to a more reasonable number.

She reached over and patted his arm. "Not long now." She hesitated, then asked, "Why is Marjorie in a care home?" She quickly added, "You don't have to tell me if you'd rather not."

"I don't mind—it's no secret." He smiled sadly. "She broke her neck playing a game of tag."

"Jeez—what happened?"

"We were down in Norfolk, visiting my daughter and her family. Marjorie was playing tag with our two little grandsons in the backyard, and she tripped on the sprinkler hose. She fell into the picnic table and hit her neck. Cervical spinal cord injury."

"Man, I'm sorry to hear that. Can they treat that?"

Richard sighed. "They're doing the best they can. Wish we lived closer to Philly—there would be better facilities there."

"Yeah. Although Letort isn't *so* far from Philly—could you take her there for treatments?"

"Transporting her is difficult. You need special equipment and people who know how to operate it to move her so it doesn't injure her neck even more."

"That's really tough ... for both of you."

Richard marshaled a smile. "She's a trouper." He sniffed, worked a handkerchief out of his back pocket, and wiped his nose. "She's been braver about this whole thing than I've been."

"I'll bet she'll be happy to see you."

Richard tucked the handkerchief back in his pocket. "I'll sure be glad to see her."

It took them only about half an hour to get from Harrisburg to Letort, and they arrived just as full darkness was falling.

Lizzy wasn't surprised that Marjorie Pearson wasn't getting better at Cedar Grove. Its scraggly landscaping and tired-looking interior didn't suggest there was money to be spent on expert staff or state-of-the-art technology.

When they reached the second floor, she saw Andy sitting on a metal folding chair next to one of the doors, Olivia standing next to him, arms crossed, leaning against the wall. Olivia straightened and raised her hand in greeting. Andy pushed himself to his feet.

"Are these your friends?" Richard whispered to Lizzy, not slowing his pace.

"Yup."

"Thank God." Raising his voice to a normal level, he greeted Olivia and Andy with a distracted *how do you do?* and disappeared into the room.

Lizzy heard an unfamiliar woman's voice from the room—"Honey!"—and a moment later, Ruby came out of the room and joined Lizzy, Andy, and Olivia in the hallway.

She hugged each of them. "Has anyone shown up? Anyone who shouldn't?" She glanced into the room across the hall, which was unoccupied. The rooms nearest Marjorie's appeared to be empty as well. "Anyone at all?" she asked uncertainly.

"Seems like occupancy is down a smidge at Cedar Grove,"

said Andy. He glanced toward Marjorie's room and lowered his voice. "I imagine anyone who has an option is going elsewhere." His voice returned to its normal register. "And as for visitors, no sign of Chapel or his men."

"That's good," said Lizzy.

"Yes. And I heard from Philip. He, Owen, and Louise are on their way to Penn U."

"I can't believe Philip ... *enlisted* that woman," muttered Olivia.

"My brother's with them, too," Andy said with a shrug.

"Philip didn't leave Owen much choice," said Olivia.

"And Philip was at the compound because of me," said Lizzy. "He saved my life."

Much to Lizzy's surprise, Andy also leapt to Philip's defense. "He saved my life, too. He's a gutsy guy."

Lizzy waited for a smartass punchline, but Andy just reached out and squeezed Olivia's shoulder.

Olivia pinched the bridge of her nose. "I know." She dropped her hand to her side and smiled wanly at Andy. "I'm just afraid that someday he's going to get himself in a bind he can't get out of."

They lingered in the hallway for another minute, then Richard popped his head out, a big grin on his face. "Lizzy, come on in and meet Marjorie!"

Lizzy and Ruby entered the room, while Andy and Olivia resumed their guard post in the hallway.

Lizzy's first impression was of hard white plastic and black straps—like a partially dressed stormtrooper—but it took only a moment for the initial impression to be banished by the woman the equipment encased. Her eyes twinkled behind her glasses, and her hair, black liberally sprinkled with gray, was pulled up into a spray at the top of her head.

"Marji," said Richard, "this is Lizzy."

"Lizzy, I'm so happy to meet you," said Marjorie, her voice scratchy but clear. "I understand you got my Richard back here from his adventures."

Lizzy smiled. "Well, I just provided the vehicle—and it wasn't even mine. He did the driving."

Marjorie arched an eyebrow. "Too fast?"

Lizzy laughed. "A little bit. He really wanted to see you."

Marjorie cast a fond look at Richard. "As long as you both got here in one piece." Her smile dimmed a bit. "And it sounds like it wasn't a sure thing. Sounds like you've been dealing with some pretty bad people."

"No bad guys are going to get past us," Andy said from the doorway.

"I guess the nurses or aides still need to come in and out," said Lizzy.

"Nope," said Marjorie. "Ruby is helping me with everything I need."

"It's no problem," said Ruby.

"They don't exactly have a full complement of residents at Cedar Grove," said Richard, "and they've been consolidating the patients to make it convenient for the staff, which I understand. But the room Marjorie would have gotten looked out onto a dumpster, and so far, we've talked them into letting her stay here. And now, with Ruby on the case, I know they appreciate not having to make a trip to this wing."

Lizzy smothered a yawn.

"You need some sleep, kiddo," said Andy. "And I suspect you're not the only one. Let's get a couple of hotel rooms nearby, and we can take shifts getting some rest. Why don't you and Ruby take the first break?" He turned to Olivia. "Is that all right with you?"

"Absolutely," said Olivia. "You guys have been here longer than I have—I'm not tired yet."

Andy got out his phone. "Richard, I'm guessing that you're not interested in going somewhere to get some sleep."

"No, sir," said Richard. "I'm staying right here."

Andy made the reservations, then Lizzy and Ruby left for the hotel. As they made their way to where Owen's old SUV was parked, Lizzy asked, "Do you mind driving? I'm pooped."

"Of course not," said Ruby, taking the keys.

As they headed toward the hotel, Lizzy asked, "How are Andy and Olivia getting along?"

Ruby's mouth twitched up almost imperceptibly. "What makes you ask?"

"Well, Andy and Philip aren't huge buddies, so Philip's feelings might have rubbed off on Olivia ... although it seems like Olivia is angrier with Philip than Andy is at the moment."

"I haven't heard Andy say a bad word about Philip since we got here," said Ruby. After a pause, she asked, "Did Andy and Olivia get to know each other when all of you were in Arizona?"

"They were both there while Uncle Owen was recovering from the knife wound, but Andy was spending most of his time with Owen, and Olivia was spending most of her time with Philip." They rode in silence for a minute, then Lizzy said, "Andy's always so flirty. I would think that might annoy Olivia."

"No flirting that I've seen."

"Maybe because he knows she's Philip's girlfriend." Lizzy rolled her eyes. "Although I've never seen that stop him in the past. I don't think he means anything by it—it's like an uncontrollable reaction to being around a woman. I've seen him flirt with—" She stopped and cleared her throat.

"Women my age?" asked Ruby, amused.

"Well ..." Lizzy laughed sheepishly. "Yes."

"It's sort of nice being flirted with by a good-looking man like Andy. Everyone knows it's just in good fun."

Lizzy was silent for another minute, then said, "Olivia and Philip are always so business-like. Well," she added, blushing, "at least when they're around other people. But maybe she just likes more serious guys. Which would mean she might like Andy more now than she would have before. He's not the same since he came back from the compound."

"They did some terrible things to him there."

"They did." After a pause, she continued. "His nose looks almost completely better, and he's recovering from the gunshot wound faster than I expected, but it seems like his hand bothers him more than I would have thought."

"He's a surgeon. His hands are his livelihood."

A lump formed in Lizzy's throat. "That's true, I didn't think of that."

"I think what happened to his hands was the worst for him, and not just for that reason."

Ruby hesitated, and Lizzy thought she'd have to prompt her again, but then Ruby continued.

"Him getting hit by the bullet was an accident, in a way—just a random shot, from what I understand. But what they did to his hands, that was personal. And the knowledge that someone might hurt you just to hurt you ... that's got to be a hard thing to live with."

Lizzy dropped her head, and a tear dripped from her chin onto where her hands lay, fingers laced together, white-knuckled, in her lap.

Ruby reached over and patted her hand. "I don't say it to make you feel bad, Lizzy. But Andy's time at the compound changed him, and it might be easier for him to be around someone who doesn't expect him to be the same flirty, unserious man he used to be."

"Yes, that makes sense." Lizzy drew a deep breath. "I sort of hope he doesn't like her *too* much—I wouldn't want him to be hurt when Olivia goes back with Philip."

As Ruby turned into the hotel parking lot, that same little smile twitched her lips. "I suppose only time will tell."

39

"Come!" Billy yelled at a knock on the door.

Tony stepped into Billy's command center, where the blackness outside the windows made the sparkle of the chandelier on the lacquered walls even more startling. "Mickey went to Rush College and asked around the lab where Pearson works. A couple of students were there, said they hadn't seen him recently, that he was on leave. If Pearson had gone to the lab, Mickey thinks they would have said so."

Billy, standing next to a window, jammed his hands in his pockets. "Send Mickey to the old folks' home and see if Pearson's there."

"What about Castillo?"

"How the fuck should I know?" snapped Billy. "It was supposed to be your job to know 'what about Castillo'!"

Tony raised a placating hand. "Sure, boss. We'll find him." He turned to go.

"Wait," Billy called after him. "You seen that Indian girl today?"

"Nope ... but you said Castillo didn't seem interested in her, and you didn't seem interested in hiring her on. I paid her cash at the end of her shift yesterday and sent her on her way."

"Stop by *Chesaperk* tomorrow—see if she's still there."

"Why, you want her back?"

"No, dumb shit," spat Billy, "I just want to know if she's still there. That okay with you?"

"Sure thing, boss."

Tony backed out of the room and eased the door shut behind him.

Billy picked up his glass from the desk, annoyed that it was empty. He stalked to the bar in the corner and grabbed a half-empty bottle, sending a shiver of sound through the other bottles on the bar. He sloshed some bourbon into the glass, then crossed to the window, watching one of the boys moving near the tree line with a flashlight. He took a sip of Woodford.

Woodford. When he had introduced Castillo to the girl at *Charm City*, Castillo had said, *They're drinking Woodford.* Why would he have said that? Billy swirled the glass, missing the clink of ice cubes that had melted an hour ago. The girl had been reaching for a bottle—he couldn't remember what it was—but it hadn't been the Woodford. It was like Castillo was warning her away from whatever she had been reaching for. And why would he be doing that?

Billy's hand tightened on the glass. Because they knew each other, and the girl had been reaching for Castillo's usual drink.

He turned and hurled the glass into one of the walls, the liquid lending another layer of sheen to the lacquer, the glass twinkling prettily on the floor.

How could he have been so stupid as to believe that two Indians, both from Arizona, just happened to show up in two restaurants right across the street from each other in Baltimore?

He yanked open the door, drawing in a breath for a bellow, and almost ran into Tony, whose hand was raised to knock.

Tony took a quick step back. "Everything okay, boss? Thought I heard a crash."

Billy pointed to the wall. "Clean that up. And tell whoever's patrolling outside that I'm going to be on the patio. I don't want some overenthusiastic asshole taking a shot at me."

As Tony pulled his phone from his pocket and began to issue instructions in a hoarse whisper, Billy went to the bar and grabbed another glass and the bottle of Woodford. He pushed past Tony and strode down the hall to the back of the house. Once on the flagstone patio, he poured two fingers of bourbon and swallowed half of it.

He replayed in his mind the scene at *Charm City*, examining it as one might probe a painful tooth with the tongue. Knob Creek—that was what she had been reaching for.

Castillo had an ally in Baltimore, and he, Billy Chapel, had missed it.

He had wanted to win Castillo over. Theo Viklund had spoken highly of him, and Theo Viklund didn't speak highly of many men. Billy was willing to force Castillo's compliance if needed, but a willing accomplice was better than an unwilling one. All he had wanted to do was give Castillo a little fun— maybe fun for the girl, too.

He downed the last of the Woodford.

No good deed goes unpunished, he thought bitterly.

40

———

The next morning, Lizzy woke feeling relatively well-rested for the first time in days—maybe weeks.

Ruby sat on the other bed in the motel room, reading on her phone.

The clock on the bedside table said nine o'clock. "Man, I keep oversleeping," Lizzy said. "You should have woken me sooner!"

"I called Andy around seven and asked him when he wanted us to take over from him and Olivia, and he said to let you sleep."

"Jeez, they must be exhausted, too. Did you get any sleep?"

"Slept like a log."

Lizzy nodded toward Ruby's phone. "Anything new about the explosion at the compound?"

"It doesn't sound like the investigators are sharing much with the press yet."

"Any sign that they found the Caravan?"

"No mention of that."

Lizzy took a quick shower, then they left for Cedar Grove, with a trip through the McDonald's drive-through to pick up breakfast. Lizzy wasn't a huge fan of McDonald's—her diet was usually a lot less meat-heavy—but it seemed like the most convenient option.

Armed with breakfast, and with Ruby again at the wheel, Lizzy called Owen to get an update.

"Louise worked through the night, testing the inhibitol," he said.

"Why all night? Is there a reason to rush?"

"We don't want to spend more time here than necessary, and working at night limits the number of people we might run into. If anyone does see us, I can say that Louise is a colleague who's helping me with a project, but if anyone questions that—or if anyone recognizes her—it would be awkward."

"What about Philip?"

"Especially since the Maryland state troopers have his Philip Riva driver's license, he's here but staying out of sight. He can't fake knowledge of neurobiology the way Louise can, so he would be harder to explain. And he's helping keep an eye on our ..." He cleared his throat. "... guest."

Lizzy grimaced. "Uncle Owen, she tried to kill you—you don't have to be polite. Just say prisoner."

When Lizzy and Ruby reached Cedar Grove, they gathered their provisions and headed up to Marjorie's room.

They found Andy barely awake on the chair in the hallway. Just inside the door, Olivia sat on the guest chair, while Marjorie snored delicately in the bed. Richard sat in a chair next to her, holding her hand.

Richard patted Marjorie's hand to wake her up, and Lizzy and Ruby distributed breakfast items. Andy rounded up two more chairs for Lizzy and Ruby, then positioned himself by the window, looking out across the parking lot as he ate his breakfast sandwich and sipped his coffee.

While they ate, Richard and Marjorie told stories about their daughter, who worked at the naval station in Norfolk, her husband, and their children.

"Every grandparent might *claim* that their grandsons are in the top ten percent in every conceivable measurement," Marjorie said with a laugh, "but I can guarantee you that that's true of Jeremy and Jamie."

Richard got out his phone and showed them some photos of the little boys, who were undeniably adorable.

When they had finished with breakfast, Lizzy collected the wrappers, but before she got to Andy, he wadded up the wrapper and tossed it toward the wastebasket.

Lizzy knew that before the injury to his hand, he would never have missed the shot, but the wrapper bounced off the basket and onto the floor.

"Good lord," he muttered, retrieving it from the floor and dropping it into the basket before anyone else could get to it. He downed the last swallow of his coffee and dropped the cup in the basket. "I'm going to catch some sleep. You guys will be okay here?"

Olivia stood. "I think I'll do that, too. There must be another room available in the hotel, right?"

"I already got two rooms ..." His voice trailed off and he glanced toward the window.

"Would you rather I stay here?" she asked, uncertain.

"No, no. That's not necessary." He turned to Ruby. "You guys will be okay here by yourselves for a bit?"

"We'll be fine," said Ruby, giving her purse, which lay in her lap, a little pat.

"Yeah," Lizzy said, imagining Ruby's purse a grandmother's treasure trove of hard candy and crayons paired with a visiting nurse's medical bag, "we'll be fine."

"Richard," said Andy, "ready for some rest? You and I can take one room, Olivia can take the other."

Richard squeezed Marjorie's hand. "No, I'm fine here."

Lizzy thought that he did look in better spirits than any of them.

Andy popped his head out the door, looked up and down the hallway, then gestured for Olivia to precede him out the door. Lizzy could tell by the way he moved that spending the night on the chair in the hallway hadn't done him any good.

As their steps receded down the hallway, Marjorie whispered to Ruby with a conspiratorial smile, "See if he takes her arm when they get to the steps."

As Ruby went to the door to the hallway, Richard rolled his eyes. "Hon ..."

Lizzy joined Ruby at the door, and they peered down the hallway.

"They just got to the stairs," Ruby whispered back into the room, then added, "He didn't take her arm."

"I'm not sure Olivia would appreciate a man taking her arm just to walk down a flight of steps," said Lizzy.

"Quite right," said Marjorie cheerfully. "Watch from the window and see if he opens the car door for her."

"Andy always opens the car door for his passengers," Lizzy said as she and Ruby hurried to the window that overlooked the parking lot.

"For his *female* passengers," Ruby corrected.

"True," said Lizzy.

"I bet he opens the door for her," said Marjorie. "He's smitten—I can tell."

Richard laughed. "Hon, are you matchmaking?"

"They'd make such a cute couple!" said Marjorie.

"Don't you think he's a little old for her?" Richard asked.

"Nonsense—I'm guessing she's around thirty, and he can't be much more than forty. That's perfectly reasonable." Marjorie turned to Lizzy and Ruby. "Richard and I met in grade school—our birthdays are only four days apart."

"Crap," said Lizzy as she gazed out at the vehicles in the parking lot, waiting for Andy and Olivia to emerge from the building. "I just remembered—at some point I have to go back to pick up the Caravan from where I left it near the compound."

"Once things settle down," said Ruby, "you and I can drive down there and get it."

Lizzy gnawed her thumbnail. "I hate to leave it there for too long—I'll bet as part of the investigation into the explosion at the lab, they'll check the area."

"We can go get it when Andy and Olivia get back."

The couple appeared and headed toward the parking lot.

"Looks like they're taking Olivia's car," said Lizzy. "I wonder what the door-opening etiquette is in that situation? I'm guessing he won't open the door since she's the driver."

"I'm guessing he will," said Ruby.

"I'm with Ruby," said Marjorie.

Andy and Olivia reached the car.

"Nope, no door-opening for the driver," said Lizzy. "I guess that would seem a little too much like he was a valet, not her escort." A moment later, she said, "But where's he going?"

Rather than getting in the passenger seat of Olivia's car, Andy was crossing to a black SUV with tinted windows.

The SUV's driver's door opened and a muscular man in a leather jacket stepped out.

Lizzy gasped, "I think that must be one of Billy Chapel's men!" She turned from the window. "You guys stay here."

Before Ruby, Richard, or Marjorie could respond, she sprinted out of the room.

41

———

By the time Lizzy reached the parking lot, Andy had crowded the man up against the side of the SUV, his words indistinct but his tone furious. Olivia stood beside Andy, a hand hovering uncertainly near his arm. The man, who was wearing a Baltimore Ravens shirt under his leather jacket, was shorter than Andy's six-foot-four but looked twice as wide. He faced Andy, his expression stony and his arms crossed … and, Lizzy noticed, one hand inside the flap of his leather jacket.

Olivia saw her coming. "Go back inside," she called to Lizzy. "We'll handle this."

Lizzy didn't stop until she was less than a dozen feet from the group. If he pulled a gun, she was pretty sure that that would be sufficient provocation for her to squeeze him, but she wasn't as sure she could do it before he could pull the trigger.

"Yes, go back inside," said Andy, his words clearly directed at Lizzy, although he never took his eyes off the man's face.

"Yeah, sweetheart," said Ravens. "Go inside and let the grown-ups work this out."

She stepped up next to him. "Do you work for Billy? Is he looking for me?"

Surprise flickered across the man's face, and he glanced over at her. It seemed clear that Billy Chapel hadn't expected the teenager from the compound to show up in Letort, Pennsylvania —or maybe he just hadn't told his henchman to expect her.

"Young lady," Andy said through gritted teeth, "step back."

Lizzy was surprised at the *young lady*, then realized Andy was trying to avoid saying her name in front of Ravens, or maybe even acknowledging that he knew her.

Ravens redirected his attention back to Andy. "Why don't *you* step back, buddy."

Andy closed the distance between himself and the man to a foot. "What are you doing here? I think it's pretty clear you work for Chapel. Here's a piece of advice: if you don't want to be connected to someone who controls drugs and prostitution in Baltimore, don't wear a Baltimore team shirt when you're visiting Pennsylvania."

Ravens flushed.

"Are you here because of Marjorie Pearson?" Andy continued. "Because she isn't relying just on a bunch of overworked aides to keep an eye on her anymore."

The man smirked. "Don't know what you're talking about."

The fist of Andy's uninjured hand pistoned into Ravens' stomach.

Ravens expelled a whoosh of air and doubled over.

Olivia grabbed Andy's arm, trying to pull him away, and only Lizzy saw Ravens' hand reach under his jacket.

Was he reaching for a gun in a holster, or just pressing his hand to where Andy had punched him?

She could feel the squeeze sputtering inside her, like the propellor of a plane just after ignition.

Andy wrenched his arm out of Olivia's grip, and she staggered back and lost her balance.

Andy pivoted toward her to grab her arm, trying to keep her from falling.

Ravens' hand cleared his jacket and Lizzy's question was answered: he was holding a gun.

The squeeze coalesced, and Lizzy could feel its power turning toward the man, but at the same time, Andy let go of Olivia, who went sprawling onto the pavement, grabbed the man's wrist, and twisted.

The gun didn't fall, but the twist loosened Ravens' grip. With his splinted hand, Andy grabbed the barrel and wrenched it out of Ravens' hand. He swung the gun and caught Ravens in the mouth with the grip.

Ravens sagged against the side of the SUV, his hand to his mouth.

Andy swung the gun the other way and this time hit Ravens in the nose.

The man dropped to his knees, and as Andy bent over him, his jacket fell open and Lizzy could see that he, too, had a gun holstered at his shoulder.

Olivia was back on her feet and once again grabbed Andy's arm. "Andy, don't. The police will come—"

Lizzy anticipated what the rule-following Olivia would say next: *Let them take care of this.*

"—and we can't let the authorities get their hands on the *young lady*," Olivia said, cocking an amused eyebrow at Lizzy.

Whatever remnants of the squeeze that remained in Lizzy's head swirled away amid her surprise. She had always assumed that Olivia's preference for dealing with a situation would be through official channels.

Andy straightened, breathing hard, and glared down at the man. "What should we do with him?"

Olivia looked toward the building, and Lizzy followed her gaze. Other than Ruby and Richard's indistinct figures in the window of Marjorie's room, there was no indication that anyone in the building had noticed the altercation.

Lizzy gave them a thumbs up, which they returned.

Lizzy suspected Andy was as surprised as she was when Olivia opened the driver's door of Ravens' SUV—Lizzy realized it was an Escalade, although an older model—and climbed in. Did she plan to run the man over with his own vehicle?

But Olivia popped open the glove compartment, felt carefully among its contents, and removed a gun and a packet of zip ties. Running her fingers under the dashboard and along the sides and underside of the seat, she discovered another gun, and then a third under the passenger seat.

"Let me get a bag," said Lizzy.

She jogged to Owen's SUV and found a cloth shopping bag from an NPR fund drive in the trunk.

When she got back, Ravens was propped against the side of the SUV and was pressing the top of his shirt to his mouth. His gun had disappeared and based on a bulge under the back of Andy's jacket, Lizzy suspected he had slipped it into the back of his waistband. Andy was cradling his splinted hand in his good hand, his features twisted into a grimace.

Olivia dumped the guns into the bag, then climbed into the back seat and began search it as well.

Lizzy stepped up next to Andy. "Is your hand okay?" she whispered.

He tried for a smile. "Pistol-whipping might not have been on my orthopedist's list of recommended activities."

She dropped her voice further. "You're carrying a gun."

He glanced toward Ravens. "You saw that?" he whispered back.

"Your jacket fell open a little when you bent over that guy.

Why didn't you use that? Not that I'm complaining," she hurried on, "but it would have saved your hand."

Andy summoned a grin. "My hand thinks it was worth it—since Lucas's lackey isn't available for a whipping, I'm happy to use Chapel's as a substitute."

Olivia emerged from the back of the SUV. "Nothing back there."

"So now what?" asked Andy. "We just let him go?"

"We could call the cops after the young lady leaves," said Olivia, "but we'd have a lot of complicated explaining to do."

Ravens followed the conversation with eyes that were already starting to swell from Andy's blows.

"Or," Olivia continued, crossing her arms and looking down at the man, "we could send him back to Billy Chapel and let him explain how badly he fucked up what should have been an easy assignment."

Ravens' eyes widened.

Andy stared down at him, considering. "How are you feeling?"

"How do you think?" Ravens honked through his shirt.

"Head hurt?"

"You just whacked the shit out of me—of course it hurts."

Andy glanced at Lizzy, then back at Ravens. "Not your face—your *head*. Do you have a headache?"

"What do you care?"

Andy, reached under his jacket, drew out the gun he had taken from Ravens, closed his good hand around the barrel, and pointed it at Ravens' leg.

Ravens raised the hand that wasn't holding his shirt in place over his mouth. "Okay, fine. Didn't know you'd care." His voice was a little more slurred than could be explained by his split lip.

"I don't *care*. I want to know if you can drive."

Ravens thought for a moment. "I have a headache."

Andy held two fingers in front of his face. "How many?"

Ravens squinted. "Three?"

Lizzy felt a roil of emotion—a sort of guilty pride that she had helped defend Andy and Olivia, alongside a guilty sorrow that Ravens counted as yet another in her tally of victims, although Andy's actions had saved Ravens from the full effect of the squeeze.

"Okay," said Olivia, "he can't drive. But we need to get him away from here. It's just luck that no one has noticed all this going on yet. We'll tie him with the zip ties and drive him somewhere else. There are plenty of woods around here. Then we can decide if we want to let Billy Chapel know where he is." She turned to Lizzy. "Can you help me with him?"

"*I* can help you," said Andy.

"No, you can't," said Olivia. "You're bleeding."

Lizzy looked at Andy, alarmed. Although Olivia might have missed the shoulder holster Andy was wearing, Lizzy herself had missed the spot of red on his shirt where it lay over the bandage covering the gunshot wound.

Andy looked down, and the sight seemed to take him by surprise, too. "Damn." He put a steadying hand on the SUV.

"Do we need to call an ambulance?" Lizzy asked.

"Get him into the SUV first," said Andy. "It's not serious—" He removed his hand from the vehicle and pulled himself straight. "—just took me by surprise."

Ravens evidently decided that, all things considered, being tied up and left somewhere in the Pennsylvania woods was preferable to some of the alternatives—or maybe Lizzy had incapacitated him with the squeeze more than she had realized —because he climbed into the back of the SUV without complaint and didn't resist having his wrists and ankles zip-tied.

When Olivia had swung the door closed on Ravens, she asked Andy, "How did you know he was out there?"

"I was watching from the window," he said as he propped himself on the driver's seat of the vehicle and began unbuttoning his shirt. "The SUV showed up sometime last night, after you guys left for the hotel, and was still there this morning. I couldn't see clearly through the windows, but I could see a light inside once in a while, probably from his phone." He eased the tape off his skin where it held a large, now bloodstained, square of gauze to his side, and examined the wound. "I just pulled out a couple of stitches—I can have that fixed at an urgent care clinic." Suppressing a wince, he pressed the bandage back in place and rebuttoned his shirt.

"Do you want me to drive you to the clinic?" Lizzy asked, concerned.

"I can do that," said Olivia.

"Actually," said Andy, irritated, "*I* can do that. After we take care of," he gestured to the back of the SUV, "this guy."

"Andy," said Olivia, "you're bleeding from a bullet wound. Let's not pretend that's not serious. You shouldn't be driving."

"I don't see how we can avoid it," he said. "Someone needs to drive the Escalade, and someone needs to follow in another car so the first someone doesn't have to hitchhike back."

Olivia ran her hand over her hair in an impatient gesture. "Damn, I didn't think of that."

"I can follow Olivia in the SUV," said Lizzy.

"Then how am I supposed to get to the urgent care center?" Andy asked with mock annoyance. Then, his tone more serious, he added, "Plus, I think it's best if you head out. I don't think anyone saw what happened, but I don't want you around here if cops start showing up."

She crossed her arms. "*I* don't want *you* around here if cops start showing up!"

He smiled with a little of his old attitude. "Are you kidding? Cops love me! I'm good at sweet-talking them."

Olivia rolled her eyes, but she was smiling. "Good thing you have a lawyer with you to advise you about when your sweet-talking is going to get you in trouble." Her smile faded and she turned back to Lizzy. "But I agree with Andy—you should head out."

"But that leaves only Ruby and Richard with Marjorie," said Lizzy. "What if another one of Chapel's men shows up?" She looked down at the bag of guns. "Should we leave one with Ruby?"

"She already has one," said Andy.

Lizzy thought of that odd pat Ruby had given her purse when Andy had asked if they would be okay if he and Olivia left.

"She's been practicing with it," Andy added. "She's a good shot."

Olivia arched an eyebrow. "Good to know."

Lizzy ran her fingers through her hair. "I hate to make things even more complicated, but Ruby was going to drive me down to the compound so I could get the Caravan before someone else finds it."

Andy waved toward the building. "Take Richard."

"He's not going to want to leave Marjorie," said Lizzy.

"He won't need to be gone for long," said Andy. "And if we end up with more vehicles than we need, maybe he can hide the extras at his house. After you get the Caravan and drop Richard back in Letort, you should go to my apartment. Owen and Philip might need some help in Philly."

"Okay." Lizzy turned toward the building. "I'll get Richard."

"You stay here," said Olivia, "just in case there's a ruckus inside. I'll get him."

Lizzy sighed. Everyone was always trying to shuttle her off to a safer assignment.

Not that it had done anyone much good so far.

42

———

Billy was in the sauna off the master bedroom of the Owings Mills house. He sometimes wondered if he should have had it installed in the basement—it might have made a better interrogation room than the cement-floored, cinder block-walled storage space he had used a time or two.

There was a knock on the sauna door. "Boss, it's Tony."

"Come!"

When Billy saw Tony's expression, he threw up his hands. "What now?"

"Mickey's not answering his phone."

"Are you fucking kidding me?"

"'Fraid not. Should I send another guy out to Letort to check on him?"

"No, I don't want you sending another guy out to Letort, you moron. First Donny, now Mickey—anything west of Baltimore is like the fucking Bermuda Triangle." He pointed to a towel hanging next to the door. "Hand me that."

Tony handed him the towel.

Billy mopped his face, then stood and pushed past Tony and strode naked into the bedroom.

Tony hurried after him.

"You and I are going to Philadelphia," said Billy. "It's where Mortensen's from, it's where that girl from the compound claimed she grew up, and it's where Andrew McNally lives."

"Who's that?"

"The guy Mortensen was holding hostage at Viklund's compound. We'll go to Philly and see what we can find out."

"Okay. I'll have one of the boys bring the Lux around back."

Billy was standing at the window, rubbing his chest absent-mindedly with the towel, then a grin spread across his face. "Bring the van ... with all the 'equipment.' If we find any of them, Mortensen or Castillo or Pearson or McNally—or the girl, for that matter—I might not want to wait until we get back to the house to ask them a few questions. And if we find more than one of them, the extra room will be handy."

"What about Mickey?"

Billy tossed the sodden towel to Tony. "What about him? Long as we get the 'Slade back, I don't much care what happens to Mickey."

Lizzy got to Andy's condo around three o'clock and carefully maneuvered the Caravan into a space in the parking garage. The pickup had gone smoothly—the official activity seemed still to be focused inside the compound—and Richard was now back in Letort with Owen's old SUV.

She took the elevator to the first floor, exchanged greetings with Sherman as she crossed the lobby, then took the second elevator up to Andy's floor. She let herself into the apartment, silenced the beeping alarm, and dropped her knapsack on the couch.

She thought about calling Owen or Andy or Ruby, but she had been checking in with them throughout the day. If anything had happened since then, they would have let her know.

It was mid-afternoon, and she hadn't eaten since breakfast. She found some leftover spaghetti in the freezer and put it in the microwave to thaw. She considered her drink choices—Andy liked chianti with spaghetti and Owen liked beer—but settled on a ginger ale. Once the spaghetti was ready, she settled down at the kitchen island with her meal, moving the stool so she could look out across the living room and through the large windows to the balcony and beyond.

The only time she had ever been alone in the apartment was when Andy had first brought her there to hide out from Louise's henchmen, and she had spent most of that time sleeping. Being here by herself was certainly a different experience than when she, Owen, Andy, and Ruby had been sharing the space.

As she twirled a strand of spaghetti on her fork, she thought about other times she had been alone: for much of the drive from Pennsylvania to Arizona, where she had planned to kill Tobe Hanrick; hunkered down in the back of the Caravan behind a West Chester Dodge dealership waiting for Andy to come and stitch up her bleeding head. She felt her throat tighten. How come so much of the time she spent alone was in the back of a van?

Then she thought of the few hours she had spent alone at Philip's Sedona casita, before the events at Oak Creek Canyon had forced him to leave his home behind. That night had ended badly, but only because she had ventured out despite Philip and Eddie's instructions for her to stay put. Yes, that had ended very badly, but the time in the casita had been lovely—paging through books from Philip's library, examining the fine woven rugs hanging on the walls and the pottery dotting the book-shelves, napping.

Things normal people did.

Leaving the spaghetti on the island, she took the can of ginger ale and moved to the doorway to the living room. She'd probably never have enough money for an apartment as nice as Andy's, but even if she did, was this the kind of apartment she'd want? She didn't think so. As elegant as it was, it didn't feel homey to her. She could imagine Andy calling up a well-known Philly interior designer, writing a check, and coming home to a fully furnished space. But she'd enjoy going to antique stores or

Goodwill and finding what she wanted in her home one item at a time. She might spend months, even years, sleeping on a mattress on the floor, but one day she'd see the perfect bed frame. Maybe brass. Maybe wicker. Her bed at her grandparents' Poconos cabin, where she and her mother had hidden out for several years, had had a brass headboard, and it looked so pretty next to the worn quilt covering the bed.

She wandered down the hall and peered into the rooms, musing on what her own version of the decor would be. Something more colorful than Andy's brilliantly white towels. Something more practical than the deep pile of the bedroom rug.

She went back to the living room, slid the glass door open, and stepped out onto the balcony. The weather continued to be pleasant, the sky a brilliant blue. She leaned against the railing and gazed down at the street. A black van idled in front of the entrance to the building several stories below. Maybe what she needed wasn't an apartment; maybe she should get a van like that and make it into a little RV. Even the Caravan wasn't too uncomfortable to spend time in, and the van would provide twice as much room—you could do all sorts of stuff with a space that big.

As she watched, a man left the building and climbed into the van. She could hear the faint sounds of conversation inside the vehicle drifting up from the street, then the van pulled away and turned right at the next intersection.

She stepped back from the railing and scanned the view. Would she live in a city? She had never imagined herself living in such a crowded place—her father had chosen the house where they had lived in Parkesburg, at the far end of Philly's regional rail service, for its remoteness. Her lips pressed in a thin line. Couldn't risk having little Lizzy run into a bratty neighbor kid and squeeze him.

But although the reason behind their secluded house in

Parkesburg pained her, she did like the country. There were so many pretty roads to explore in Chester County. She took a sip of ginger ale. Maybe when this was all over, she'd get a bike and take a road trip.

Her fingers tightened on the can. *When it was all over.*

She couldn't imagine it ever being all over.

44

———

Tony climbed into the van's driver's seat and slammed the door. "You'd think it was goddamned Fort Knox."

"No way to get up to the apartments?" asked Billy.

"Nope. Chatted with the guy at the security desk—told him I was looking for a restaurant that's actually around the corner. Then asked him how he got the gig—that I wouldn't mind having a job where I could sit around reading magazines all day. He didn't take kindly to that—told me he was National Guard and that he got the gig because he takes keeping people safe seriously."

Billy sighed. "If you want to get info from people—and you can't use your fists—try not to piss them off right off the bat, Tony."

Tony threw up his hands. "Who knew he was going to be such a hardass about his job?"

Billy rolled his eyes. "If we strike out at the other places, we'll come back when another guy's on duty, and I'll see what I can find out. I can be charming if I need to be." He got out his phone. "Drive around the neighborhood for a couple of minutes. Maybe we'll have the luck of the Irish and see McNally or one of his buddies coming in or going out."

"Show me that picture again."

Billy opened the phone's browser to a photo of five men and women standing in front of Children's Hospital of Philadelphia and zoomed in on a tall, slim man with reddish hair, beard, and mustache. "That's McNally."

"Got it." Tony pulled away and turned right at the next intersection.

Billy pulled up the search he had done on the way to Philly on *Andrew McNally Philadelphia*. He had already read through the first couple of pages of results, which included not only the article about McNally's affiliation with CHOP but a number of references to conferences at which he had spoken and papers he had published.

He adjusted his search to *Andrew McNally Philadelphia medicine* with much the same result, then *Andrew McNally Philadelphia university*.

This brought up results for *McNally Philadelphia university*, although without *Andrew*, including an article in the *Philadelphia Register*. He clicked on it.

The article, from two years earlier, included a photograph of a man standing with a few other academic types on a podium. Like Andrew McNally, he was red-haired, fair-skinned, and tall. Unlike Andrew McNally, he was probably a hundred pounds overweight.

"Goddamn," Billy muttered.

"What?"

Billy turned the camera toward Tony. "If that isn't Andrew McNally's brother, I'll tar and feather myself."

Tony glanced over. "Brothers for sure. Who is he?"

Billy scanned the article. "Owen McNally. Neurobiologist

and a professor at William Penn University." Billy tapped in another search, scanned the results, and grinned. "I think we may have found Mortensen's backup lab."

45

Philip sat in a chair next to the glass door leading from the lab to the hallway of the Penn U. science building. One benefit of the positioning was that Philip was out of the line of sight of anyone glancing through the door, which he hoped would prevent him from having to fake a knowledge of neurobiology for the benefit of any visitors. It also reduced the chances that someone would recognize him as the man who had fled the scene of a suspicious explosion in Western Maryland.

It also enabled him to keep an eye on Louise. His position could theoretically enable him to intercept her in the unlikely event she made a dash for the door, although he was less concerned about that than he was about her sneaking away when she left the lab to use the restroom. For those trips, Owen accompanied her to the door of the women's room and then loitered in the hallway outside, pretending to peruse the offerings in the vending machine that had provided their meals for the last twenty-four hours.

Philip hadn't slept since the morning of the previous day, and only the copious amounts of coffee that Owen kept brewing in the department break room was keeping him awake. Louise and Owen had each taken a couple of cat naps in Owen's office, but in view of the concentration their work required, they were probably even more exhausted than Philip was.

In fact, at that moment, Owen sat back on the stool next to Louise's and rubbed his hands down his face. "I think we've done all we can do."

"You want to take a break?" asked Louise.

"No. I think we've done all *we* can do, period."

Louise raised an eyebrow. "You're satisfied with the safety of the drug?"

"Not entirely, but Andy and I can conduct further tests."

"Can he come do that?"

"Not at the moment, but I don't see that there's a huge hurry. We wanted to get *your* work done here as quickly as possible, but Andy and I can take our time running the tests."

"There are still a few tests I'd like to run," Louise said, her gaze sliding toward Philip.

He understood what she was trying to tell him—she might have completed the assignment that Owen knew about, at least to Owen's satisfaction, but not the assignment that only she and Philip knew about.

"It's not necessary," said Owen, levering himself off the stool. "Plus, I wouldn't trust any results either of us got, as tired as we all are. We should all get some rest and then decide on next steps."

"If Mortensen wants to run more tests," said Philip, "maybe we could come back after we've rested up."

"No," said Owen. "Andy and I can do whatever additional testing is needed." He went to a supply closet and removed what looked to Philip like an elaborate Tupperware container with a handle and began transferring the half-dozen vials of the material Louise had produced into the container. "We'll go to my house in Lansdowne, get some rest, and decide what to do next.

It's close by. I got quite a fancy burglar alarm installed. And I need to water my plants—assuming any of them are still alive." He glanced into the case. "These have different-colored stoppers —is that significant?"

Glancing again at Philip, Louise said, "No, you can treat them all the same." She stood. "Do you really think it's safe to go to your house?"

"As far as I know," Philip said, "Owen hasn't hit Billy Chapel's radar. Do you know otherwise?"

"No." She arched an eyebrow. "But you would know more about who is on Billy Chapel's radar than I would."

Philip massaged his eyes with his thumb and fingers and thought with longing of the actual bed that might be available at Owen's house. "Well, Chapel saw Andy at the compound, and he knows his name, but as far as I know, that's all he knows." He sighed. "Okay, let's go to Lansdowne."

46

———

Half an hour later, Owen was coasting the Lexus slowly down the alley behind his house. He rolled to a stop and pointed to the next house in the block. "That's mine."

From the back seat, Louise shifted to peer through the darkness at the house. It was a two-story Craftsman, its solid construction reminding her of its owner. Its back yard was illuminated by a light burning near the back door.

After a few moments, Owen, his voice hopeful, said, "Looks okay."

"How can you possibly tell?" she said. "It's not as if Chapel is likely to announce his presence."

"How could he know where I live?" asked Owen. "He doesn't even know who I am." He cast a baleful look back toward Louise. "It's *your* man who broke into my house."

Louise shot a look toward Philip. "Well, we don't have to worry about him anymore, thanks to Philip and Lizzy."

"He shot first," said Philip. "And put a bullet in my shoulder. If you hadn't locked us in the basement and set your house on fire—"

"Okay," interrupted Owen, "let's just agree that the sooner we don't have to have anything to do with each other, the better we'll like it."

Philip sighed. "Sorry."

They were all silent for a few beats, still staring at the house.

"Nothing has triggered the alarm system," Owen ventured.

"I suppose it would be possible to disable it," Philip said, "but the back porch light is working, so we know the power is on." He unfastened his seatbelt. "Only one way to find out. I'll check the house."

"It's my house—I should check it," said Owen.

Philip pulled back the flap of his jacket, removed the gun from the shoulder holster, and held it out grip-first to Owen.

Owen looked nervously at the weapon. "Maybe we should both go."

Philip returned the gun to the holster "I'm not leaving Mortensen in the car. And if there *is* anything up inside, I want her right there facing it with us."

"Charming," said Louise.

"Should we put the car in the garage?" asked Owen.

Philip considered. "No, let's park it behind the garage in case we want to make a quick getaway."

Owen nodded and pulled up behind his detached garage.

The two men swung their doors open and climbed out of the car.

Louise reached out her hand, and Philip helped lever her out of the car's tiny back seat. She reached back in and retrieved her overnight bag.

A rattle of metal came from behind them, and the three spun, Philip's hand going for his gun, but a second rattle revealed the source: a cat jumping along a line of garbage cans behind one of the houses.

"Good lord," muttered Owen. "My nerves are frazzled." He

popped open the trunk, removed the sample transport case, and pressed the trunk closed.

"I'll go first," Philip whispered, drawing the gun, "then Louise, then Owen."

Louise had no issue with being placed in the middle of their line—it meant a body between her and anyone who came out of the house or anyone who came up behind them.

They passed through a gate next to the garage. When they reached the door, Philip whispered to Owen, "Unlock the door but don't open it."

Owen moved past Philip and unlocked the door.

"Are the controls to the alarm system right inside the door?" Philip asked.

Owen nodded.

"Follow me in and turn off the alarm, but you and Mortensen stay by the back door."

Philip opened the door and, leading with the gun, stepped inside.

Owen and Louise followed, and Owen silenced the alarm's beeping. Philip disappeared into a hallway leading toward the front of the house, while Owen and Louise waited by the back door.

After half a minute, he appeared again in the doorway. "So far so good, but stay here until I check the rest of the house. And don't turn on any lights."

As Louise listened to Philip move through the second floor and then descend to the basement, she scanned the kitchen. It was the space of someone who loved to cook: a bookshelf devoted to cookbooks, a well-stocked spice rack over the counter, a set of well-seasoned cast-iron pans hanging from hooks over the stove. It was also the kitchen of someone who had taken care to preserve its authentic craftsman details: a backsplash of handmade clay tiles, paneled cabinetry, beautifully wrought hardware on the door leading to the hallway.

A minute later, Philip stepped back into the kitchen, holstering the gun. "All clear."

Owen closed and locked the back door, re-set the alarm, and dropped the car keys into a wicker basket near the back door. Then he turned to Louise. "I assume the vials don't need to be refrigerated?"

She considered. "It couldn't hurt."

He opened the refrigerator and rearranged some items to make room for the case, then closed the refrigerator and opened the freezer. "We've been subsisting on vending machine food for too long." He removed a container from the freezer. "I could thaw some chicken noodle soup. It's homemade, and there's enough for three."

"Thank you, but I'd rather get some sleep," said Louise.

"Me too," said Philip.

Looking disappointed, Owen put the container on the counter. "The bedrooms are upstairs. Louise, you can use the guest room—it's the one with two twin beds. Philip, I'm afraid the only other room is Ruby's, but I'm sure she wouldn't mind."

"I'd rather stay downstairs," said Philip. "The couch in the living room is fine."

Owen brightened. "Yes, the couch. It's actually quite a nice Stickley mission oak settee."

"Oh," said Philip. "Um ... would you rather I not sleep on it?"

"Oh, no—it has served as guest accommodations in the past. Quite comfortable, from what I've been told. I'll make it up."

"Don't bother."

"I believe there's a quilt hanging over its back. Amish. Very fine work. Also fine to use," he added hastily. "Why have anything if it can't be used?"

Philip went to the door to the hallway and flipped on a light, then said to Louise, "Coming?"

She followed him down the hallway to the living room. The curtains were closed, but by the light from the hallway it appeared that Owen McNally had furnished his entire home with craftsman antiques.

She started up the stairs.

"Don't get any ideas about leaving," Philip said. "I'm a light sleeper."

"I couldn't leave anyway—Owen set the alarm."

As she continued upstairs, she heard Philip return to the kitchen. Maybe he had changed his mind about the soup.

She found the guest room and put her overnight bag on a vintage luggage rack whose straps were embroidered in an arts-and-crafts floral design. She was exhausted but so keyed up from nerves—and from the extra-strong coffee Owen had brewed back at the lab—that she doubted she'd be able to sleep. The room was stuffy—maybe some fresh air would help. She opened the curtains, cranked open the casement window, and drew in a deep breath. She turned a straight back chair to face the window and sank onto it.

The residential street was quiet except for the *chir, chir* of crickets and, once, the hoot of an owl. It was surprising. Here they were, barely outside one of the largest cities on the East Coast, and they might have been in some sleepy suburb in some mid-sized Midwestern city.

A quarter of an hour passed, and she caught a whiff of the chicken soup. Her stomach rumbled, and she briefly thought of going back downstairs for something to eat, but the thought of sitting at the kitchen table eating soup with a man she had tried to have killed dampened her appetite.

Her eyelids were drifting closed. Perhaps she could get some sleep after all.

47

Lizzy roused at the ping of a text on her phone. Since she had Andy's apartment to herself, she was taking advantage of the fold-out couch in the media room rather than her usual air mattress in the living room, and she picked up her phone from the end table.

Pumpkin, we did all we could at WPU so we came to Lansdowne —I'll call you in the morning. XOXO

She checked the time—just after midnight—then dropped the phone back onto the table and lay back.

She knew Philip had been trying to keep her and Louise apart to save Lizzy from the temptation to squeeze Louise. She thought it was an unnecessary precaution—experience had shown that unless someone demonstrated an immediate threat to Lizzy or someone she cared about, she was unlikely to be able to squeeze them. Her stomach clenched as she thought back to the most recent times she had been forced to use the squeeze: in the compound conservatory, a second before Donny would have shot Philip in the face; in the parking lot of Cedar Grove, a second before Ravens would have shot Andy or Olivia. It wasn't a conscious act. It was more like being tapped on the knee and having your leg swing out—a reflexive response to immediate danger, not a measured decision.

She hoped that Philip—and Owen, of course—were managing the situation with Louise so that immediate danger wouldn't be an issue.

But if Lizzy was in Louise's vicinity and on the juice, maybe she would be able to eavesdrop on her thoughts. Even if Owen and Philip were enforcing Louise's cooperation now, they couldn't believe that she would share any information with them beyond what was required to keep them helping her. What if she could tell them what Louise was really thinking?

She threw back the covers and swung her legs off the bed.

She'd go to Lansdowne, take the juice, and see what Louise's thoughts had to tell them.

And just to make sure that Louise didn't erect any mental barriers, Lizzy would go now, while it was dark, to make sure Louise didn't know she was there.

48

The sound of a vehicle outside woke Louise. It was a testament to how quiet the street was that it had broken through her sleep, but she was on a higher level of nervous alert than normal. She stood up from the chair where she had fallen asleep and looked out the window in time to see a black van reach the end of the block and turn out of sight.

She debated whether to change into the nightgown she had in her overnight bag. It would be more comfortable than her dress, but also seemed vaguely disrespectful. It wasn't as if this was a normal overnight stay and she a normal guest. Perhaps she would just take off her dress so that it didn't get more wrinkled than it already was.

She slipped off her shoes and was massaging her feet when the sound of a vehicle once again caught her attention. The vehicle moved into her line of sight, then slowed and stopped in front of the house next to McNally's.

It was the same black van. The windows were tinted, making whoever was inside invisible. No one emerged from the vehicle —it just sat at the curb, idling.

And, perhaps, allowing whoever was inside to observe her standing in the window.

She snatched up her shoes and backed into the shadows of the room. She reached for the overnight case, then changed her mind. Easing the door to the hallway open, she slipped out of the room and made her way down the stairs, wincing at a squeak. The dim light filtering in from the kitchen revealed a quilt-covered shape on the couch.

Shoes still off, she crept toward the back of the house, glancing back just before the couch fell out of view. The shape hadn't moved.

In the kitchen, she found Owen seated at the table with a bowl of soup, a magazine open next to him.

"I need to get something out of the car," she said.

He patted his mouth with a napkin. "Don't you have what you need in your overnight bag?"

"Something's missing. It must have fallen out in the car."

"I can probably provide anything you need. What fell out?"

"A ... feminine item."

Owen blushed and glanced toward the door to the hallway. "Can't it wait? I think Philip would want to go out to the car with you and he needs to sleep." He glanced at her feet. "And why aren't you wearing your shoes?"

"I didn't want to wake up Philip when I came down the stairs."

"Well, there you go."

She crossed her arms. "Fine." She scanned the kitchen. "I'll just get a drink of water before I go back upstairs."

Owen made a move to rise. "I'll get you a glass."

"Not necessary—I see one in the dish drainer."

"Really? I thought I put everything away," he said, now on his feet. He turned toward the sink.

She stepped to the stove, grabbed a cast iron pan off its hook, and swung it into the side of Owen's head.

He staggered, reached for the counter to try to steady himself, missed, and fell to the floor with a joist-rattling thump.

Louise slammed the door to the hallway and turned the lock. She opened the refrigerator, grabbed the sample case, then stepped over to the wicker basket, reaching for the keys to the Lexus.

The basket was empty.

"Damn!"

She heard footsteps from the hallway, then Philip's voice. "Owen?"

"Philip," Owen groaned from the floor. "Louise—"

She stepped to the alarm and pressed in the numbers she had seen Owen enter when they had arrived. The alarm chirped off. She wrenched the back door open, stepped outside, and, shoes in one hand and sample case in the other, ran.

49
———

Philip snapped to wakefulness. What had woken him? A thump?

He heard movement from the back of the house, then an interior door slamming.

He threw back the quilt and ran down the hall.

The door to the kitchen was closed—he tried to turn the knob—and locked.

"Owen?" he called.

"Philip," he heard a bleary voice call. "Louise—"

He heard some movement, then a chirp that must be the alarm being disarmed.

He banged his shoulder against the door, but it was as well-constructed as the rest of the house appeared to be.

He stepped back and slammed the heel of his stockinged foot into the door.

The door shivered. The latch wasn't as solid as the wood, but he wasn't going to be able to kick it in in stocking feet.

He ran back to the living room, jammed his feet into his boots, then ran back down the hall.

The door popped open on the third kick. Owen was on his

knees, gripping the edge of the counter and trying to pull himself up.

Philip knelt next to him. "Are you okay?"

"Yes," muttered Owen. "Just stunned." His hand went to his head. "I'll be okay." He waved toward the back door. "Go after her."

Philip jumped up and sprinted outside. When he got to the alley, he scanned both directions. There was no sign of Louise.

If he picked the right direction, he could easily catch her on foot. But if he picked the wrong direction ...

From his pocket, he pulled the Lexus keys, which he had removed from the basket in the kitchen when he saw Louise eying them. He jumped into the car, started it up, and drove to the end of the alley.

To his left, the deserted residential street stretched away into the dark. To his right, he could see a brighter gleam of light—maybe a commercial district with more options for evading pursuit. He turned right.

He caught up with Louise just a few blocks away, on a block of small shops, restaurants, and offices. She was hurrying along with the sample case in one hand and her shoes in the other. He pulled up beside her and slowed the Lexus to match her pace.

She looked over, her fearful expression moderating to anger when she recognized him.

He buzzed rolled down the window. "Don't piss me off by making me chase you."

She stopped and looked up and down the street, but the buildings housing the shops, restaurants, and businesses were all connected, and there was no alley or opening for her to escape into. She returned her gaze to Philip. "What do you plan to do—force me into the car?"

"I will if I have to, but that would be even more annoying. Just get in the car, Louise—we need to talk."

"Back at McNally's house?"

"Not necessarily."

She scanned the street again—was she looking for someone to intercede?—then, with a sigh, slipped on her shoes and got in the car, holding the case on her lap.

"Much more comfortable up here than the back," she said pointedly.

"Why did you pick now to try to run?" he asked.

She folded her hands on top of the case. "I want to get away from here. I don't think I'm going to be safe anywhere in the Philadelphia area. Not only might Chapel think I would come back here, but I have the Philadelphia authorities looking for me, too."

"What did you plan to do—walk to Delaware?"

She raised an eyebrow. "I got from the airport where Lucas dropped me off with no money and no ID to a lovely suite in a Main Line hotel. Don't underestimate me."

"Good point. So, where did you intend to go?"

"Harrisburg."

"And what were you going to do in Harrisburg?"

"Arrange to meet you so that I could fulfill my end of our bargain."

He gave a derisive snort. "Honor among thieves."

"If we go to Harrisburg, we can run a test at the motel where you met up with me and Richard. And at some point, I need to pick up the rental car I left there. Now that Owen has what he wants—the inhibitol for Lizzy—he might have decided to turn me in." She glanced nervously into the side-view mirror.

"Who are you looking for?" he asked. "The cops Owen called when he couldn't even get off the floor? The attorney general's representatives that he contacted at," he glanced at the clock in the dashboard, "almost one in the morning?"

She returned her gaze to him. "I'm not looking for anyone in particular."

He glanced at the case in her lap. "We need to get that somewhere we can keep it cool, right? You said to Owen it couldn't hurt to have the vials refrigerated."

"I just said that so he'd put the case in the refrigerator and not lock it away somewhere."

His mouth twisted in a reluctant smile. "Clever. And what's the status of the drugs?"

"For the inhibitol, just as I said at the lab. I confirmed it's harmless but haven't been able to test its efficacy."

"How about the other drug you told me you were working on?"

"The V-2."

"V-2?"

"I called the drug that I created to increase what Ballard calls 'the squeeze' Vivantem gammadexasone," Louise said, "or V-sone for short. I thought it made sense to call this variant, intended for use by subjects who were ..."

"Not the result of unethical experimentation?" Philip suggested sourly.

She scowled. "People born without scientific intervention. I call it V-2." She shifted in her seat. "When McNally wasn't hovering over my shoulder, I was able to finish the work on that."

"And were you able to run tests on that?"

"No."

"What would you need to do that?"

She raised an eyebrow. "I'd need the lab facilities."

He sighed. "Yeah, I figured." After a pause, he asked, "What's your assessment of its safety?"

She hesitated. "It poses some risks."

"Great." He ran a hand down his face. "More risks that trying to get past Chapel's men to put a bullet in his head or a knife in his gut?"

"No," she said drily, "perhaps not more risk than that."

"Would you try the V-2 yourself?"

"Not without further testing."

"Which we don't have any way to do."

She was silent.

He dropped his head back against the seat. "I think I've got to try it."

"There's no other way to dispose of Chapel?"

He gave a bitter snort. "Dispose of. Like garbage."

"Yes. Like garbage."

He was silent for a beat, then said, "Not a bad analogy, I suppose."

"And you're willing to take an untested drug because you consider it to be a marginally safer method of killing Billy Chapel?"

He turned to face her. "It's not just Chapel. If I'd had this drug when I first met Lizzy, I would never have sent her to Arizona to kill a man she had never met before—I could have *disposed of* Tobe Hanrick myself. And I could have done it without getting her kidnapped, not to mention getting a friend of mine killed in the process. To be frank, I wouldn't have had to rely on her to kill your errand boy, George Millard. Billy Chapel is a bastard, but there are a lot of bastards in the world, and I don't like the idea of relying on a teenage girl—or anyone else, for that matter—to deal with them."

They sat in silence for a few moments, then Louise said, "So, what now?"

He raised an eyebrow. "Under other circumstances, I'd say we had to go back to the house to check on Owen."

"I didn't hit him hard—it was a glancing blow to the side of the head, and I intentionally avoided his temple. I don't think it even broke the skin. It shouldn't cause any lasting damage."

"You'll forgive me if I don't rely on your assessment of how much damage you did," Philip said, getting his phone out of his pocket.

"What are you going to tell him?"

Philip stared through the windshield for a few moments. "I am getting so goddamned tired of lying to people who deserve better."

"McNally."

"Yes."

"And Ballard."

"Yes." After a beat, he said, "I'll tell him that there's something in Harrisburg that you need to finish work on the inhibitol."

"He'll want to come along."

"I'll tell him he should stay in the area and keep an eye on Lizzy."

Louise raised an eyebrow. "It seems more realistic to say that Ballard would need to keep an eye on McNally."

Philip opened his contacts app. "They'll keep an eye on each other."

"And when we've gotten what we need in Harrisburg, you still intend to let me go?"

He didn't look up from the phone. "Sure."

50

Lizzy reached Lansdowne around one o'clock and pulled over a couple of houses before Owen's—she wanted to make sure Louise didn't see her if she happened to be looking out a window, and Owen, Philip, and Louise had been keeping such a strange schedule, she didn't want to assume they were asleep. She climbed into the back of the Caravan, got out the case that held a vial and a couple of syringes, and injected herself with the juice.

As she waited for the drug to take effect, she examined the house. At first, she thought everything was dark inside. If they had all gone to bed, would Lizzy be able to read Louise's mind if she was asleep? Then she noticed a light visible behind a drawn shade at the back of the house—she thought it was the kitchen. Maybe the three of them were sitting around Owen's kitchen table ... but doing what? Maybe Owen and Louise were talking about medical topics.

She considered what she had heard ever since first taking the juice—from Owen and Andy and Philip and Olivia—about the dangers of a teenage girl taking a steroid-based drug. She knew Owen had lowered the concentration of the drug as much as he could, and she downplayed her own concerns about it. But she sometimes wondered if she'd experience any long-lasting symptoms if she overdid it. Would she be fine for years, then pay the price—whatever that might be—down the road? She was willing to take the risk to try to find out what Louise Mortensen had in mind, and so far, had been willing to take the risk to be able to reduce her financial dependence on Owen by bringing her drug-induced ability to the poker table, but she'd far rather be in a situation where taking the juice was no longer necessary.

Soon she began to experience the heightened sensory sensitivity that was one of its side effects—the foghorn-like hoot of an owl, the strident thrum of peepers, loud even through the closed windows. She climbed out of the Caravan and eased the door closed, then crept across the neighbors' lawns and toward the lit window of Owen's house.

She squatted down under the window, wondering if her juice-induced ability would work through the wall between her and her target.

There were definitely people in the kitchen—not only could she sense their thoughts, but she could hear the voice, although not the words, of one of them. As she listened, her gut clenched —that slight Southern drawl could only be Billy Chapel.

There was another man in the kitchen ... she thought it was Tony, the man who had shown up after closing at *Chesaperk* to pick up a cold brew for Billy.

But the thoughts that were most clear to her were Owen's, and his interior monologue was an inventory of the appliances and utensils in his kitchen, along with a frantic assessment of the damage each could do if wielded by ill-meaning hands. But his thoughts were even more jumbled than might be explained by his horrible situation—there was a haziness that Lizzy thought might reflect some physical cause. Had Billy hit him in the head?

She had no sense of Philip or Louise being part of the gathering in the kitchen, and although she wouldn't be surprised at her inability to access the thoughts of either of them—she suspected Louise's mental defenses were as impenetrable as Philip's—she would have expected at least to be able to sense if they were there.

What she could hear—actually hear—from the three men in the kitchen was no more than a murmur, but the juice filled in the blanks in her mind. And although she hadn't been able to read Chapel's thoughts at the compound, that had been because her own thoughts had been disrupted by Louise's highly concentrated version of the juice. Now his thoughts were horribly clear.

"I'll ask you again," said Billy. "Where is Mortensen?" *That bitch.*

"I don't know!" said Owen. "She hit me on the head with a pan and ran out!" *The pan that's now sitting next to the knife block ... dear God ...*

"When?" *Maybe a broken finger would focus his attention, like it did for his brother.*

"I don't know—the blow to my head is making things confused. Maybe an hour ago?" *Please don't let Philip come back right now—he'd have no warning they're here.*

"Were you upstairs tonight?" *Good thing we made another swing by the house.*

"Uh ..." *Why in the world is he asking that?*

Lizzy jumped at a yelp from Owen—Billy had kicked him in the shin.

"Don't lie to me," said Billy. "I saw someone up there. We drove by earlier and the house was dark, the curtains and the windows were closed. We drove by just now, and the upstairs curtains and window were open. Someone was standing at the window."

"Oh. That was me." *We should have told Louise not to open the window ...*

"You sure gained a lot of weight between then and now—the person we saw in the window was a lot skinnier than you." *Maybe Castillo, but it looked more like a woman.*

Owen's mind was blank with terror.

"I know you were at the university, using the lab," Billy continued. "We found a pretty talkative janitor, although we couldn't get into the building without university IDs." *They must have left by a door we didn't see.*

"*I* was at the lab. I'm a neurobiologist, I'm working on a study of how neuronal networks encode and process information—"

There was another kick to the shins from Billy and another yelp from Owen, although Lizzy could tell Billy was just playing with him ... and she could see what Billy planned as next steps if Owen didn't give him what he wanted.

"You know where Mortensen is?" Billy asked.

"No." *Oh, God, the meat cleaver is hanging right next to the knife block ...*

"You know where Castillo is?"

"Who?" *Should I know who Philip is? I need a minute to think ...*

Owen's yelp in response to the resulting kick was louder this time, and Lizzy could tell Billy was losing patience.

Heart pounding, Lizzy frantically sorted through her options. She couldn't squeeze Billy and Tony while she was on the juice. Should she call the police and leave an anonymous tip about a man being held hostage in his own home? She suspected that by the time she convinced them to take the call seriously, it would be too late for Owen. Maybe she could throw a rock through a window. She knew that Owen's alarm system triggered at the sound of breaking glass ... but then she realized that the system must be disengaged if Billy and Tony were inside. Owen had a fire alarm as well, but even if she could get inside, and even if she could bring herself to set a fire in Owen's beloved house with him sitting in the kitchen, she had no idea how she would light it.

She had no weapon, and even if she did, could she bring herself to shoot at Billy and Tony? A report of gunshots in this quiet residential neighborhood would definitely bring the police around in a hurry, but the last thing anyone—including the police—needed was for them to take Lizzy into custody. They might be protected from the squeeze by the effects of the juice for a while, but the juice would wear off. She didn't want to think about what would happen if, with the squeeze fully operational, she found herself the subject of an aggressive interrogation or, God forbid, thrown in prison with a bunch of violent criminals.

But, she realized, she didn't need an actual gun to bring the police to Owen's house.

She sprinted back across the neighbor's lawn to the next house on the street. She couldn't see any sign of a camera at the entrance, which was lit by a porch light. She ran to the door and unscrewed the bulb, singeing her fingers. She dropped the bulb to the porch, where it shattered, then she banged on the door. An agonizing half-minute ticked by. She pounded again.

She was starting to wonder whether she would have to try another house when she sensed more than heard someone approaching the door.

"Who's out there?" called a woman's tremulous voice.

A thought drifted through the door to Lizzy: *No way I'm opening this door in the middle of the night.*

The woman wasn't going to open the door? This was even better than Lizzy had hoped.

"Call the cops!" she said in a voice she hoped was loud enough to carry through the door but not loud enough to be heard in Owen's kitchen. "I saw two guys carrying guns and wearing ski masks going into that Craftsman house two doors down."

"Doctor McNally's house?" Nervousness was replaced by alarm. *That nice man?*

"I don't know whose house it is—just call the cops!"

"I'll call right now!" *Should have brought my phone downstairs with me.*

Lizzy heard steps hurrying away from the door, and she turned and ran down the street, away from Owen's house.

A little further down the block and on the other side of the street, one of the houses had a *For Sale* sign in the yard, and its windows were dark. A hedge ran along the sidewalk. She slipped behind the hedge and knelt on the ground.

One minute ticked by ... then two ... then three. What might Billy and Tony be doing to Owen in the kitchen? Should she risk confronting them—squeeze-less—after all?

Then she saw figures moving through the darkness near Owen's house toward a black van parked in front. Had her plan been unnecessary? Were Billy and Tony leaving? And what were they leaving behind in Owen's kitchen?

Then she saw that the figures were not just Billy and Tony but Owen as well. The realization hit her like a punch in the gut: they were going to take Owen with them, and the police, if they arrived at all, would arrive to nothing but an empty house.

Then she heard the distant wail of a siren. It grew nearer second by second, but Lizzy doubted they would arrive before the two men forced Owen into the van.

Then Owen went sprawling onto the lawn. Her breath caught—had they hurt him? Had they acted on one of the awful ideas she had seen passing through their minds in the kitchen?

Billy and Tony each grabbed one of Owen's arms and tried to pull him to his feet, but he was deadweight. He had slimmed down a lot over the preceding months, but they obviously weren't going to be able to get him on his feet without considerable effort.

Billy bent over, his mouth inches from Owen's ear.

Then he snapped an order to Tony, and they dropped Owen's arms. They ran to the van, jumped in, and disappeared around the corner just as a police car, lights strobing and siren wailing, turned onto the street.

51

As the cruiser pulled up in front of Owen's house—Lizzy could now hear a second siren approaching—Owen climbed unsteadily to his feet.

The siren warbled into silence, and an officer got out of the cruiser, her gun drawn. "Sir," she called to Owen, "keep your hands where I can see them."

Owen popped his hands in the air.

"We have a report of someone carrying a gun in this area," said the officer. "Do you have a weapon?"

"No, ma'am."

"Have you seen anyone with a weapon?"

After a brief pause—he was obviously still rattled by the encounter with Billy and Tony—Owen said, "No, I haven't."

If there was more conversation, Lizzy couldn't hear it over the wailing arrival of another cruiser and couldn't sense it from this distance. The second car pulled up behind the first, the siren silenced, and an officer emerged from the car, also with his gun drawn. He and the first officer consulted, and Lizzy withdrew further behind the bush.

Along the street, lights were coming on. At a few houses,

occupants were appearing backlit in open doorways. Lizzy checked the windows of the house in whose yard she was hiding and was relieved to see they were still dark.

While the female officer covered Owen, whose hands were still in the air, the male officer patted him down. He gave a thumbs up to the woman, and they holstered their guns.

There was some conversation among the three of them. Owen got out his wallet and showed them what must be his driver's license. The male officer said something, and Owen nodded and waved toward the house. The officer disappeared around the back of the house, and behind the closed curtains, Lizzy could see dim rectangles of light illuminating window after window as he moved from room to room. When he reached the guest room, whose curtains were open, the light spilled into the front yard.

By the time he emerged a few minutes later, a number of people were standing on their porches. The female officer went to her cruiser, and a moment later, her amplified voice came from the vehicle.

"Please go back inside and lock your doors. We received a report of two armed men in the neighborhood and are investigating. Please go back inside and lock your doors."

The neighbors retreated into their houses, appearing moments later at their windows.

The male officer went to the house two doors down and knocked. Almost immediately, the door was opened by a gray-haired woman in a housecoat, and she stepped out onto the porch. She and the male officer chatted for a few minutes, the woman pointing to the bulbless porch light and then at the remains of the bulb on the porch. The words *teenaged girl* and *prank* drifted over to her.

A third cruiser arrived, and after some consultation between its driver and the female officer, rolled away. Lizzy could follow its slow progress around the surrounding blocks by its flashing light.

Leaving Owen sitting on his front steps, the first two officers began knocking on the doors of the other houses near Owen's, holding brief conversations with the homeowners.

Lizzy couldn't very well be hiding behind the hedge when they reached this house, especially since, based on the gray-haired woman's report, they would be on the lookout for a teenage girl.

She hoped they didn't run the plates of the vehicles parked along the street ... although, she realized, the plates on the Caravan would just lead them to its official owner, Ruby, who lived in Owen's house. There should be no issue there.

She got out her phone and called Owen's number.

He jumped at the buzz of his phone, then fumbled it out of his pocket. He checked the screen, then tapped, and his lowered voice came over her phone. "Pumpkin?"

"I'm just down the street."

He scanned the street. "Where? The police are here. Billy Chapel and some other man—"

"I know what happened, and I saw them search the house. Do you think they're going to go back in?"

"I don't see why they would."

"I think it's a better place for me to be than the bush I'm hiding behind. I think I can get to the back door without anyone seeing me."

"Okay. Be careful."

They ended the call.

LIZZY ASSESSED HER OPTIONS. She couldn't just stroll across the street—the officers canvassing the neighborhood were drawing closer every minute.

The houses on Owen's side of the block all had detached garages or fences separating the yards from an alley, but she seemed to remember from long-ago walks with Owen that many of the other properties in the neighborhood had backyards that ran uninterrupted into the backyards of the houses on the next street. If the *For Sale* house was one of these, she could sneak through to the next street, then make her way to Owen's alley and his back door. If it was *not* one of these, she'd probably have to climb a fence, but at least for now, the officers seemed focused on interviewing the residents at their front doors, not exploring the properties.

She checked the windows of the house—still dark—and moved toward its side yard.

She could hear a voice, but the windows in the next house, only a dozen yards away, were open, and the lights were on. It was probably people discussing the current excitement—or more likely someone on the phone, since she could hear just one voice, a woman's. She caught only snatches of conversation, and the distance meant that the juice didn't help her fill in the blanks.

"... prank ... just got her to sleep after the sirens ... Rob's in Arkansas... sorry to have missed the excitement ... glad to hear everything's okay there ... bye-bye."

Should Lizzy run past the lit window now or wait until she knew the woman was occupied with the officers at the front door? It sounded like hers would be the next door they would knock on. She couldn't wait here in the side yard, she decided—she was too exposed. She'd at least get to the backyard of the *For Sale* house and scope out the situation. If there was a fence and climbing over it seemed too risky, maybe there was a shed she could hide in or a porch she could slip under.

Lizzy scuttled toward the back of the house ... and froze as the porch came into view.

On it stood a young woman wearing an oversized terrycloth robe. Her back was to Lizzy, and she was joggling a baby on her shoulder and murmuring "Stay ... a ... sleep ... stay ... a ... sleep." It was the voice Lizzy had thought was coming from the house next door. The woman was only about a dozen feet from Lizzy—close enough that Lizzy could pick up her thoughts. *Stay ... a ... sleep ... stay ... a ... sleep.*

But the baby, a chubby-cheeked toddler, was wide awake, and its round, curious eyes, peering over its mother's shoulder, were fixed on Lizzy.

In the hand not supporting the baby, the woman held a phone. She was walking slowly away from Lizzy, synchronizing her steps with the joggling of the baby. Her eyes were on the phone, her thumb tapping the screen, then she lifted it to her ear. "Stay ... a ... sleep," she chanted.

The baby broke into a toothless grin and raised its pudgy hand to Lizzy.

In a moment, the woman would reach the end of the porch and turn around. Then she'd see Lizzy and scream, the police would come running, and Lizzy would be thrown in the back of the cruiser and then into a jail cell.

She frantically scanned the yard. Any potential hiding places were too far away.

She threw herself onto the ground and scuttled across the grass toward the porch.

The baby let out a delighted crow.

"Oh, no," said the woman, "I thought you were asleep." Lizzy could tell that she had turned and was now facing where Lizzy lay. "No, sorry, Greta, I was talking to Polly. It's Jen—I'm just calling around to the neighbors, making sure everyone's okay. ... Yes, I'm fine. Seems like it was just a prank. Rob's in Arkansas looking for a place for us—he's going to be so sorry to have missed the excitement."

The area under the porch was enclosed in lattice, and Lizzy pressed herself against it as Jen walked slowly toward her. Jen reached the edge of the porch—if she looked down, she couldn't help but see Lizzy—and set Polly on the railing, one arm wrapped firmly around the baby's torso. "Do you know what happened?" *I'd love to know what happened.*

Polly leaned forward against Jen's arm, looked down at Lizzy, and gurgled happily.

"Someone told me they saw the police pointing their guns at that nice Doctor McNally," said Jen, "but then the officers started going from house to house, and they left him on his front steps, so I can't imagine Doctor McNally has done anything wrong." *He's such a nice man.*

Rarely had Lizzy experienced a person whose speech and thoughts were so perfectly in sync. In other circumstances, she would have found it refreshing.

Polly opened and closed her hand in greeting. "Bye-bye," she said.

"Not bye-bye quite yet, sweetie," said Jen. "Polly's saying *bye-bye*, Greta. ... Yes, she can say it quite clearly. Rob thinks she's saying *papa*, but I think it's *bye-bye*." *She's such a smart baby.*

Lizzy pressed herself harder against the lattice, hoping she didn't break through and go rolling under the porch—the sounds of splintering wood would certainly grab Jen's attention.

"We packed up all the lamps—that wasn't so smart!—I only have lights in the kitchen and bathroom and bedroom. I have to get around the other rooms at night with a flashlight." *What a goof I am.*

Lizzy almost yelped at the sound of a firm rap on the front door.

"Oops!" Jen laughed. "Actually, I think Polly's clairvoyant— maybe it is time to say bye-bye. the police just got to my house."

"Anybody home?" someone called from the front of the house.

"I'll talk to you tomorrow, Greta," said Jen. "Bye-bye."

"Bye-bye," said Polly.

"Back here!" Jen called. She lifted Polly off the railing,

Lizzy heard a click ... and a light suffused the backyard. Jen must have had the flashlight in the pocket of her robe.

Jen began descending the stairs that led from the porch to the lawn, just a few feet from where Lizzy lay.

At the same time, another flashlight illuminated the side yard, held by someone approaching from the front.

If Lizzy jumped up now and ran—Jen's yard did connect with the yard of the house behind it—could she outrun the officer? And even if she could, would she be able to evade the search that was sure to follow?

The two pools of light from the flashlights merged a dozen feet from where Lizzy lay.

"Good evening, ma'am," said the new arrival. "I'm Officer Thorpe. Is everyone okay here."

"Oh, yes, I was just out back with the baby. She likes when I walk with her on the porch."

"We're asking everyone to stay inside. There was a report of a couple of men with weapons. It might have been a prank, but better safe than sorry."

"Yes, of course," said Jen. *Better safe than sorry.*

Polly raised her hand to Lizzy. "Bye-bye."

"Smart little thing," said the officer. "Can we speak inside, ma'am?"

"Of course. Let's go around front. The kitchen is a *disaster*—I wouldn't want you to have to contend with that! My husband's in

Arkansas looking for a house for us. He got transferred to Little Rock …"

Her voice faded as they moved toward the front of the house, Polly still waving placidly to Lizzy as the group moved out of sight.

Lizzy scrambled to her feet and ran.

SHE REACHED the alley behind Owen's house about ten minutes later, having had to detour to dodge the patrolling cruiser. She was glad to see that he had turned off his porch light—she could get across the yard unseen. She was considering whether she should call or text him to confirm that the coast was clear, when the door opened and Owen stood in the doorway, beckoning her toward him.

She ran across the lawn and slipped into the house.

"How did it go?" he asked, closing the door behind her. "I didn't expect it to take so long—I was frantic!"

"I almost got given away by an overly friendly baby," she said with a breathless laugh. "Polly."

"Jen and Rob's baby? How in the world—"

They both jumped at a knock on the front door.

"It must be the police again," Owen whispered, although there was no way anyone at the front door could hear him. "Hide in the basement!"

He opened the basement door for her, flipped on the light, and stood watching from the top of the stairs until she reached the bottom. "Ready for lights out?" he whispered, then, in response to a louder knock at the front door, yelled, "Coming!"

Lizzy gave him a thumbs up, and he flipped off the light.

Standing in the darkness, she tried to picture Owen's base-ment—she had enjoyed playing down here when she was little

—and to think of where she could hide if the police decided to search the house again. She didn't think she'd be able to fit into her favorite place under the stairway anymore.

But the murmurs of conversation she could hear emanating from upstairs never moved away from the front door. After a minute, she heard the front door close, and Owen's steps return to the kitchen. The basement door opened, and the light came on.

"All clear," he said.

"What did they want?" she asked as she climbed the stairs.

"Just to tell me that they think it was a prank, but that they'll keep an extra patrol on through the next day or two. Why are you here? Not that I'm not very grateful ..."

She dropped into one of the kitchen chairs. "I thought I might be able to read Louise's mind and give you guys some useful information."

She filled him in on her eavesdropping outside the kitchen window, her ploy to summon the police, and her encounter with Jen and Polly.

Owen, in turn, described Louise's escape from the house, Philip's pursuit of her, and Billy and Tony's arrival while the alarm was still deactivated. She could sense most of it a second before he said it, but the effect of the juice was fading, and she preferred to hear it the normal way. She did her best to tune out his thoughts and focus on his words.

"I guess Louise must have seen Billy and Tony coming," she said when he finished his update.

"That's what I think, too."

"Good thing the police showed up before they got you into the van. And lucky you fell."

"I just pretended to fall," he said, with some satisfaction. "I was too scared to fight back, but I figured a little passive resistance was in order. Sometimes carrying a few extra pounds is an advantage."

"Good idea. What did Billy say to you right before they left?"

His expression sobered. "That if I told the police that he had been in my house, Andy would pay the price."

"Oh, no," Lizzy said, dropping her face into her hands. "Like poor Andy hasn't already paid a big enough price for the trouble I've gotten myself into."

He patted her hand, then, after a moment, said, "Speaking of Andy ... Philip has the Lexus, and Louise has the drugs she had been working on at the Penn lab."

"Philip!" Lizzy got out her phone and tapped a name on her Favorites list. After a moment, she said, her voice tight with concern, "He's not answering."

"I did get a call from him not long after he ran out, asking me if I was okay. When I told him I was, he said Louise needed something from her car in Harrisburg related to the inhibitol, and he ended the call before I could ask any questions. He didn't pick up when I called him back. Maybe he saw the police and went away to lay low."

"Maybe he was under duress. Did Louise have anything she could have used as a weapon against him?"

"Not that I know of ... although I suppose she could have grabbed a knife." He got up from the table and examined a knife block on the counter. "All accounted for." He opened and closed a few drawers. "Nothing I can think of that she could have grabbed as a weapon is missing."

"You said she hit you with a pan."

"You think she threatened Philip with a pan?"

"No, I'm worried about your head. Sit down—I want to check it."

He resumed his seat at the table, and she rose to examine his head.

"It's fine." He gestured to a bag of frozen peas on the table, surrounded by a puddle of condensation. "I've been icing it. I really think she just wanted to put me out of commission long enough to get out of the house—she could have done a lot more damage if she had hit me in the temple or in the neck."

"Jeez, Uncle Owen," Lizzy said, exasperated, "she tried to kill you and you're making excuses for her." She picked up the bag. "This one's not cold anymore. I'll put it back in the freezer so it cools down again." She got out a bag of frozen lima beans and handed it to him. "Do you need to see a doctor?"

"I *am* a doctor. I've self-diagnosed. I'm fine."

"We could call Andy ..."

"He would ask me to describe my symptoms, and when I did, he would tell me that I'm fine."

She dropped back into her chair. "Considering you guys are doctors, you sure put up a fuss about seeing one."

They sat in silence for a few moments, then Lizzy said, "Philip wanting to avoid the cops makes sense, and it is a little hard to imagine Louise coercing him in some way, but why he isn't answering his phone?"

Owen hesitated. "Do you think she and Philip are ..."

Lizzy had enough of the juice left in her system to see the unwelcome question forming before he said it. She glared at him. "Are what?"

He shrugged, embarrassed. "You know ... in cahoots."

"Why would Philip be in cahoots with Louise—" She stopped, then continued, her voice still angry. "Although I guess it's not too big a leap from the three of you palling around at William Penn to the two of them running off together."

"I wouldn't call it palling around ... we wanted Louise to finish testing the inhibitol for you."

She sighed, her anger draining away. "I know. I'm sorry. It's just so confusing."

"I'm not going to be much help—I'm so tired I can't think straight. What I really need is sleep, and I imagine you could use some sleep, too."

She ran her fingers through her hair. "Yeah, I think you're right about that. Do you think we should go somewhere else, like a hotel?"

"As long as we keep the alarm on, I think we'll be okay. And with all the police that showed up, I can't imagine Billy and Tony will come back, at least tonight. Let's get a couple of hours of rest, then let's go to Letort and help those guys keep an eye on Marjorie."

She marshaled a smile. "I don't know if that room is big enough for two more bodyguards." She sighed. "But it's better that just hanging around here doing nothing."

Owen cast a longing look around his kitchen. "I can't wait until we can just hang around and do nothing."

52

"Who the hell called the cops?" sputtered Billy from the passenger seat of the van as they sped south on 95 toward Baltimore. "You sure there was no one upstairs or in the basement?"

"I'm sure, boss," said Tony.

Billy had to admit that, despite Tony's deficiencies, if he said there was no one other than McNally in the house, then there was no one other than McNally in the house. Tony wasn't a fuck-up like Donny ... or, evidently, like Mickey, who was still incommunicado. He glowered at Tony. When Billy was pissed, it always helped to have a fuck-up around to take it out on.

"And we still have no idea where Castillo is," Billy muttered.

"That janitor at the university didn't mention seeing a guy with McNally, just a woman."

"Castillo could just have been staying out of sight."

They rode in silence for several minutes, the industrial land-scape south of Philly giving way to stretches of woods as they neared Wilmington.

The only thing better than having a fuck-up around to take

his frustrations out on was having someone around who had crossed him ... or, failing that, someone close to them.

He had no doubt Castillo was involved in whatever Mortensen and the fat McNally brother were up to—it was too much to hope that the cops would find his body at the compound, maybe dead in the explosion that had destroyed the lab. And he suspected Castillo cared about what happened to the girl—Lizzy Ballard—more than he was letting on. Billy had never really bought Castillo's story that he had had a casual hook-up with the girl he claimed to have thought was Theo Viklund's niece, but it had been fun watching him try to tap-dance around the truth. But Billy wasn't in the mood to play games anymore.

He got out his phone and hit a number in his contacts list.

"It's Chapel. ... Don't tell me it's late in Arizona—it's three goddamned hours later on the East Coast. Listen, you have a guy in Flagstaff, right? ... Well, I have a way you can pay me back for that favor I did for you last year. Send him down to Sedona. I want him to pay a visit to a retired cop. That's right, a cop. You like cops? ... I didn't think so, so you're going to enjoy this assignment."

53

———

Philip unlocked the door and stepped into the second of four adjoining motel rooms he and Louise had booked. Louise followed him in. He was carrying the sample transport case and a Walmart shopping bag. She was carrying a satchel she had gotten from her rental vehicle.

This room was where he would become the first test subject for the V-2. The rooms on either side were a buffer space—"Just in case there's any noise," she had said. The fourth room was where Louise would monitor his reaction.

The sky was just beginning to glow with the impending dawn. He flicked the light switch next to the door. "Couldn't you just stay in one of the buffer rooms?" he asked, trying to maintain a matter-of-fact tone. "It's not like it's a problem if *you* hear any noise I might make."

"I'd like a little more distance between us when you take the V-2." She nodded to the Walmart bag he was carrying. "Why don't you set up the monitor."

He got the baby monitor out of the bag and unboxed it. Despite his nerves, he almost smiled at the memory of accompanying Louise Mortensen into the Walmart to buy their supplies.

It was clear she had never been in a Walmart before, and although she obviously found the setting distasteful, she also seemed fascinated, as if she were visiting an exotic country.

Louise set the satchel on the desk. "Despite the precautionary measure of having an intervening room between us during the test, the goal today won't be to test your ability to squeeze someone, just to test your tolerance for the drug. I'll give you quite a low concentration, at least for this first test."

"Fine." He plugged in the monitor. "How long will the effect last?"

"I haven't any idea."

Philip had just barely come to terms with the idea of allowing Louise Mortensen—who, among other crimes, was responsible for the deaths of Lizzy's parents and the attempted murder of Owen McNally—to inject him with a drug. He had convinced himself that if she wanted him dead, it would have been easy enough for her and Lucas to kill him during his earlier visit to the compound, and even easier to make sure his body was never found.

But the idea that Louise really had no idea what the side effects of the drug might be reignited his doubts. He could easily have just forced Louise to give him a vial of the drug, and then taken it to someone else to undergo the test. But who?

Owen McNally had watched Louise like an eagle through her tests of the neuroinhibitol at Penn U. and so probably had almost as good an understanding of how that drug worked as Louise herself did, and there must be some similarities between that drug and the V-2. But he doubted Owen McNally would agree to be part of a plan to give Philip a deadly ability, even if Philip's target—at least, his *initial* target—was Billy Chapel.

Philip suspected that Andy McNally wouldn't balk at helping him kill Chapel, since Chapel had been at least partially responsible for the treatment Andy had received at the compound. But Andy had suffered enough for his involvement in Philip's business. Philip didn't intend to drag him into it any more than he already had.

And who better to treat whatever adverse reaction to the drug Philip might have than the person who had formulated it?

While Louise busied herself at the desk, he wandered the room, looking in the closet and the drawers of the dresser.

"What are you doing?" Louise asked.

"Looking for a safe."

"You have something valuable that needs to be locked away?"

"No," he said, nodding toward the sample case, "*you* have something valuable that I don't want you leaving with."

"Any luck?"

"No safe in the room."

"It doesn't matter. If I can't take the vials with me, I can always make more of the drugs."

"You'd need to find another lab, and I don't want to make things any easier for you than I can help."

"Do what you feel is necessary." She had lined up one of the drug vials, a syringe, and a sharps container on the desk. "Bare your bicep."

He shrugged out of the navy sport coat he had picked up at the compound and dropped it on the bed, then unfastened the shoulder holster and put it on the bedside table. It wasn't worth keeping the weapon away from Louise. If she wanted to kill him, in just a few minutes she'd have the perfect opportunity to do it in a much tidier way than a gunshot. "Do I need to take off my T-shirt?"

"No." She removed a roll of duct tape from the Walmart bag. "Do you want to be lying down or sitting up for the test?"

He picked up the sample case and put it on the floor, then pulled out the desk chair and put it over the case at an angle, so that the case was trapped between the chair's legs. He sat down. "Sitting."

She pulled a length of tape off the roll. "I'll tape you to the chair, so you won't fall over."

"And so I can't come after you if the V-2 really does work."

"That, too."

He raised his arms and Louise applied a few turns around his torso and the chair back. She stepped back and examined her work. "I should secure your hands, too."

"Why?"

"So you don't hurt yourself if you have an adverse reaction."

"What do you expect me to do—punch myself?"

"Well …"

He raised his eyebrows. "Seriously?"

She looked uncomfortable. "You're the one who expressed a willingness to try out an untested drug."

"Jesus Christ," he muttered.

He lay his forearms along the arms of the chair, and she secured his wrists.

She got an alcohol wipe from the satchel and pulled up the sleeve of his T-shirt to swab his arm, revealing the bandage over the gunshot wound Donny had inflicted. She raised an eyebrow. "You should get a tetanus shot." She glanced over at the satchel. "I don't carry tetanus toxoid vaccine with me, since it needs to be refrigerated."

"I have to say that lockjaw is not at the top of my list of concerns at the moment. Plus, Lizzy cleaned it up."

"Very well." She switched to the other arm, swabbed it, then returned to the desk and drew fluid from the vial into the syringe.

"Back at Penn," he said, "Owen mentioned that the vials have different-colored stoppers. Is that for a reason?"

"The red vials are the V-2. The blue vials are the inhibitol."

She returned to where he sat, bound and sweating. "Are you ready?"

"As ready as I'll ever be."

She leaned toward him, then straightened. "If things go badly, I don't have any way of reversing the effects. Do you want me to call emergency services?"

He raised his eyebrows. "You're telling me you'd call 911?"

She shrugged. "As long as I knew I could be well away before anyone got here."

He forced a laugh. "You're a piece of work, Doctor Mortensen." He shook his head. "No, don't call 911."

After a pause, she said, "Very well."

She bent again and gave him the injection, and Philip was oddly grateful for how painless it was.

She dropped the syringe into a sharps container, returned the container to the satchel, and snapped the satchel shut. "I'll leave this here in case it's needed." She picked up the Walmart bag. "I'll be monitoring you from the other room."

She left the room, and in a moment, he heard the faint thud of the door two rooms down closing.

He tried to assess his condition objectively. His heart was pounding, and he could feel a trickle of sweat making its way from his forehead down the side of his face, but that wasn't necessarily the effect of the drug.

A minute passed, and Louise's voice came from the monitor. "Can you hear me?"

"Yes."

"Are you experiencing any effects yet?"

He tried to look past what he could chalk up to extreme stress to something more, something different ... whatever that might be. "There's ... some pressure in my head."

"More like a tension headache or more like a migraine?"

"More like a tension headache, I guess. I've never had a migraine."

He winced at a quick stab of pain that seemed to shoot from his temple to the front of his skull. "Shit," he hissed.

"What's happening?"

"It's getting worse." Suddenly the light in the room seemed extraordinary bright, as if someone had turned a pair of high-intensity interrogation lamps in his direction. "The light ..."

"What about the light?"

He dropped his head, trying to block out some of the light. "It's everywhere. It's coming from everywhere."

"What's coming from everywhere? The light?"

"Yes," he said through gritted teeth. Was it his imagination, or was there an edge of panic in Louise's voice?

"Are there any other symptoms besides the headache and light sensitivity?"

To call the cacophony pounding away in his head a headache seemed laughable. In fact, he would have laughed except he had a sudden vision of the action sending his skull exploding in shards into the walls of the room, red and gray runnels of brain slipping down the walls. His stomach flipped, and he was afraid he was going to vomit.

"Philip?"

He had to cover his eyes—he had to get his hands free. He strained at the tape and felt the arm of the chair give slightly, but the movement escalated the pain in his head, and now it was as if someone was forcing a needle from the top of his spine into his brain.

"Jesus Christ, Mortensen," he gasped, "what did you give me?"

And then it all came crashing down, as if he had been trapped between a pair of cymbals wielded by a giant. And everything went black.

54

From the monitor, in the room two doors down from Philip, Louise heard a low, long groan, a sharp intake of air, and then a guttural, animal sound.

Was the V-2 giving Castillo the stroke that she intended its recipient would be able to inflict?

She went to the door of her room and put her hand on the knob.

But even if he was in distress, he still might be able to wield whatever power the drug could give him.

She withdrew her hand from the doorknob and returned to the monitor.

Her fingers were laced together, her grip tightening until her knuckles were white. "Philip?"

There was no response.

"Philip—can you hear me?"

She heard another groan, then a heavy thump.

"Philip? Do you need help?"

Silence.

She made another circuit between the door and the monitor. "Philip?"

She twisted the wedding ring on her finger. "Philip, I'm coming to the room, and I want you to remember that I'm there to help you, not hurt you. Do you understand?"

Nothing.

She left her room and hurried down the walkway. She pressed her ear to the door of Philip's room but could hear nothing.

She opened the door and stepped inside.

The chair was on its side, Philip still duct-taped to it, although one of the chair's arms had been pulled loose. His head was bent toward his chest, less like it had fallen forward on its own than as if he were ducking down to avoid some threat, like a man in a foxhole. His features were twisted, his eyes screwed shut. Sweat stuck his T-shirt to his body.

She knelt beside him. "Philip?"

"What—" Whatever he had been about to say was cut short by another groan, and he pulled his legs up, as if protecting himself from a beating.

She went to the satchel, got a pair of scissors, and snipped through the tape binding his torso and his wrists.

He rolled into a ball, his fists at his head, his wrists pressed to his temples.

She reached for his wrist. "Let me take your—"

"No!" he snarled.

"I need to—"

"No ..." This time it was more like a whimper.

She returned to the satchel and considered her options. She wanted whatever she gave him to work quickly. There was no reason for him to continue to suffer.

After a moment, she selected a vial and a syringe. If his thigh had been uncovered, she would have injected him in the vastus lateralis, which would be preferred for a dose as large as she planned to administer, but the deltoid muscle would have to do.

She filled the syringe and knelt by him again.

"I'm going to give you something that will help."

"No ..."

It was barely a gasp.

She pulled the sleeve of his T-shirt up and injected him.

In a moment, his features fell slack, and his hands dropped from his head.

She returned to the satchel, dropped the syringe in the sharps container, and snapped the bag shut. Then she pulled the bedspread off the bed and draped it over his body.

She considered the gun lying on the bedside table. It was the gun Philip had taken from Donny at the compound, and she had no desire to risk being found with a weapon that could be traced back to Billy Chapel. Even if she had been willing to risk that, she couldn't picture herself shooting someone. She left it where it was.

She picked up the sample case, now accessible next to the overturned chair. She hurried out of the room and pulled the door closed behind her.

She went to her room, unplugged the monitor, and dropped it into the Walmart bag, then, carrying the bag and the sample case, went to where the Navigator was still parked. Tossing the bags into the back, she got in and started the car.

Then she turned it off.

Where was she to go? She had money and fake IDs—she could go anywhere.

She and Gerard had enjoyed visiting the vineyards of Sonoma. Paris was beautiful ... but everyone went to Paris. She had heard good things about Prague. Perhaps a cruise? It would certainly be difficult for Billy Chapel to catch up with her on a ship.

But all those destinations would have been so much more enjoyable with Gerard. He had loved planning trips.

She twisted her wedding ring on her finger.

She didn't want vineyards. She didn't want the Eiffel Tower. She didn't want to make polite conversation with strangers in a cruise ship dining room.

There was only one thing she wanted, and she had exhausted her options for getting it ... or *almost* exhausted them.

But she had a call to make first.

55

———

Lizzy tried to relax as the SUV sped through one of the construction-area cattle chutes that seemed to be an inevitable part of any trip on the Pennsylvania Turnpike, the rising sun a fiery ball in the rear-view mirrors.

"I hate these," she said. "I always picture that I'm going to scrape one side and then bounce off and hit the other side—back and forth until eventually the Caravan is stuck crosswise in it."

A moment later, Owen glanced over at her. "I wish you hadn't described that—now it's all I can think about."

His phone buzzed in his pocket.

"Damn," he muttered. "I'll pull over once we're out of this."

"Who do you think it is?" Lizzy asked. "Andy?"

"No, I have a different ring tone for him."

When they were clear of the construction, he stopped at an emergency pull-out and got out his phone. His eyebrows rose. "It was Louise. And she left a voicemail."

He opened the message and put the phone on speaker.

"Owen," Louise's clipped voice came from the phone, "I'm at the motel in Harrisburg where you picked up Richard and me.

Philip is here as well—room 207. He's in some distress. He volunteered to be a test subject for a drug I'm developing—a drug he knew hadn't yet been tested for safety—and he had an adverse reaction. Before I administered the drug, I offered to call emergency services for him if it went badly, and he declined. Afterwards, I gave him ten milligrams of diazepam. I left my medical bag in the room. The door is unlocked."

The call ended.

Lizzy and Owen stared at each other wide-eyed.

"What's happening?" said Lizzy. "What drug that she's developing did she give him—the inhibitol? I thought you said that was safe."

"It should have been. It must have been something else."

"What was the other drug she gave him—diazepam?"

"It's Valium. It would help if he was agitated ..." He ran his hand over his head. "Or if he was experiencing convulsions."

"Convulsions? Uncle Owen!"

"Let's not panic—we don't know what's actually going on there."

"I'm panicking *because* we don't know what's actually going on there!" She pulled out her phone. "Do you think Louise was telling us the truth about what happened?"

"She wouldn't have had to call us at all, so I'm thinking she was."

She stabbed Philip's number in her contact list. "No answer," she said her voice anguished. "You put the address of the motel in your map app, and I'll keep trying him."

Owen entered the address and put the SUV in drive, then put it back in park.

"What are you waiting for?" said Lizzy. "Let's go!"

"Louise said Philip didn't want her to call 911 if things went badly, but you know him better than I do. Even assuming he actually told her that, do you think that's really what he would want?"

Her voice cracking, Lizzy said, "Yes, I do. The police would get involved, they'd realize who he is, and they'd prove he killed Tobe Hanrick in Sedona. They might even blame him for the other two guys who died in Oak Creek. He'd go back to prison."

"Going back to prison is better than dying."

"Not for Philip. He told me that one time—that he'd rather die than go back. And he wasn't exaggerating. He meant it literally."

Owen nodded sadly. "Having gotten to know Philip a little better, I think you're right." He glanced at the route on his map app. "Forty-five minutes." He put the SUV in drive. "Let's make it in forty."

THEY MADE IT IN THIRTY-SIX.

Lizzy sprinted from where Owen had pulled up next to the stairs to the motel's second floor and toward room 207.

The only light in the room came from a narrow gap in the curtains, and as her eyes adjusted from the brightness of the morning, she could see a form on the floor covered in a bedspread.

She rushed across the room and knelt next to him. "Philip?"

He was curled on the floor, his hair plastered to his skull, his skin waxy.

When she had told Owen that Philip would rather die than go back to prison, she hadn't truly believed it was a possibility. What if she was responsible for his death because she had talked Owen out of calling an ambulance?

But then his eyelids flickered, flickered again, and opened, although his eyes were unfocused. "Who—?" he rasped.

She grasped his hand. "It's Lizzy. And Owen," she said, her voice thick with a combination of horror at his condition and almost paralyzing relief that he was alive.

Owen had reached the room and joined Lizzy at Philip's side, puffing slightly. "How are you feeling, Philip?"

"—hell," Philip croaked.

Lizzy sat on the floor next to him. "You *look* like hell."

He summoned the shadow of a smile. "Better now."

"Let's get you up on the bed, Philip," Owen said.

Lizzy pulled the bedspread off Philip, alarmed at how his T-shirt stuck to his body, the neck ringed with white from the salt from his sweat.

Owen got one of Philip's arms looped around his neck and hoisted Philip to his feet and onto the bed. Lizzy helped swing his legs up.

"Louise said she left her medical bag," Owen muttered, then spotted the satchel on the desk. He brought it and the over-turned chair, to which cut strips of duct tape were stuck, over to the bed, and sat.

He checked Philip's pulse and scowled. He peered into the satchel, removed a blood pressure monitor, and slipped it on Philip's arm. He read the measurement off the display. "Hmph. Philip, can you touch your finger to your nose."

"Rather not."

"Why's that?"

"Hurts."

"Can you tell us what happened?" Owen held up a hand. "Actually, let me tell you what Louise told me, then you can correct as needed." Owen related the message from Louise. "Is that what happened?"

"Yes."

"Can you tell us anything more?"

"Uncle Owen," said Lizzy, "can we let him rest now?"

"I don't know, Pumpkin. Philip, is there anything we need to know right now?"

Philip was silent for a few long moments. "Don't think so."

"Are Andy and Ruby and the rest in danger because of what happened here?"

"Not from Mortensen."

Owen sighed. "Okay. You rest now. But I want to know as soon as possible what's been going on."

56

Lizzy sat on the dresser, watching Philip's long, slow breaths. Owen sat in the desk chair, texting with Andy.

She checked the time on her phone. It was early afternoon and Philip had been sleeping—or, maybe more accurately, unconscious—for almost eight hours. If he didn't wake up soon on his own, they would need to wake him up and see if he could give them any more information about what had happened with him and Louise.

She jumped when her phone buzzed in her hand. She checked the caller ID, and her heart skipped a beat. This couldn't be good news.

"Eddie," she whispered to Owen. She jumped off the dresser and stepped outside.

"Hey, Eddie," she answered. "Is everything okay?"

"You bet," he said, sounding even more cheerful than usual. "Just called to let you know that I got to have a little law enforcement fun last night—actually, early this morning—old geezer though I am."

She allowed herself to relax a bit. "You're not an old geezer. What happened?"

"When you warned me there might be danger of an increase in crime in Sedona, I thought maybe you meant someone would try to break into Philip's casita, so I staked it out. In the middle of the night, I heard someone sneaking around outside, but when I peeked out, they weren't sneaking around the casita— they were behind my rancher. And you know what they were doing?"

"No, what?"

"Pouring gasoline around the foundation."

"Oh my God!"

"Planned to have quite a bonfire, too, because there were a bunch of cans."

"What happened?"

"I called a buddy of mine on the force and told him what was happening. I didn't want to wait for the official cavalry to arrive because by that time they had poured out almost all the cans, and I didn't want to give them a chance to strike a match."

Lizzy was alarmed but also a little amused, because it was clear from Eddie's tone that the story was going to have a happy ending. "And ..."

"Clobbered one of them over the head with his own gas can and winged the other one in the leg with my Smith & Wesson Shield." He laughed. "Can you say 'winged' if it was in the leg?"

Lizzy laughed as well, although hers was a little shaky. "Good for you, Eddie."

"The cavalry arrived a few minutes later and took them away.

"Any idea who they were?"

"Couple of punks from Flagstaff."

"Any ties to the East Coast? Specifically to Baltimore?"

"Not that I know of, but I'll have my buddy check that out." He continued, his voice slightly more sober, "You know, that rancher isn't much to look at, but I would have been sorry to lose it. It suits me." After a pause, he added, "Just like that casita suited Philip."

"Yeah, it did." She took a deep breath. "Well, I'm so glad to hear you and your house are okay."

"And how about you, Lizzy, friend of Philip. Are you okay? You and your friends?"

She glanced back toward the motel room door. "Yes, we're pretty much okay."

He waited for more, but when she was silent, he said, "Do I need to be on the lookout for any more unusual crime activity or is that it?"

She sighed. "I'm not sure. I think the danger will pass eventually but keep a lookout just in case."

"Will do, Lizzy. You and your friends do the same."

"We will."

They ended the call, and Lizzy stood looking at the uninspiring view of fast-food joints and parking lots available from the motel's walkway. It was disheartening to think that Billy's reach extended all the way across the country to Arizona.

She turned when the room door opened, and Owen popped his head out. "Philip's waking up."

She hurried back into the room and over to the bed.

His color was better than it had been and his features were more relaxed, but his eyes were squinted against the light.

She turned down the already dim bedside light. "How are you feeling?"

"Better." He licked his lips. "Thirsty."

Owen had joined her at the bed. "Let's get you sitting up. Easier to drink."

While Owen got Philip propped up against the headboard, Lizzy opened one of the bottles of water Owen had gotten on the shopping trip she had sent him on and handed the bottle to Philip.

He managed a few swallows, his hand trembling.

"Better?" she asked.

"Yes." He ran his fingers through his hair and winced. "Jesus, I'm disgusting. I need a shower."

"How about food? We could get delivery while you shower."

He groaned. "No food."

"While you were asleep, Uncle Owen went out and got you some clothes—more like the kind you usually wear. But," she said in a loud stage whisper, obviously audible to Owen, "I think they're going to be a little big."

Owen said good-naturedly, "Hey, what do I know about buying clothes for other people?"

"Thanks, Owen," said Philip.

Lizzy stood, and Philip swung his legs off the bed, managed to stand, then promptly dropped back onto the bed.

"Want some help?" Lizzy asked.

"Please, no," he said with a grimace. "Leave me some dignity."

He managed to stay standing on his second attempt, and made his way to the bathroom, keeping a steadying hand on the wall and spotted surreptitiously by Owen. Owen gave him the bag of clothes, and soon they heard water running in the shower.

"How does he seem to you?" Lizzy whispered to Owen.

"Actually much better than I would have expected, based on his condition when we first got here."

When Philip emerged from the bathroom, he was much cleaner but somewhat ridiculous-looking in his too-large clothes: blue T-shirt, zip-up sweatshirt, jeans held up by a canvas belt, and sneakers.

"Thanks for getting these for me, Owen," he said, easing himself onto the desk chair, which Owen had vacated. "And I appreciate you guys being patient about hearing what happened. I feel a lot more coherent now." He took a sip of water, and when he spoke, he addressed himself to Lizzy. "When Louise accidentally formulated a drug at the compound that would temporarily inactivate the squeeze, it seemed clear that if we could confirm it was safe, it would be a great option for you. We know the juice inactivates the squeeze, but I think we all agree that you taking a steroid drug is not a great idea. And even if the juice wasn't steroid-based, you'd always be having to deal with the mental chatter of the people around you, which I can't imagine is pleasant. This was a chance for you to live a more normal life."

"Philip," she said, "I appreciate you looking out for me, but—"

He raised a hand. "Let me finish—then you can decide if you appreciate what I did." He took a deep breath. "While she was at the Penn lab, she also finished work on a drug that can produce the squeeze in regular adults who aren't the result of the experiments she was conducting at Vivantem. She calls it V-2."

Owen scowled. "I could see she was doing something other than testing the inhibitol. I let her continue because I wanted to see what she was doing. I should have put a stop to it."

Philip smiled ruefully. "You did sort of put a stop to it—by proposing that we leave the lab and go to Lansdowne."

"And that meant that she had formulated the drug—the V-2 —but hadn't tested it," Owen said.

"Yes."

"And you became her test subject."

Philip nodded.

"Voluntarily?" Owen asked, skeptical.

"Yes." He looked back at Lizzy. "The agreement she and I made at the compound is that if she did develop the V-2, she would give it to me so that I could go to Baltimore and squeeze Billy Chapel. And having some insider perspective into how heavy the security presence around him is, I thought that being able to squeeze him was a less dangerous option that using some more old-fashioned method."

Lizzy's eyebrows rose. "Safer than letting Louise give you an untested drug?"

"Yes, I believed it was safer than that. *Still* believe it, because," he raised his hands, "here I am—a little worse for wear, but alive."

"Does that mean you have the squeeze now?" Owen asked, alarmed.

"Right now? I don't think so—although you'd probably have to pretend to attack me to find out. But this time wasn't meant to test that, just to see if—"

"—if you survived?" asked Lizzy pointedly.

"Yeah, pretty much. But Louise was in the room with me after I took the drug, and it doesn't sound like she suffered any ill effects. I'm guessing that even if the drug would have given me the squeeze, I was too out of it for it to work."

"You couldn't even stand up," added Lizzy. "And you're still wiped out—just telling that story has tired you out."

Philip sighed. "Yeah."

"Oh, I almost forgot—Eddie just called. Two guys tried to burn down his house, but he caught them and they're with the police now."

Philip groaned. "Goddamn. Well, *that* can't be an accident. Thank God you warned him."

"Chapel has men in Arizona?" asked Owen.

"Well, he was in some kind of partnership with Viklund," said Philip, "and we know Viklund had ties to Arizona. Chapel probably just called in a favor with another ... business associate." He shook his head. "Bastard," he said tiredly. "That's just one more reason to want him out of the way."

"And where do you suppose Louise is now?" asked Owen.

Philip drew a deep breath and let it out slowly. "Haven't a clue."

Owen got out his phone. "I'm going to call Andy and give him and the rest of the folks in Letort an update." He sighed. "Although I hope Louise Mortensen has better things to do than harass them and the Pearsons."

"It's Chapel they need to watch out for," said Philip.

Owen nodded. "It's who we *all* need to watch out for."

"Just until I'm back on my feet," said Philip. "Seems like the squeeze isn't going to be in my arsenal, but there are other ways I can take care of Billy Chapel."

57

S itting in the passenger seat of the car Owen had rented, Lizzy checked the time on her phone for the fifth time in almost as many minutes: almost ten o'clock. "Ruby's been in there for a while. Maybe Billy doesn't plan to eat dinner at *Charm City* tonight." She tapped a text message into her phone, and a reply pinged back a few moments later. She sighed and looked over at Owen in the driver's seat. "Ruby says he's still talking with some people at the bar."

"Well," said Owen, sounding hopeful, "if he doesn't eat there tonight, we can try again tomorrow."

Lizzy dropped the hand holding her phone onto her lap and looked out at the nearly deserted street, eerie in the sodium-vapor glow of the streetlights. "How many nights can Ruby eat at *Charm City* before it starts looking weird? It probably already looks weird—it's not the kind of place people go on their own, especially not this late." She gnawed her thumbnail. "Maybe I should just meet up with him at the bar. There would be plenty of witnesses to see—or to think—that I didn't do anything to him."

"No. We agreed that if he's already eating dinner when you

arrive, it's more likely he'll stay at the restaurant and not decide to go somewhere else, like that private room where Olivia saw Philip." He shuddered. "Or his house."

"Yeah, I know." Lizzy didn't mention that after her surreptitious trip to Owings Mills, she was even less enthusiastic than Owen was about the possibility of Billy deciding to take her there.

"Want to review the plan?"

"I know the plan, Uncle Owen."

"Review it for my benefit, then."

She shot him a look. "Really?"

He summoned a smile. "Come on. Humor me."

She sighed. "Tell Billy I'm there because I'm looking for Philip." She thought for a moment, then brightened. "I know—I'll tell him that I'm pregnant and Philip's the father."

"Good grief," muttered Owen. "It seems like there are all sorts of ways that could go wrong. Let's keep the lies as close to the truth as possible."

She sighed again. "Yeah, you're probably right."

"Do you think Chapel thinks Philip is alive?"

"I don't know. Other than Donny, the Maryland police haven't found any bodies at the compound—" She grimaced. "—any fresh ones, anyway. But if Philip had been in the lab when it blew up, there probably wouldn't be much to find."

"True."

"I also need to try to find out who might take over from Billy if he's not around anymore, and if we would have anything to worry about from them." She ran her fingers through her hair. "Man, I wish I could read minds and squeeze at the same time. Maybe I should take the juice—"

"Absolutely not—you need to be able to squeeze him."

"Yeah." After a moment, she continued. "He has the recording of me reading Edmund Rinnert's mind at the compound, but Edmund was obviously drugged. Philip suspects that Billy thinks I could only do it *because* he was drugged. Plus, it was pretty obvious I couldn't read Billy's mind at the compound, so he probably thinks he's immune. If that's really the case, then it removes one reason he might refuse to meet with me. And if I can't squeeze him, I need to figure out a way to convince him that he doesn't have anything to worry about from you or Andy or Ruby or Richard or Marjorie ... or Olivia, if he suspects she's anything other than some barista from *Chesaperk* who worked a shift at *Charm City*."

"How do you plan to do that?"

She looked over at him with a forced smile. "I'll think of something." She turned her eyes back to the nighttime scene. "And once I've done all that, then engineer a situation where I can squeeze him."

They both sat in silence for some time, then Owen said, his big hands twisting on the wheel, "You'll need to make him mad."

"I might not have to work too hard to make him mad. He's probably already pissed off about almost getting caught in Lansdowne—" She laughed shortly. "—and by the fact that Eddie surprised those guys in Sedona."

"I wish I could do something to help you other than drive the getaway car. I'd feel better if it was me instead of Ruby in the restaurant sending status reports." He smiled and nudged her in the arm with his elbow. "I read the *Charm City* reviews online. The food is supposed to be top notch, and I bet I'd appreciate it more than Ruby will."

She forced a laugh.

His smile faded. "And I wish I was the one helping you get out of there once the deed is done."

Lizzy felt the thump in her gut that accompanied any thought of what she was about to do. *Once the deed is done.* At least it sounded better than *once you've intentionally killed a man.*

She patted Owen's arm. "I can't imagine Billy Chapel wouldn't notice the man from Lansdowne sitting at his bar. Plus, you know how good Ruby is in these kinds of situations—she'll help me get away. And if Billy has what looks like a stroke or a heart attack at the table, there's going to be so much commotion that nobody will be paying attention to me." Her phone pinged and she checked the text, then sat up. "Ruby says he just sat down at a table, and he must have told the bartender what he wanted because the server already brought out an appetizer."

"Maybe give him a couple of minutes to settle in," said Owen.

"Yeah, yeah, that makes sense." The knot in her stomach twisted. "I wonder how Philip is doing."

"Olivia will contact us if there's anything we need to know."

When Philip, clearly still exhausted, had fallen asleep again after their conversation in the Harrisburg motel, Lizzy had told Owen her plan: to take care of Billy Chapel herself.

As she had expected, Owen had argued against it, but he couldn't argue against her underlying position: someone had to get Billy Chapel out of the way, and she was the one best equipped to do it and get away with it.

They had called the contingent in Letort and explained only that Lizzy and Owen needed to leave Harrisburg, and Olivia had driven to the motel to keep an eye on Philip. Waking up to find Lizzy and Owen gone and Olivia in their place must have been quite a surprise for Philip—largely a happy one, since she knew he'd be glad to see Olivia, but an awkward one as well, since he had a lot of explaining to do.

With Ruby now in Baltimore with them, that left only Richard and Andy guarding Marjorie—and each other.

This was no way for her friends to live.

She needed to end this tonight.

She handed him her phone. "I can't wait anymore." She reached for the door handle.

"Are you sure about this, Pumpkin? Maybe if we take another day or two to think through our options—"

She turned back to him. "Uncle Owen, taking another day or two gives him time to think through his options as well—and maybe act on them in a way that would be bad. We need to take care of this now." Her voice dropped almost to a whisper. "I want to get it over with."

Owen's face was even paler than usual. "I understand. Please be careful, Pumpkin."

"I will."

She leaned over and kissed him on the cheek, then climbed out of the car. She tugged down her dress. It was a size smaller than she would normally get ... actually, it was probably two sizes smaller than she would normally get. She hoped it would make it clear to Billy and his men that she wasn't wearing a wire —she wasn't carrying a purse for the same reason—and might encourage him to speak more freely. And she was wearing high heels to complete a look she hoped would improve her chances of not being turned away by the men who served as Billy's bodyguards.

Owen had parked the car around the corner from the restaurant, and she was relieved to reach the gate over which the words *Charm City Diner* arched without tripping or twisting her ankle. She hated high heels. She passed through a now-empty patio area and entered the dining room.

There was a group of a half dozen at the bar, and four of the tables in the dining room were occupied. Sitting at a table near the entrance to the dining room, Ruby studiously ignored Lizzy, her fingers hooked through the handle of a seemingly untouched cup of coffee. At a second table, a couple gazed dreamily across the table at each other, fingers intertwined between empty dessert plates. At a third, two men in their thirties were passing a cell phone back and forth, laughing at whatever its screen showed.

Billy Chapel sat at the fourth, near the back of the restaurant, chatting with Tony.

Lizzy started across the dining room toward him.

The bartender stepped out from behind the bar. "Sorry, miss, we're not seating for dinner anymore—" He sized her up. "—although you're welcome to sit at the bar if you're over twenty-one."

"I'm here to see Billy," she said, and continued toward his table.

The exchange had attracted Billy and Tony's attention, and Tony moved to put himself between Lizzy and Billy.

As Lizzy neared the table, Billy grinned. "Don't worry about her, Tony. She and I are old friends."

"Old friends?" Tony asked, surprised.

"Yes indeed," Billy said as Lizzy reached the table. He leaned back and hooked his arm over the back of his chair. "You remember Theo Viklund, Tony?"

"Sure, boss."

"Well, the claim was that this was his niece—Rey Viklund's little sister."

"That was the claim, eh?"

"That was the claim."

"You want to talk to her?" Tony asked, gesturing at the chair facing Billy's.

"Absolutely."

Tony pulled out the chair, and Lizzy stepped toward it.

Billy wadded up his napkin and tossed it onto the table next to his plate. "But not here. Somewhere a little more private." He waved toward the patrons still in the restaurant. "And it's closing time—get these people out of here."

58

Lizzy had known that being taken to the private room where Philip had seen Olivia was a possibility—a likelihood, even—although she had downplayed the chances with Owen and Ruby. She still believed *Charm City* was the best place for the meeting with Billy. According to Olivia, it was the only place other than his house that he seemed to spend any time, and Lizzy had no intention of going willingly to his home. And a chance encounter on the street wouldn't give her the time she needed to get the information she wanted.

As Billy and Tony escorted her through the dining room toward the stairs, she could sense the eyes of the men in the room on her—along with Ruby's, although for a very different reason.

When they reached the second floor, they passed a few darkened rooms, and at the end of the hallway, Billy opened a door labeled *Private*. The three entered.

Billy waved to a table. "Have a seat."

Tony followed Lizzy to the table, pulled out a chair for her, then, once she was seated, pushed it in again—a little tighter to the table than she would have liked.

Billy went to a drink cart in the corner and picked up two glasses and a bottle.

"Want me to stay, Billy?" Tony asked.

"Nah. I can grab her if she tries to scamper away." He sat down opposite Lizzy. "And it's not like she's hiding anything dangerous under that dress." He smiled, but his eyes were as flat as a snake's. "At least nothing more dangerous than any good-looking girl hides under her dress. I'll yell if I need you."

Tony crossed the room and stepped outside. The door clicked shut softly behind him.

"New haircut, I see," said Billy. "Maybe you couldn't wash the blood out—had to cut it out. Blood can be a bitch to get rid of."

"You'd know." She interlaced her fingers in her lap to keep them from trembling.

His eyes drifted to her arm, where the scars from where he had cut her with the broken champagne bottle were still visible, then his gaze returned to her face. "When I saw you and McNally leaving the compound on the chopper, I figured that would be the last I'd see of you."

"That was what I hoped."

"Although it looked like you might have been planning to let the chopper leave without you once you got McNally onboard."

"He needed to get to a hospital."

"Good Samaritan, are you?" He grinned. "At least in comparison to me."

"You set a pretty low bar."

He laughed. "So, how is ol' Andy?"

"Recovering."

"Got hit by a stray bullet, did he?"

"Yes. He also had his nose broken and two fingers dislocated."

He shrugged. "Not by me."

"Maybe not. But I'll bet there are plenty of Andy McNallys in your past." As anger began to displace fear, she felt the stirrings of the squeeze ... but it was too soon—there was information she needed to get from him.

He leaned back and raised his hands, as if in surrender. "Me? Nope. I never get my hands dirty with that shit."

It was as good an opening as she would get to find out more about his dealings, and who might take over from him if he wasn't around anymore. "What shit *do* you get your hands dirty with?"

He grinned. "A little of this, a little of that."

"Anyone looking to take any of that over from you?"

His grin faded. "Not anyone who knows what's good for them." His eyes narrowed. "Why?"

She shrugged. "Isn't someone always trying to muscle in on whoever's on top?"

"Sure, but I make sure they know it's not a good idea."

"Not Tony?"

He barked out a laugh. "Tony is strictly for steppin' and fetchin'." He picked up the bottle and poured a golden liquid—Woodford bourbon—into the two glasses. He pushed one across the table to her.

She pushed it back. "I don't drink."

"I think you will today. You come to my restaurant, you follow my rules." He threw back his drink, banged the glass down on the table, and stared at her.

She picked up the glass, then put it back down. "I can't. I'm pregnant." She realized as she said it that this story posed some issues—for example, she'd have to be barely pregnant not to be showing in her tight dress—but she hadn't foreseen the need to avoid having to get drunk with Billy Chapel.

Billy's eyebrows shot up melodramatically. "You don't say! Who's the lucky guy?"

She was silent, her face blazing.

"Andrew McNally?"

She shook her head.

He grinned. "Castillo?"

"Yes." She twisted her fingers together, and the nervous move was only partially an act. "That's why I'm here. I need to let him know. My baby needs a dad. I thought you might know where he is. He works for you, right?"

His grin morphed into a scowl. "*Worked*, past tense."

She widened her eyes. "He's dead?"

He regarded her. "You tell me."

"I don't know—that's why I'm here."

He turned his empty glass on the table, looking at her speculatively. "How do you know Louise Mortensen?"

She sorted through the information Philip had been able to give her, based either on the facts he had gathered during his time with Billy or on the theories he had developed.

"She made me be able to read minds when she gave me a drug, and when she drugged the person whose mind I was supposed to read."

"And what were these drugs?"

"How should I know? I just took what she gave me."

"Why?"

"She threatened me if I didn't."

"Threatened you with what?"

"She said she'd have Lucas do something to me if I didn't cooperate. Like he did to Andy."

"Where is Mortensen now?"

She pushed her chair back and stood. "I don't know where she is, and I don't care. I came here looking for Philip, and you're obviously not going to tell me, if you even know."

"Sit down!" he snapped, all traces of good humor gone.

For half a second, she considered running for the door. But she knew Tony was probably stationed outside ... and this was what she had planned for, wasn't it? To make Billy Chapel angry?

It seemed she was succeeding in that, at least.

She lowered herself back down on the chair.

"You want Philip," said Billy. "I want Mortensen. You help me, I'll help you."

"How could I help you? I already told you—I don't know where she is."

"But she might come out of hiding if she knew her little guinea pig, Lizzy, was in danger."

She swallowed. "*Am* I in danger?"

He shrugged, some of his nonchalance returning. "Could be. Wouldn't necessarily have to be *real* danger, as long as she believed it." He leaned forward and refilled his glass. "Wouldn't necessarily *not* be real danger. That would be up to how cooperative you are."

"And then you'd put me in touch with Philip? Or help me find him?"

"Because your baby needs a daddy?"

She squirmed a little—among all the lies she was telling, this one was the most uncomfortable. "Yes."

He tossed back his drink and sat forward again, his forearms resting on the table. "Well, Lizzy, maybe you should re-think the benefits of having Philip Castillo be around to help raise your little bastard, because he's not a good guy."

A chill raised gooseflesh on Lizzy's skin, and she crossed her arms. "What do you mean?"

"You don't like me, Lizzy. I don't have to be a mind reader to see that. After all, I offered to break Phil's fingers when he tried to keep me from teasing you a little back at the compound—a regular knight in shining armor, that boy."

Lizzy's stomach flipped again as she thought of the argument between Billy and Philip and Billy's threat: *I swear to God,*

Castillo, if you say another word without being asked, I'll bend your finger back until it snaps. She felt the squeeze begin to surface again, like the shifting surface of an almost-boiling pot of water.

"And after all," Billy continued, "I did cut you a couple of times with that broken bottle."

Lizzy suppressed a shiver, not so much at the wounds Billy had left on her arm, but at the memory of her terror that he would thrust those razor-sharp spikes into her face. The bubbles of the squeeze trembled, almost ready to burst through the thin remaining vestiges of control.

"I had my reasons for doing those things," he said, as if they were discussing the latest Baltimore sports team scores, "but maybe you don't agree with my philosophy that the ends justify the means."

She dug her fingernails into her palm. If she could hold off for a few more moments, maybe she'd improve the chances that the force would build to a level that would be guaranteed to kill him. "No, I don't."

"And that some lives are worth more than others."

"I don't agree with that either."

He shrugged. "You don't need to agree with me, but I'm not sure your friend Philip would disagree. You see, ol' Phil and me, we're not so different." He grinned. "We should go into business together. *Chapel and Castillo.* Church and castle. Catchy, eh? Sounds like a fucking law firm."

"You make it sound like you were already in business together."

He shook his finger at her, scolding, his good humor seemingly restored. "No, no, no. Phil was my boy, not my partner ... although not always a *good* boy. You know Donny?"

Her heart jumped—the man she had squeezed in the conservatory. She frantically tried to think of any reason Billy would think she knew him. "I know a couple of guys named Donny, but I doubt they're the ones you're talking about."

"Probably not," Billy said agreeably. "Donny's one of my boys. *Was* one of my boys—cops found him dead at that damn compound. I think Phil was responsible."

Lizzy thought it was best not to let Billy know that she herself had been responsible for Donny's death.

"Donny was such a jackass," continued Billy, "I can hardly blame Phil. I might have popped Donny myself, given the right opportunity." He shook his head ruefully. "Yeah, Phil could sometimes be a pain in the ass, but I foresaw great things for him if he had stuck with me."

"Like what?"

"Oh, based on what I saw he was willing to do, almost anything. A man who's willing to do what he's done is a valuable asset."

Lizzy tried to avoid shifting in her seat. "What did he do?"

He leaned back, smiling. "You know Lucas, Theo Viklund's head of security?" He waved a hand. "Of course you do—he was on that helicopter with you and McNally. You know what happened to him?"

"No."

"Tony!" Billy bellowed, sending Lizzy's heartbeat skyrocketing.

Tony stepped into the room. "Yes, boss?"

Billy gestured to Lizzy. "Tell my friend here what happened to Lucas."

Tony's gaze shifted from Billy to Lizzy and back. "Everything?"

"Yup, everything. I think we can trust little Lizzy."

After another glance at Lizzy, Tony said, "We caught up with him at BWI, about to board a flight back to Sweden. Brought him back to Baltimore."

"And why did we do that?"

"Needed some information from him."

Dread wrapped itself around Lizzy's heart, and she wondered if there was anything she could say to change the subject.

"We knew Lucas would be a little hesitant to share that information," Billy said to Lizzy, then turned back to Tony. "So what did we do?"

Tony shifted uneasily. "You mean, specifically?"

"Jeez, Tony, when I said we can trust Lizzy, that's what I meant. No need to beat around the bush." Without waiting for a response from Tony, he turned to Lizzy. "I knew Donny would be happy to ... *encourage* Lucas to share what he knew. So I let Donny have his fun." He turned back to Tony. "And what kind of shape was Lucas in when Donny was done with him?"

Lizzy tasted bile in the back of her throat.

"Not good, boss," said Tony.

"No, not a pretty sight." Billy topped up his glass, took a sip of bourbon, and considered Lizzy. "But you probably want to know what this has to do with your pal Phil."

No, Lizzy wanted to say, *I don't want to know.*

Billy pushed his glass to one side and leaned forward, lacing his fingers together on the tabletop. He locked eyes with her. "When Donny had gotten everything we were going to out of Lucas, Phil put a gun to the back of Lucas's head and pulled the trigger."

She felt her thoughts jumbling, the shock dissipating the power of the squeeze. Whatever she had thought Billy was leading up to, it wasn't this.

Then she remembered the comment Philip had made when she asked about whether the man Donny tortured had survived: *No, he didn't. But that's a story for another day.*

Was it possible Billy was telling the truth?

"He—" She tried to swallow down the lump in her throat. "He wouldn't do that." Her words were barely audible. "Not just like that. That's like ... an execution."

"Oh, but he did. Didn't bat an eye. A man like that, who can put a gun to the head of a man who never did him any real harm and pull the trigger—like, I said, a valuable asset."

Lizzy's heartbeat was pounding in her ears. She cleared her throat. "He wouldn't do that," she said, a little louder than was necessary.

He laughed. "Oh, but he would. A cold-blooded killer, that's what Philip Castillo is. Is that the man you thought you knew? Is that the man you want to help raise your baby? Is that—" His voice rose to a nerve-grating falsetto, "—the man you love?"

Lizzy's power coalesced. It reached out like spectral fingers, wrapped itself around Billy's brain, and squeezed.

Billy's eyes widened. He coughed explosively.

"Boss?" Tony said from the door.

"Jesus—" Billy wheezed.

Lizzy's mental fingers tightened.

Billy let out a strangled yell and used the table to pull himself to his feet, sending his chair clattering to the floor. He pointed a trembling finger at Lizzy. "Tony ..." he managed, his voice choked. "Get her ..." He squinted his eyes shut, and his words deteriorated into a groan. "Oooowww ..."

Tony hurried across the room. "Okay, boss, I'll get her out."

"No ... I ..." Billy staggered and crashed to the floor.

Lizzy knelt next to him and bent her face toward his, almost as if she were going to kiss him. "I can't just read minds," she hissed in his ear. "I can crush them."

59

By the time Tony got to Billy's side and knelt next to the stricken man, Lizzy was on her feet, backing away, a look of horror—not entirely faked—on her face. "What's happening to him?"

Tony loosened Billy's already-loose collar, then ran back to the door, threw it open, and bellowed, "Ricky!"

A moment later, she heard footfalls pounding up the stairs, and the bartender appeared at the door. He took in the scene. "What the fuck—?"

Tony, who was getting out his phone, nodded at Lizzy. "The boss wants her out of here."

Ricky crossed the room, grabbed Lizzy's upper arm, and turned her toward the door.

"No—" Billy groaned.

"It's okay, boss," said Tony, jabbing his phone. "You just take it easy. I'll call the doc."

Billy tried to say something but only a choked garble came out. He grabbed Tony's arm and tried to pull himself up, but instead almost pulled Tony down on top of him.

"Don't worry, boss," Tony said, struggling to maintain his

balance. "Help is on the way." He glanced back at Ricky. *"Move it!"*

Just before Ricky pushed Lizzy through the door, she turned and met Billy's eyes. He was still conscious, although he wouldn't be for long. And she could tell he was still aware enough of what was happening to understand that she was responsible for taking his life.

Ricky jerked Lizzy out of the room and hustled her down the hallway to the stairs. She stumbled and was saved from a fall only by his iron grip on her arm. When they reached the main floor, the bar and dining room were empty, although she saw that a sweater hung over the back of the chair where Ruby had sat. In her panic, she almost offered to take it to its owner. She barely stiffed a hysterical laugh.

Ricky propelled her through the courtyard. When they got to the front gate, he spun her so she faced him. "You didn't see anything tonight, right?"

"Right," she said, barely able to speak.

"In fact, you weren't even here tonight."

"That's right—I wasn't here."

He turned her and pushed her through the gate. "Take a hike —and don't come back."

He stepped inside, slammed the metal gate closed, and ran back into the restaurant.

Lizzy started down the block in the direction of Owen and the car, trying to keep her steps unhurried, but it was clear that she was so unsteady that she couldn't remain upright long on the high heels. She slipped them off and hooked the straps over her fingers.

She kept to a walk only through sheer force of will. She promised herself that when she got to the corner, she'd run.

She almost shrieked when she felt bony fingers on her arm.

She turned to see Ruby beside her.

"Young lady," said Ruby, "I seem to have had a little too much to drink. I'd be so grateful if you would help me find my car. I'll just have a little nap in the back before I try to drive home." She dropped her voice to a whisper. "It's less likely for Chapel's men to pick two people off the street than one."

They reached the corner, and there was the car, Owen at the wheel, only a dozen yards away. Lizzy was ready to break into a run, even if it meant dragging Ruby along beside her, when she saw the two men she had seen in the dining room—they had been laughing over something on a cell phone—emerge from the alley just a few yards ahead of where the car was parked. Now she could see the telltale style of all of Billy Chapel's henchmen: a cheaper and flashier version of Chapel's own wardrobe.

"Hey," said one of them, "that's the girl that wanted to see Billy."

"And that's the old lady who was eating alone," said the other.

Lizzy and Ruby froze, the two men between them and the car.

The car door swung open, and Owen climbed out. "Mom—you found her! Thank God! Sweetheart, what are you doing in Baltimore?" He hurried past the two men and slung one arm around each woman and herded them toward the car. "I've been worried sick about you. Thank goodness your grandmother found you." He opened the back door of the car and pushed them inside. "Let's get you home to your mother right away!"

As the two men stood gaping at the scene, Owen hurried to the driver's door.

"Kids!" he exclaimed to the men, shaking his head. "You can never tell what they'll get in their heads to do."

He dropped into the driver's seat.

"Go!" said Ruby.

He fumbled in his pockets as the two men approached the car.

"Hey," yelled one of them, "what's up? What were you two doing at *Charm City*?"

Ruby slapped the locks down on the back seat doors. "Doctor McNally ..." she said, her voice taut.

"I had the keys one second ago," stammered Owen.

"We need to get out of here. Right. Now."

Owen held up the keys. "Got them!" He jammed the keys in the ignition, revved the engine, and shot out of the parking space.

Lizzy looked back to see the two men standing in the otherwise deserted street, looking after the rapidly receding car.

"Ruby, you left your sweater ..." said Lizzy, her voice thready.

"I know. I figured it was a good excuse if I needed to go back ... as I should have done sooner. Is Chapel ...?" She let the question hang.

"He's dead. Or he will be soon." Lizzy swallowed back a sob.

Owen reached back and squeezed her hand.

"Keep your hands on the wheel!" snapped Ruby.

Owen returned his hand to the wheel. "What now?" he asked.

"Letort?" said Ruby, looking to Lizzy for confirmation.

When Lizzy was silent, Owen said, "I think so. I hope we don't have anything to worry about from Chapel's men, but better safe than sorry. Let's go to Letort, circle the wagons, and keep our eyes peeled." He looked back at Lizzy in the rearview mirror. "How does that sound, Pumpkin?"

Lizzy let her head drop back against the headrest, no longer bothering to hold back her tears. "Yes, let's do that."

A moment later, Owen pressed a handkerchief into her hand. "You did what needed to be done, Pumpkin."

"I know," she whispered.

Billy's taunting words as he described what Philip had done drifted through her mind like a horror movie flickering on a theater screen: *the ends justify the means … some lives are worth more than others. … a cold-blooded killer … we're not so different.*

Turned out she wasn't so different from Billy Chapel, either.

60

———

Philip forced his eyes open and cranked his head to one side, expecting to see Owen in the desk chair and Lizzy sitting on the dresser.

Instead, Olivia sat in the chair, her eyes on him, her fingers interlaced in her lap.

"I was starting to think you were going to sleep until the morning," she said.

He tried to sit up, groaned, and fell back onto the bed. "What time is it?"

She glanced at her phone. "Almost midnight."

"What are you doing here? Not that I'm not glad to see you, but I thought you were in Letort. And where are Owen and Lizzy?"

"I'm here because Owen and Lizzy had to leave."

"Where?"

"I don't know. They were very secretive about it."

His heart sank. He had a pretty good idea of where they had gone: to Baltimore, to take care of Billy Chapel, since Philip was too feeble to do it himself.

"Can I get you anything?" Olivia asked. "Let me get you a fresh glass of water." She stood.

He managed to sit up. "I can get it. I need to use the bathroom anyway."

"Need some help?"

"I think I can manage."

Her mouth quirked up in a smile. "I meant help with *getting* to the bathroom."

"Yeah, I figured. I think I can manage the whole thing on my own."

She gestured to a bag on the dresser. "I brought your duffel. Your box from Sedona also."

"Thanks." He shuffled to the dresser and got a leather toiletry kit out of the duffel. "I'll be back to my old self in no time."

She raised a skeptical eyebrow. "You'll need a lot more than toiletries for that. You look awful. As Dad would have said, 'You look like a bulldog took you out for a worry and a chew.'"

He smiled wanly. "Apt. It hasn't been a good ..." He struggled through the calculation. "... twenty hours or so."

"So I hear."

Philip brushed his teeth and splashed his face with water. Shaving seemed like way too much trouble. He made his way back to the bed and sat heavily on it, leaning against the backboard.

"So, Owen and Lizzy told you what happened?" he asked.

"Yes. How come I keep hearing what you're up to from other people?"

He dropped his head back against the wall. "Things have been a little too crazy for much conversation. But we have time now." He considered. "Although if you talked with Owen and Lizzy, I think you're all caught up." He raised his head and looked at her. "What have you been doing?"

"Just helping to keep an eye on Marjorie Pearson."

"How's she doing?"

"Fine. She's a lovely woman. I couldn't be that cheerful in her situation." She smiled. "And she and Richard are such a sweet couple." Her smile faded. "Do you think Chapel will really come after them?"

"If he's given a chance."

She was silent for a beat, then said, "Do you think he'll be given a chance?"

"Not if I can help it."

"What does that mean?"

He let his head fall back again. Without looking at her, he said, "I don't think you want to know."

"And why wouldn't I want to know?" Her tone was icy.

He was silent for almost a minute. Then he raised his head and met her eyes. "Olivia, you and I have known each other a long time—long enough for us to understand what drives the other person."

She crossed her arms. "And what drives me?"

"The desire to use the tools that society gives us to right wrongs."

"And ..." She cleared her throat. "And what drives you?"

"The desire to use any tools I have at my disposal to right wrongs."

"I see. And what tools do you have at your disposal?"

He was silent.

Her fingers tightened on her biceps. "And you'd use whatever these tools are in order to protect Marjorie and Richard."

"Yes. And you. And Owen and Andy and Ruby—"

"And Lizzy."

"Yes. And Lizzy."

She uncrossed her arms and took a deep breath. "When I

found out that you had lied to me about where you were going when you went to the compound with her ..."

"I'm sorry."

"I hate being lied to."

"I know."

She drew a deep breath. "Do you love her?"

"Liv, she's seventeen—"

"That's not what I asked."

Suppressing a wince, he swung his legs off the bed and moved so he was sitting as close to her chair as he could. "I've only loved three people in my life. Lizzy is one. Oscar was one. You're one."

She crossed her arms and dropped her eyes.

"Liv, I've loved you since the moment Oscar engineered an introduction. I remember seeing you in the visitor waiting room at Williams and knowing you were Oscar's daughter just by the way you held yourself. I remember you'd brought him a book of poetry he had asked for, and I remember that you didn't make me feel like an idiot for never having heard of the poet. I even remember what you were wearing—a white blouse, a denim skirt, and a squash blossom necklace. You were wearing leather sandals, and there was a little drop of white paint on one of them. I remember wondering what you were painting, and whether I could help you with it." He smiled. "What were you painting?"

She raised her eyes, and they glistened with tears. "The fence behind the grammar school. I remember being so pissed that I hadn't put on my old sneakers."

"I would have liked to have helped you paint that fence, if I had been a free man."

"I would have liked to have had you there."

They sat in silence for half a minute, Olivia periodically

wiping away tears with the back of her hand. Eventually she spoke. "But …?"

"But I don't think we're right for each other."

"Because I'm limited by the tools society provides," she said bitterly, "and you're not limited by anything."

"Liv, you're doing the right thing. I'm doing the wrong thing. That's why we're not right for each other."

"You know," she said, her voice barely audible, "I always thought that the way we met made a relationship extra hard. Dad wanted us so much to be together, and then all his friends at Williams expected it." She smiled blearily. "It was almost like an arranged marriage."

He returned her smile. "I know what you mean."

"Maybe it would have been different if he had gotten out. Not quite so much riding on us being a couple."

"Maybe."

She met his eyes. "He loved you so much."

Philip dropped his head and sat, his eyes on the floor, tears burning behind his lids, for a full minute. When he finally looked up, Olivia's face had relaxed into almost contemplativeness.

"What are you going to do once you don't have to worry about the Pearsons anymore?" he asked.

"Go back to Arizona, I guess. I can't do as much good there as I could at the BIA in D.C., but I can still do some good."

"You can do a lot of good."

"Actually, Andy had some really good ideas for how medical care could be made more available to people on the res. He said that—" She glanced over at Philip and blushed. "You don't want to hear all the details."

"I do. Andy's a smart man. And a good guy. The two of you together—you'd be unstoppable."

"In terms of getting medical care to people on the res ..." she said uncertainly.

"Absolutely." He reached out and covered her hand with his. She didn't draw away. "Tell me your plans."

61

The female anchor straightened the prop papers in front of her on the news desk and turned toward the camera. "We begin tonight with news from Letort, Pennsylvania. Authorities were alerted by an anonymous tip about a man in a vehicle who required assistance. Upon arrival, police discovered a man bound with zip ties in the back of a Cadillac Escalade hidden behind bushes off State Route 34. He was reported to be hungry, dehydrated, and somewhat confused, claiming not to remember how he had gotten there, but seemingly otherwise unharmed. He was transported to Letort General Hospital for assessment. Upon further investigation, authorities discovered that the man was wanted for violating parole after serving a four-year sentence for extortion at the Jessup Correctional Institution. The vehicle he was found in is registered to Billy Chapel, a Baltimore figure known in law enforcement circles as 'Teflon Billy' for his ability to evade prosecution for his alleged crimes."

The camera switched to the male anchor. "In related news, Kristi," he said, "just days ago, an explosion at the estate of reclusive Maryland billionaire Theo Viklund linked yet another vehicle to Billy Chapel. The blast destroyed an outbuilding, apparently a lab of some sort. As authorities searched the property looking for possible victims of the blast, they found a number of bodies of men thought to be part of Viklund's security staff throughout the property. Many had been dead for some time, but one victim is reported to have died fairly recently. Authorities have not yet released the identities of the victims. Authorities also found an Escalade, also registered to Chapel, on the property. They made one more gruesome discovery: a severed hand stored in a refrigeration unit in the home."

"And that's not the oddest part about this story, Keith," said Kristi. "Billy Chapel's reputed associates are not the only ones suffering odd or fatal incidents. Chapel himself suffered what appears to have been a stroke late last night at his Baltimore restaurant, *Charm City Diner*. He was rushed to Johns Hopkins Hospital but died en route. We will continue to follow this developing story closely, bringing you updates as they become available." She tapped her papers. "Up next, our meteorologist Judy Chetham has your forecast, including what to expect if you're planning outdoor activities this weekend. Stay with us."

The red light went off.

"Weird, weird stuff," Keith said as a production assistant patted his nose with a powder puff.

Kristi took a sip of water. "One of my friends knows the sister of one of the EMTs who was with Chapel in the ambulance. They said he was conscious almost until they got to Hopkins and kept saying what sounded like 'izzy' and 'weez' and 'castle.'"

Keith shook his head. "Maybe a stroke? My granddad died of a stroke, and they said he had trouble talking at the end."

"Maybe." Kristi shook her head as she retouched her lipstick. "I'll bet the folks in Baltimore are glad to have Chapel out of the way."

"Yeah." Keith sighed. "Wonder who will take his place?"

62

Lizzy turned off the newscast on the TV in Marjorie's room.

"Well," said Owen from his chair in the corner of the room, "I *think* it's a good thing that the police are finding a connection between Billy Chapel and Theo Viklund."

"Although since Chapel and Viklund are both dead," said Andy, leaning in the doorway, "I can't imagine we have too much to worry about. Did anyone get the sense that either of them had someone they were grooming to take over?"

"I think the most likely person in Theo's case would have been Lucas," said Lizzy, "and he's dead. Billy clearly didn't see Tony as next in line. I'm guessing whoever takes over in Baltimore won't be someone Billy would have confided in, so I can't imagine that person would know about us."

"So," said Ruby, from her chair next to Marjorie's bed, "no worries from Theo Viklund or Billy Chapel. That leaves Louise Mortensen."

"I really don't think that Richard and Marjorie have anything to worry about from Mortensen," said Olivia from where she stood next to Andy in the doorway, "so we needn't burden them with speculation on that front."

Richard, perched on the side of Marjorie's bed, raised a hand. "That's fine with me—the less I know, the better."

"That's what I think, too," said Marjorie.

"I understand you have other things to keep you busy," Owen said cheerfully.

"Yes," said Marjorie. "Olivia is working on getting my insurance company to reassess my treatment, and Andy is working on getting me moved to a better facility." She smiled at the two. "Nothing like having a lawyer and a doctor on my team."

"And I'll probably be working on that from D.C.," said Olivia. "My boss said I can have my job back at the BIA."

Lizzy smiled. "That's great news."

"And guess who else is going to be spending some time in D.C.," said Marjorie, grinning at Andy.

In a first, as far as Lizzy was concerned, Andy blushed. "I'm not going to be much good on rounds or in an ER until my hand is better," he said. "Olivia thought that the Bureau of Indian Affairs could benefit from some consulting on medical issues, so I'll be making some trips down there," he looked at Marjorie with mock severity, "from my apartment in Philadelphia."

Marjorie laughed. "You don't need to explain the arrangements to me—I'm not your chaperone."

Olivia smiled. "Until we can get Marjorie transferred elsewhere, a friend of my father's is taking a job in the maintenance department here at Cedar Grove. It's not exactly 24/7 security, but he'll be able to keep an eye on things."

"Is it one of your friends who doesn't mind cracking some heads?" Richard asked with a laugh.

"If I had any fear that any heads would need cracking," said Olivia, "I *would* arrange for 24/7 coverage."

Owen stood. "I imagine Marjorie and Richard are going to be relieved not to be sharing the room with five extra people."

"I've enjoyed it!" said Marjorie. "The more the merrier."

"But I'm sure all of you are looking forward to sleeping somewhere other than on a chair or a hotel bed," said Richard.

"Yup," said Owen. "Olivia will be heading back to Bethesda. Lizzy, Ruby, and I will go back to Lansdowne. And Andy can go to his apartment—and have a little privacy for a change."

They exchanged farewells, and the visitors headed downstairs.

They had managed to accumulate four of their five vehicles in Letort: Owen's old SUV, which he would be driving; his new SUV, which Ruby would be driving; Andy's Lexus, which Olivia had driven back from Harrisburg, and about whose scratches Andy had been remarkably calm; and the Caravan for Lizzy. Andy would be driving Olivia back to Harrisburg to pick up her rental.

After exchanging farewells, they dispersed to the various vehicles, Owen and Lizzy heading for the Caravan.

"So," Owen said, "off to see Philip?"

"Yes. I texted with him a little while ago, and he said he was feeling a lot better, so I don't think you need to come to check up on him."

"Okay—but if it looks like he could use a medical opinion, give me a call."

"You? Not Andy?" she said, her tone teasing.

They looked over to where Andy and Olivia were laughing over something as they climbed into the Lexus.

Owen smiled indulgently. "No, maybe not Andy. If he and Philip weren't on the best of terms before, I can't imagine the current situation would improve that." He and Lizzy waved to Ruby and then to Andy and Olivia as they pulled out of the lot. Then Owen's smile faded, and he looked back to Lizzy. "Do you really think we don't have anything to worry about from Louise?"

She sighed. "So far no one has come up with what seems like a good reason for Louise to come after us. The only reason I can think of is if she thought we would turn her in to the authorities, but she knows that would be as risky for us as for her. We have as much to hide as she does."

"Yes, I agree. And she knows we don't have any reason to come after her ourselves. We have what we wanted from her: the neuroinhibitol ... or at least the wherewithal to create it. Once Andy and I run a few more tests to make sure it's safe, you can try it and see if it's effective as well."

"Yup."

"What's the first thing you're going to do if you know you can interact with people without putting them at risk?"

She considered. "Take some kind of class."

Owen perked up. "A college class?"

She laughed. "I doubt I would qualify. I haven't been in a classroom since Happy Hours Montessori, and that hardly counts."

"You could get a GED."

She grimaced. "Not without a better fake ID than I have."

"Yes, I suppose that might put you on official radar screens. Maybe something a little more informal." He smiled. "I know you've done an impressive amount of reading in neurobiology thanks to your ever-enthusiastic godfather. Maybe you could audit one of my classes at Penn U." He smiled ruefully. "You do know a good deal more about brain function than most of my students." This time his smile was bright. "We can carpool to class together!"

"You're really comfortable with me staying with you and Ruby in Lansdowne?"

"Absolutely. I already talked about it with Ruby—she can't wait to have you there."

"I can't wait either." She stepped forward and gave him a hug, then stepped back. "Actually, Philip is going to need somewhere to go, too. He can't very well stay in the motel. He doesn't even have a car. Maybe—"

But Owen was already shaking his head. "I don't think that would work out, Pumpkin."

"I think we should at least make the offer—"

"Philip and I have already talked about it. I told him it wasn't possible. He understands."

"He understands? What does he understand? What did you talk about?"

"Ask him when you get to Harrisburg. I think it's better that you hear it from him directly."

63

Lizzy knocked on the door of the Harrisburg motel room. She heard movement from inside, and after a moment, the door opened to reveal Philip.

He didn't look as bad as he had when she had first discovered him in the room. He didn't even look as bad as he had when she and Owen had left on their mission to Baltimore. But he didn't look good. He was still pale, and he must have lost some weight, even in the short time since he had taken the V-2. Olivia must have bought him clothes that were more his usual size, but even these hung loosely on him.

He stepped back to let her into the room, and she saw that, in the hand hidden behind the door, he held a gun.

He slipped the gun back into the shoulder holster he was wearing. "I am really, really glad to see you."

"I'm really, really glad to see you, too."

They hugged and she realized she was right—he had lost weight. His shoulder blades were too prominent under his shirt.

When he released her, she stepped back. "Do you think you still need that?" she asked, gesturing to the gun.

He tried for a smile. "Better safe than sorry." He pulled out the desk chair for her and sat on the bed, his elbows on his knees, his hands clasped between them. "But I can't imagine I have too much to worry about, since you took care of Chapel."

"It worked out fine. Have you had anything to eat recently?"

"I'm not hungry."

"It doesn't matter—you need to eat something. Do you want something healthy, like a salad, or something filling, like a pizza?"

He smiled, and this time it was more relaxed. "Let's go for something filling like a pizza."

Lizzy searched on her phone for a pizzeria that delivered and placed an order for a large cheese pizza and two lemonades.

"So, tell me about Baltimore," he said when she was off the phone. "I want to hear how you pulled it off."

She shrugged. "I just got him mad and then squeezed him."

"I'm guessing it wasn't quite that straightforward."

"I don't want to talk about that part right now."

He raised his hands. "Completely understandable."

"But Owen and Ruby were there with me. Owen drove the car, even though he wanted to do more, and Ruby was in the restaurant so she could tell me when I should come in. She was supposed to wait in the car after she left the restaurant, but then she got worried about me and was coming back when she ran into me. She had left a sweater behind so she'd have an excuse to go back in."

Philip smiled. "Good idea."

"And then I thought we were screwed because a couple of Billy's guys happened to be outside, near the car where Owen was waiting for us. You should have seen him talk us past them —classic Uncle Owen."

"You have a good group of people around you, Lizzy Ballard."

"I know I do."

They passed the time until the pizza arrived by reviewing the news coverage of the events in Baltimore, Letort, and Sedona on Lizzy's phone. When there was a knock at the door, Philip unholstered his gun and checked through the peephole before giving Lizzy the thumbs up to open the door to a teenage boy in earbuds bopping to a rhythm only he could hear.

When Lizzy had had three pieces of pizza and Philip one, he said, "I have something for you." He opened the bedside drawer, took out an iPad, handed it to her, and resumed his seat on the bed.

She took it. "What's this?"

"Louise's medical records. It has information about the work she did at the compound. I thought you and Owen and Andy might be able to do something with it."

She turned the iPad uncertainly in her hands. "What could we do with it?"

He shrugged. "I'm not sure, but I figured if anyone was holding that information, it should be you."

"Do you think we should send it anonymously to the police, or maybe the Attorney General's office?"

"That wouldn't be my recommendation. First of all, you'd need to make very sure that there was no reference to you, but I think the information could lead the authorities to Vivantem, and who knows where that could go. You're probably in the official Vivantem records as well as the unofficial ones. I think sending it to the authorities, even anonymously, would be a big risk for not much payoff ... and might disrupt the lives of a lot of other people as well."

"Yeah, I agree." She set the iPad on the desk. "But I'll have Uncle Owen and Andy take a look at it."

He pulled a flash drive from his pocket and handed it to her. "There's no question about sharing the information on this with the authorities—this has Louise's records about you on it. Or at least that's the claim."

She held it as if it might be radioactive. "How did you get this?"

"A messenger service brought it by this morning."

"From Louise?"

"Yes."

Lizzy put the flash drive on top of the iPad. "I don't know what I'm going to do with that information." She grimaced. "I don't think I even want it."

"You don't have to look at it now—maybe ever. I think, with Owen's help, you will decide what the best thing is to do, or not do, with it."

She nodded, uncertain. "Why would she give it to you? She must have known you'd pass it on to me, wouldn't she?"

"I think she would have." They were both silent for several seconds, then Philip continued. "You know, despite all the terrible things Mortensen has done, in her own way, she has looked out for you. You told me she kept Lucas from shooting you in the lab at the compound."

"That's true," she said reluctantly. "Although I don't much like the idea of being in Louise's debt, and it's not much, stacked up against all the bad things she's done."

"No argument there. But there's something ..." He leaned forward, elbows on knees. "I don't know how else to express it: I think she cares for you—at least, she cares about what happens to you. She thinks of you as ..."

"As her creation," finished Lizzy, her voice leaden. "Like Doctor Frankenstein and the monster."

"Yes. But maybe more than that. Almost like a daughter."

Her eyebrows shot up. "Her daughter?" She managed a somewhat unhinged-sounding laugh. "You're joking, right?"

"No, I'm not. I admit that she certainly doesn't love you like any normal mother would her daughter." He shrugged. "It's just an observation, but it's one I didn't think you would see for yourself. It might be useful someday."

Her features twisted in a grimace. "Thanks. I think."

"It's nothing you have to worry about right now."

Eager to change the topic, Lizzy asked, "What are you going to do after you've recovered from the V-2? Hopefully you won't have any long-term effects from it."

He took a sip of his lemonade.

"Right?" she prompted.

"This might not be the last time I take it."

"What?" she said, aghast. "Why do you say that? Look what it did to you!" She stood and, without waiting for an answer, she hurried on. "And how would you do that anyway? Louise didn't give you a supply ... did she?"

"No. But if it got created once, it could get created again. And it could probably be modified so that it wouldn't have such an extreme effect, just like Owen modified the juice to reduce the side effects for you."

"But ... it's only good for squeezing people. No doctor—at least no doctor other than Louise—would make a drug that had that purpose!"

"Andy would."

"How do you know?"

"I asked him. Owen has told him enough about what he saw Louise doing that he says he thinks he can replicate it."

"Does Owen know about this?"

"I told Andy I'd leave it up to him how much he wants to tell Owen ... but I think Owen suspects."

She felt tears spring to her eyes. "Is this why Owen doesn't want you coming to Lansdowne? Because you're going to take a drug that gives you the squeeze? And he doesn't want anything to do with that?"

"I think it's more that he doesn't want *you* to have anything to do with that."

She glared at him through her tears. "This is so screwed up!"

"I know. I—"

"I need to ask you something."

He sat up, surprised. "Okay."

"When I was with Billy at *Charm City*, he said that Donny tortured Lucas. Is that true?"

"Yes."

"You told me that, too—when we were at the compound."

"Yes."

"How do you know? Did Billy tell you that?"

He was silent for a long moment, then said, "I was there when Billy was questioning Lucas."

"In the same room?"

"Yes."

"Billy said ..."

She stopped. Did she really want to know the answer to the question she was about to ask? It might change everything ... but not knowing, always wondering, would be worse. She dropped her eyes. "He said you killed Lucas."

The silence was longer this time. Then he spoke. "I did."

Her eyes snapped up. She hadn't imagined the answer would be so straightforward—and so awful.

Philip dropped his face into his hands. Then his hands fell, limp, between his knees. His eyes stayed on the floor.

"Billy said he wanted me in the room while they interrogated Lucas. I was never sure if he did it to test my willingness to go along with whatever he decided to do, or because he thought he could learn something by my reactions to whatever Lucas said. Either way," he continued, his voice bitter, "I guess I passed the test. And then Billy decided he—he and Donny—had gotten everything they were going to out of Lucas, and he wanted Lucas put out of his misery. He picked me to do it." He finally met her eyes. "Lizzy, that was the worst moment of my life—and the moment I'm most ashamed of. I justified what I did by convincing myself that Lucas was going to die anyway and that it didn't much matter who pulled the trigger. In fact, I told myself it was better if I did it, because who knows what Donny would have done to stretch out the 'fun' a little more—take off the top of Lucas's head but not kill him immediately, maybe. I also told myself that the longer I seemed to cooperate with Billy and let him think I was on his side, the more I could learn and the better I could protect you and Owen and Andy and Ruby. But when it comes right down to it, I did it because I knew if I didn't, Billy would let Donny have some more fun with me."

By the time he finished talking, tears were streaming down Lizzy's cheeks. "Oh, Philip. I'm so sorry." One of her hands reached out toward his, hesitated, then dropped back into her lap.

"Me, too. But Lizzy, I don't want you thinking what I did was noble, or even justifiable. I'm ashamed of the circumstances of Lucas's death: that Billy forced me to do something because I was afraid of what would happen to me if I didn't. And that's why I want the V-2. I never want to feel that powerless again." He stood, walked to the window, and cracked the curtain enough to look out. Then he turned back to Lizzy. "You know I've killed men before. I killed that rancher's son when I was a teenager, although that was an accident. I killed Tobe Hanrick, and that was no accident. I would have killed Donny if you hadn't taken care of him for me. And if I had been able to kill Billy Chapel and Donny the minute they walked into that basement room with Lucas, I wouldn't have spent a moment regretting it." He crossed the room and knelt in front of her. "Do you understand, Lizzy? What I did—and what I plan to do—isn't noble, and Owen is right not to want me around you or him or Ruby."

"So …" She cleared her throat. "So what are you going to do?"

He sighed, straightened, and sat back down on the bed. "I don't know. But I know that I should do whatever it is far from all of you."

"So you just fall off the map, and Louise just falls off the map, and we're supposed to pretend like everything's normal?" she said, her voice bitter.

He marshaled a smile. "Let's do everything we can to make things normal—for all of you, but mainly for you, Lizzy. You deserve that."

They sat in silence for half a minute, Lizzy's eyes on the floor, her heart torn between sadness and frustration, between pity and anger. She could feel Philip's eyes on her. Finally, she took a long, shuddering breath. "I guess I better go." She looked up, then dropped her eyes again. "Do you need anything. Groceries?"

"No. But thank you."

She stood and walked to the door.

Philip followed her.

"Bye, Philip."

"Bye, Lizzy."

She stepped out the door and went down the steps to the parking lot, gripping the handrail because the stairs swam in her vision. She didn't hear the door close, but she forced herself not to look back. When she got to the Caravan, she thought for a moment that she should wait until she was calmer to drive away, but the idea of sitting there, knowing Philip was watching her— it was unbearable. She started up the Caravan, backed out of the space, and turned into the road.

She was halfway to Lansdowne and Owen and Ruby when she realized that she and Philip hadn't bumped fists.

64

———

Louise Mortensen finished the last of her excellent coffee and patted her lips with the linen napkin. She had been to this restaurant years ago with Gerard when she had been in D.C. for a conference, and she had managed to get the same table where they had sat. She recalled Gerard had been especially impressed by the wine list, although since she had been scheduled to give a talk later that day, she had gotten sparkling water. Today, she had ordered a glass of champagne.

Whether she had reason to celebrate or whether this would be her equivalent of a last meal would soon become clear.

She slipped some bills into the check folder—the server would certainly be pleased with his tip—then rose, retrieved her handbag, and left the restaurant.

She was about to walk down the alley that ran alongside the restaurant when she noticed a woman just down the street, shapeless in layers of clothing, one hand gripping the handle of a shopping cart filled to overflowing with black plastic trash bags, the other holding out a huge, battered Starbucks cup.

Louise double checked the contents of her handbag: a

wallet, a lipstick, a comb, a packet of tissues, hand sanitizer. She removed the driver's license identifying her as Louise Gerard from the wallet and slipped it into the pocket of her dress. She walked down the sidewalk to the woman and held out the handbag.

"There you go," she said. "There are a few dollars in the wallet, and you could get quite a bit of money for the handbag."

The woman tentatively took the bag and gazed at it, her eyebrows rising. "*Lewis Vweeten?*"

"*Loo-ee vee-tahn,*" said Louise.

"What?"

"It doesn't matter."

The woman's eyes narrowed. "The real thing?"

Louise raised an eyebrow. "I certainly hope so." She turned and walked down the sidewalk.

It was a lovely day out—a few puffy white clouds against a bright blue sky, a faint breeze blowing in from the Potomac. The rhythmic click of her heels on the pavement pleased her—she had treated herself to a new pair of low-heeled Louboutin pumps. Her old ones had been getting quite shabby looking.

She entertained herself imagining Philip's reaction when the flash drive with Elizabeth Ballard's medical records had arrived at the motel, and she wondered what he would do with it. Keep it? Give it to Ballard? She really didn't care—she just didn't want to be holding it when she reached her destination. And she had pored over those records so many times, she practically had them committed to memory.

Elizabeth Ballard: her most successful experiment. Louise would never have imagined that the scared young woman she and Gerard had held hostage in their Pocopson home would be the person who dispatched Billy Chapel, because it couldn't be a coincidence that Chapel had died of a stroke. Yes, Ballard had done them all a favor.

Had she regretted doing it? Louise felt certain she had. In fact—her mouth twisted in a grimace at the thought—Louise suspected Ballard regretted having killed Gerard, although even Louise had to admit that it probably wouldn't have happened if Gerard hadn't been shooting at the girl.

Yes, the connection with Ballard had ended Gerard's life and set Louise's on a trajectory she would never have chosen for herself ... and yet ...

And yet, there was a part of Louise that couldn't help but feel proud of the young woman Ballard had become.

It took her only a few moments to reach her destination. She briefly thought of circling the block, but to what end? Better to know sooner than later how her plan would play out. Plus, the building took up the whole block, meaning she'd be treated to a view of its brutalist ugliness the whole way.

She went through the revolving door and crossed to the security checkpoint.

"Everything out of your pockets," said the man staffing the machine, handing her a small plastic tray. "And you'll need to put your handbag through the scanner."

"I don't have a handbag."

He raised an eyebrow. "You'll need an ID."

She removed the driver's license from her pocket and put it in the tray, then handed the tray back to him.

"Okay," he said. "Step through the scanner."

She passed through without triggering any alerts—she had chosen a fabric belt rather than one with a metal buckle, just to be on the safe side—then retrieved the license and crossed the utilitarian lobby to one of the reception stations.

The man behind the bulletproof glass looked up. "Welcome to the Federal Bureau of Investigation. How can I help you?"

She drew a deep breath. "I have some information that

would be of interest to the FBI. May I speak with someone in charge?"

END OF BOOK 5

DID you enjoy *Drawing Dead* (Book 5)? If you did, I would be so grateful if you would take a moment to leave a rating and review on your favorite online platform. For inspiration, check out what other satisfied readers have said!

Thank you!

Matty

ALSO BY MATTY DALRYMPLE

The Lizzy Ballard Thrillers

Rock Paper Scissors (Book 1)

Snakes and Ladders (Book 2)

The Iron Ring (Book 3)

Kill Box Checkmate (Book 3½)

Scare Card (Book 4)

Drawing Dead (Book 5)

The Lizzy Ballard Thrillers Ebook Box Set

The Ann Kinnear Suspense Novels

The Sense of Death (Book 1)

The Sense of Reckoning (Book 2)

The Falcon and the Owl (Book 3)

A Furnace for Your Foe (Book 4)

A Serpent's Tooth (Book 5)

Be with the Dead (Book 6)

The Ann Kinnear Suspense Novels Ebook Box Set - Books 1-3

The Ann Kinnear Suspense Shorts

All Deaths Endure

Close These Eyes

May Violets Spring

Ministers of Grace

Our Dancing Days

Sea of Troubles

Stage of Fools

Write in Water

Non-Fiction

Taking the Short Tack: Creating Income and Connecting with Readers Using Short Fiction with Mark Leslie Lefebvre

The Indy Author's Guide to Podcasting for Authors: Creating Connections, Community, and Income

From Page to Platform: How to Succeed as an Author Speaker with M.L. Ronn

Collaborate to Create: A Guide to Coauthoring Nonfiction with M.L. Ronn

ABOUT THE AUTHOR

Matty Dalrymple (DAL-rim-ple) is the author of the Lizzy Ballard Thrillers, beginning with *Rock Paper Scissors*; the Ann Kinnear Suspense Novels, beginning with *The Sense of Death*; and the Ann Kinnear Suspense Shorts, including *Close These Eyes*. She is a member of International Thriller Writers and Sisters in Crime.

Matty also podcasts, writes, speaks, and consults on the writing craft and the publishing voyage as The Indy Author. Her non-fiction books include *Taking the Short Tack: Creating Income and Connecting with Readers Using Short Fiction*, *The Indy Author's Guide to Podcasting for Authors*, and *From Page to Platform: How to Succeed as an Author Speaker*. Her articles have appeared in *Writer's Digest* magazine. She serves as the Campaigns Manager for the Alliance of Independent Authors.

Matty lives with her husband, Wade Walton, and their dogs in Chester County, Pennsylvania, and enjoys vacationing on Mount Desert Island, Maine, and Sedona, Arizona, and these locations provide the settings for her novels.

Go to www.mattydalrymple.com > About & Contact for more information about Matty's fiction work and to sign up for her occasional email newsletter.

Go to www.theindyauthor.com/ > About & Contact for more information about Matty's non-fiction work and to sign up for her weekly email newsletter.

facebook.com/matty.dalrymple

ACKNOWLEDGMENTS

My heartfelt thanks to everyone who generously shared their expertise to help shape this story:

As always, Wade Walton, for being my most ardent supporter, and Mary Dalrymple, for being my most enthusiastic fan.

Jon McGoran, for lending his expert editorial eye to the story.

Marc Bjorkman, for his guidance on Richard Pearson's field of study.

Thomas Dunne, for invaluable advice on the mechanics of fire and explosions.

Ken Fritz, for his insights into the medical aspects of the story.

Jane Kelly, Lisa Regan, and Kaylin Tristano for unfailing cheerleading.

Jerri Williams, for providing the details of the lobby of the FBI's D.C. headquarters.

And my trusty advance reader team, including Mike Bassick, Marc Bjorkman, Sandra Carey Cody, Babs Labenberg, Rhonda Taller, Linda Triegel, and AnnaMarie Vnucak.

Any deviations from strict accuracy—intentional or unintentional—are solely the responsibility of the author.